EVERYTHING BUT YOU

NEWBERRY SPRINGS SERIES
BOOK THREE

HARLOW JAMES

Copyright © 2023 by Harlow James
All rights reserved.

No part of this book may be reproduced in any form or by any electronic or mechanical means, including information storage and retrieval systems, without written permission from the author, except for the use of brief quotations in a book review.

This is a work of fiction. Names, characters, businesses, places, events, locales, and incidents are either the products of the author's imagination or used in a fictitious manner. Any resemblance to actual persons, living or dead, or actual events is purely coincidental.

Paperback ISBN:

Cover Designer: Abigail Davies
Editor: Melissa Frey

To those of us who understand that second chances are opportunities to grow, learn, and never stop fighting for what we want.

And remember that in love, sometimes we lose people just to find them again.

"True love has a habit of coming back."

Unknown

CONTENTS

Prologue	1
Chapter 1	19
Chapter 2	38
Chapter 3	65
Chapter 4	84
Chapter 5	96
Chapter 6	110
Chapter 7	121
Chapter 8	141
Chapter 9	162
Chapter 10	185
Chapter 11	198
Chapter 12	209
Chapter 13	228
Chapter 14	238
Chapter 15	252
Chapter 16	273
Chapter 17	282
Chapter 18	289
Chapter 19	305
Chapter 20	320
Chapter 21	338
Chapter 22	341
Chapter 23	352
Chapter 24	357
Epilogue	371
More Books by Harlow James	385
Acknowledgments	387
About the Author	391

PROLOGUE

Shauna

Age Eighteen

"Come on, slow poke!" Glancing over my shoulder, I see Forrest struggling to keep up with me as I push Bodi, my favorite horse on the Gibson Ranch, to increase his speed. "You gonna let a girl beat you?"

"You fail to realize I'm not losing anything! I've got a front-row seat to your ass as you ride away from me!" Forrest calls out, the wind carrying his words to me. "And I can't wait to get my hands on it!"

"Who says I'm going to let you touch it when we stop?" I toss back as his laugh echoes out around us.

Facing forward once more, I focus on the run-down shack in the distance that we're headed to, our place of solitude that allows the two of us some quiet time away from his family and my mother. And it's the perfect place to have this conversation that I've been avoiding but know I can't put off any longer.

Right now, time alone is a rare occurrence, especially with Forrest's younger twin brothers around and college looming in the future. I love Wyatt and Walker dearly, but they're like his little shadows, which is rather cute but annoying when I want to make out with my boyfriend and do other things not suitable for young eyes.

I pull on Bodi's reins, urging him to slow down as the distance between us and the shack lessens. Bodi comes to a stop, and the ringing in my ears from the wind begins as he trots to the door we always use to enter. The sun is about to set in the distance, lighting up the sky in pinks and oranges that remind me of rainbow sherbet.

Damn, now I wish I had some to share with Forrest while we're here.

"Jesus, woman. In a rush to get me naked?"

I smirk at Forrest over my shoulder as I hop off the saddle. "Always."

He shakes his head at me and dismounts his horse, Malakai, landing on the solid ground beneath him before standing to his full height. Taking both horses over to the hitching post, he secures them before moving to unlock the door. My eyes trail him the entire time.

I remember when I first saw Forrest Gibson. I was in my junior year of high school and had just moved to Newberry Springs with my mom. It's been just the two of us since my dad left when I was three. My mom was offered a job as a receptionist at a law firm in Texas, so we packed up all of our belongings and left Little Rock, Arkansas, landing in this small town smack dab in the middle of nowhere. I was beyond pissed that she made me leave my friends and the only home I ever knew. But then, on the first day of school, I walked into English class and saw Forrest sitting in the back row with a stoic scowl etched on his face, assessing the entire room as if he were sizing everyone up.

I was drawn to him; there's no other way to explain it. And when our eyes met and he dipped his eyes up and down my body, I felt something I'd never felt before: *lust*.

It didn't take long for us to get together, and now, two years later, I'm nervous about what this next chapter of our lives might hold. I love Forrest with every fiber of my being, but there's something else I'm finally ready to explore, and I know it could alter our future. My mother doesn't seem to think Forrest and I have much of one anyway, since the first time she dabbled in young love left her with heartbreak and a child to raise on her own and me wondering why my father didn't bother to stick around to get to know me.

Looks like I might be able to find that out sooner rather than later.

"We've gotta replace this lock," Forrest grumbles as he fights with the key to turn. His father thinks he's kept us out of here by locking this place up, but Forrest copied the key months ago and keeps it with him so we can go out here when we want to be alone. This is also where we lost our virginities to each other almost a year ago, so the place holds sentimental value as well.

"Well, in a few months, it won't matter." I rub his shoulder from behind as he finally wiggles the lock loose and opens the door, leading me inside and shutting the door behind me.

"Exactly. We'll have our own place in College Station within the year, and then we won't have to worry about sneaking around." Forrest pulls me into his chest and places a kiss to my forehead. Every time he does that, I melt. It's so simple, but it makes me feel so cherished, so close to him.

Moments like this make me terrified of what the future holds because I don't want to lose him.

We stay like that for a moment, but then I start running my nails up and down his back. He lets out a groan before slamming his lips to mine as the smell of dirt and wood fills the air. "Fuck, I can't wait, Shauna," he mumbles between kisses. "I can't wait to marry you, come back here after we earn our degrees, take over the ranch for my parents, and start our lives together."

These aren't new thoughts. We've talked about our future many times before. However, the idea of following that plan has my heart galloping and my stomach bottoming out. It's been happening more and more lately, especially after we graduated a month ago. And given the email I received a few weeks after that, I've changed my mind about a lot of things.

"Actually, there's something I need to talk to you about," I venture as Forrest peppers my skin with kisses, licking and sucking on my neck, distracting me from what I need to say.

"Sex now, talking later," he mumbles before finding my lips again and reminding me how strong our connection is.

God, I'm going to miss him.

It's not that I don't want the same things as him. I do. But we're only eighteen, and if I don't follow through with my decision to go to the University of Nevada, Las Vegas and try to establish a relationship with my dad now, I know I'll regret it.

The thing is, I can't tell Forrest exactly why I'm going there instead of Texas A&M like we planned because he won't understand. Or worse, he'll tell my mom, and then all hell will break loose. He thinks my father is the scum of the earth just like my mother does because he left her and me to fend for ourselves, but I'm pretty sure Forrest's jaded opinion of him only exists due to the heavy influence of my mother—which is ironic, since he and my mom don't exactly get along, either.

Mom spent most of my childhood avoiding the topic of my father. Every time I brought him up, she told me we were better off without him, but if I pressed her too hard, she'd go off about how he cared about no one but himself and that's why he left. And for a while, I believed her. I never felt a lack of love or affection from her and considered myself lucky to at least have a mom who loved me enough for two lifetimes. But deep down, I've always felt like a part of me was missing—and that her reason for him leaving was lacking.

So a few months ago, I set out to find him. I couldn't ask my mother if she knew where he was because if she found out I was looking for him, she'd blow a gasket. But at least I knew his name, so I had something to go on.

It only took a few days of social media sleuthing for me to locate him in Las Vegas. And I sat on that knowledge for a while before I decided that the scholarship offer I got from UNLV would be the perfect excuse to move out there and try to get to know him.

After contacting him and hearing the surprise in his voice when I called, I knew I had to take this chance. A person only gets one father, and I've missed out on having mine in my life for the past fifteen years. I want to remedy that for the next fifteen, if possible.

When Forrest's lips meet mine again, I shove down the thoughts of our impending conversation and focus on the man encasing me in his arms, his biceps so big and strong I can't help but feel safe, and remind myself that Forrest and I are meant to be.

This man loves me; I don't doubt that for a second. But I also don't know who I am without him, and that's terrifying.

That's another reason I think the space will do us some good—allow us to figure out who we are without the other person and give us the opportunity to truly decide what we want to do with our lives.

I know Forrest thinks he has everything figured out, but I still have doubts, questions, and a desire to explore a bit more before we settle down and create a life together.

And I also have an estranged father who I'm desperate to know.

"Fuck, Shauna." His lips travel up my neck, waking up every nerve ending on my skin. "I need you, baby."

I let my body take over and reach down to the button of his jeans, knowing nothing can beat sex with him. And now that we're here, I know that's what I need. It will help ground me and remind me of how perfect we are together and that we can make it through anything.

"Make love to me, Forrest," I command as I pop the

button on his pants and pull down his zipper, palming his erection through his jeans.

"Get naked then." He steps back and reaches behind him, pulling his shirt up and over his head, revealing his muscular chest and shoulders. Playing football has been a blessing to this man's body, and his college scholarship to Texas A&M was well-earned. Forrest doesn't want to play professionally, but I think he could if he changed his mind. But that would interfere with his desire to take over his parents' ranch eventually, and I respect that. His family means the world to him, and I know that wherever he lands, he'll be successful.

I admire the trail of dark hair leading down from his belly button and disappearing into his jeans, his hip bones that frame his abs that I love to trace with my tongue, and that five o'clock shadow on his jaw. Forrest is the definition of tall, dark, and handsome with his deep brown hair and eyes, and right now, they're looking at me like I'm the center of his universe.

A girl can't complain about that.

So I yank my shirt off as well, popping the clasp on my bra behind me and letting it fall to the floor, eager to let him devour me.

"Fuck, you're perfect," Forrest declares as he closes the distance between us, grabs my chin in one hand and my right breast in the other, and kisses me desperately before backing us up to the air mattress in the corner. Luckily, it's still holding air from the last time we came out here a few days ago, so we carefully crawl on top of it after discarding our jeans and underwear.

Forrest rubs his length along my slit, teasing me as his crown hits my clit. "I'll never stop wanting you, baby, but I'm just warning you: This might be quick, because just touching you like this has me wanting to come already."

"Wouldn't be the first time you went quickly," I tease him.

He pinches my ribs as I squeal. "It's not my fault you're so sexy. Plus, stamina takes time, Shauna. But I think I've proven I can last when it counts."

"Oh, God, Forrest," I murmur as his crown hits me perfectly on my clit, over and over again. "Yes, you have." Desire takes over, and I claw at his back as he teases me.

"I love you, Shauna," he whispers in my ear before leaning down and pulling my nipple into his mouth.

"I love *you*. Now get a condom . . . please."

Chuckling, he reaches for his pants, grabs a condom from his wallet, and covers himself in record time. I lean up and capture his lips again, biting down on his bottom lip, which I know he loves.

Forrest lets out a low growl and then peers down, lining himself up to my core. As he pushes inside, we both gasp as we connect.

"Jesus, you feel so fucking good," Forrest grits out as he reaches my end, holding still while he allows me to adjust to him. Forrest is thick, and it still takes me a minute to relax when we have sex, but then it feels incredible when I do. "Every time it just gets better and better."

Clawing at his shoulders, I take in a shaky breath. "Move, Forrest. Please."

"Fuck," he whispers as he thrusts in and out, gliding through me like smooth velvet. "So good."

Our bodies grind and bump as Forrest finds his rhythm, taking us higher and higher to ecstasy. He sucks on my nipples, grips my hips tightly, and increases his speed when I start to clench around him. I reach between us to find my clit, stirring my own orgasm to life. Forrest loves when I do this, which is evident when his eyes dip down to the sight and light up.

"I'm gonna come," I whisper as my orgasm starts to bloom.

"Right there with you, babe. *Fuck*," he grits out as I shatter, and he follows me over the edge.

With his head buried in my neck, he says, "God, I love you. You know that, right?"

Tears build behind my eyelids. "I know. I love you too."

Once we catch our breath, I rest my head on his ribs as we lie there naked. The humidity in Texas is here for the summer, and we're both beyond sweaty. But this time together is precious, so we deal with the uncomfortable parts just to absorb each second.

"I want some rainbow sherbet," I mutter, still fixated on the craving I had earlier.

Forrest laughs. "What else is new? You know that shit isn't ice cream, right?"

I rest my chin on his chest and look up at him. "Says who? It's in the ice cream section, correct?"

"Yeah, because there isn't a sherbet section. I don't know how you eat that crap." He shudders, but this argument isn't anything new. The first time we went out for ice cream on a date, he gave me shit about my favorite flavor and hasn't stopped since.

"Well, at least it has more pizzaz than just chocolate. That's like the most boring flavor you can choose."

He scoffs. "Chocolate isn't boring. It's a classic."

"It's an old-man choice."

He tickles my ribs, making me squeal. "Take that back!"

"I'm with an old man!" I scream as Forrest tickles me until I can't breathe. "Okay, okay! You win!"

"Tell me chocolate is the best flavor," he commands.

"Rainbow sherbet is the best flavor," I say instead.

He pinches my ass, making me shriek again, and then settles me back on his chest. "Stubborn ass."

"You love it," I reply, sighing as I relax into his arms once again.

"I do." He kisses the top of my head. "I can't wait to grow old with you, Shauna. I'm going to build us a farmhouse like my parents' on the ranch, a house big enough that we can fill it with a bunch of kids."

"With white wood and blue shutters?" I tease him,

quoting *The Notebook*. Forrest thinks that chick flicks and romantic movies are stupid, but I know he pays attention to them more than he lets on.

"Sure, babe. Whatever you want."

"I want a porch swing, too, then." My head rests on his chest again. "A bench one, big enough that we can sit side by side and cuddle as we watch the sunset."

"Then I'll make sure to put one on the porch."

"And a small wedding. Just family and a few friends. Weddings are a waste of money."

"Noted."

Sighing, I get lost in the vision of making a life with Forrest in a house so beautiful, it looks like it belongs in a magazine. We both grow quiet as we lie there, enjoying each other's company. But then I remember what I came out here to do, the thing that could potentially ruin that entire vision. That could potentially ruin everything.

"So about that thing I wanted to talk to you about . . ."

"Uh-huh," he mumbles, his eyes closed as I look up at him.

Time to rip off the Band-Aid. "I think I'm going to go to UNLV after all."

His entire body shoots up from the air mattress, knocking me off of him. "What? Why?" His eyes are wild as he stares down at me.

"Well, I can't pass up that scholarship, Forrest." That's a huge part of the decision, and the main one I'm going to use for now to explain my choice to him. "And I think some space might be good."

"It's just money, Shauna . . . and space? Why the fuck do we need space?"

"First of all, it's a lot of money, Forrest. You have a scholarship to Texas A&M; I don't. I'd be paying out of pocket, and besides, I'm getting a degree in communications. It doesn't make sense to pay for one when I can get one for free. And second, I think going to school out of state will be good for me. I've only known Arkansas and Texas for the last two years. I want to see somewhere new." I hope he buys this. I hope he doesn't press me to explain this any further.

His furrowed eyebrows tell me he's still confused. "Where did this come from? I thought we were happy and on the same page. What about everything we were just talking about? What will this mean for us?" He reaches for my hand, bringing it to his lips to press his mouth to my skin.

"We *are* happy. I *do* want a future with you, but for right now, we can do long distance . . ."

"I don't want that." He cuts me off. "I can't imagine not seeing you every day."

"I know," I say, staring down at my lap now. "But we will be so busy, anyway, between classes, your practices, and working." I lift my eyes to meet his once more. "We can talk every day on the phone, fly back and forth once a month—"

"This is really what you want?" he asks, and the pain in his eyes is making me want to change my mind.

But I've already contacted both universities. And my dad knows that I'm coming. I have to see this through, and part of the reason I made those changes before we had this conversation is that I knew Forrest would try to get me to change my mind.

I want to tell him the truth, but I can't yet. Not until I see how things go once I get out there, and again, I know he'll say something to my mom. If stuff doesn't work out with my dad, I can always leave. It's not the best choice, but it is an option I have if I need it.

"I do. I love the campus. And it's Vegas. There will be so much for us to do when you visit."

He flops back on the mattress, staring up at the ceiling. "It feels like my heart is being ripped in two, Shauna. You're my girlfriend. I love you. I don't want to be away from you."

I lie back down next to him. "I'm sorry. But I do think it's the best option for me, Forrest. I know it will be hard, and at times it will suck, but we can get through this. We can." I lean over and reach for his face, turning him toward me so I can kiss his lips.

"I don't want to lose you."

Staring up into his brown eyes, I reassure him. "You won't. This is just temporary. Four years will fly by . . . we'll be back in Newberry Springs before we know it."

He nods but doesn't say anything. And as much as I

want to keep talking, I know I shouldn't. It won't be easy leaving him behind, but my heart tells me I have to do this. I don't want to live the rest of my life wondering *what if*.

We lie there together for almost fifteen minutes before he finally speaks again. "You know . . . I say we keep this shack once we take over the ranch," Forrest says as he rubs his hand up and down my arm.

"We won't need it if we have our own house, though," I counter, grateful that he is able to still think about our future after I just altered our road to get there.

"I know, but I want to have it just in case. Maybe one night, we can come out here for old times' sake or something . . . you know, when we're older and have kids." He shrugs. "I just don't want to forget our beginnings, Shauna. I want to remember where we started."

He turns his head down so our eyes connect again.

"I want to remember where we came from and how crazy we are about each other. I want to remember our beginning because falling in love with you has been the best thing that's ever happened to me. And even though we're gonna be apart for now, I know we'll find our way back here because we're meant to be. I know that in my soul." He pounds his fist on his chest.

Smiling, I lean up and press my lips to his. "Me, too, Forrest. I'll always love you."

He pinches my ass again and finally cracks a smile. "You'd better."

Squealing, I try to roll off of him, but he pins me down on the air mattress, hovering over me. "We should get back," I tell him, staring up into his deep brown eyes, pushing his unruly hair off his forehead. He's in desperate need of a haircut, but part of me loves the longer length on him because I can run my hands through it more easily. In a few months' time, he's going to look a little different every time I see him. My heart contracts at the thought.

"Just one more round," he whispers in my ear, growing hard against my thigh again. "I can be quick. If you're going to leave, we've got to take advantage of every opportunity we have to be together."

"Earlier, you were offended by my reminder of how quick you were."

He tickles my ribs again, making me shriek. If someone was riding by outside, they would definitely know we're here by now. "Do you want my dick or not, woman?"

Playfully rolling my eyes, I relent to his suggestion. But really, I would always want this man over and over again, and deep down, that should be reassuring . . . but it's terrifying, too. "Fine, but I'm gonna time you, then."

After he puts on a condom, he pushes forward once more, connecting us in the most exquisite way as he shuts me up with his mouth, showing me just how fast he can be. But of course, he gets me off first before finding his own release.

We were naïve to think that the next few years would be easy, that Forrest and I could survive the distance and the secrets. In fact, we didn't even last two years before life took a turn and led us down a path that neither one of us saw coming—one that both of us were too stubborn to bounce back from and one that created so much distance between us that I figured we'd never cross paths again.

Until we did.

CHAPTER ONE

Forrest

Present Day

"And what does the budget look like so far?" I stare across the table at Javier Montes, my lead project manager, trying not to clench my jaw too hard because it's only going to make this headache worse. I hate these goddamn profit and loss meetings—P&L for short—but they're necessary each week to make sure this company I own is actually making fucking money.

"Well, last week, we ran into a few issues that set us back in materials and labor. As of right now, we're breaking even, but if more unexpected expenses come up, we might take a loss on this building."

I pinch the bridge of my nose and sigh. "Fuck. This project was supposed to be a piece of cake."

Javi nods. "I know, but these young assholes on the crew keep fucking up. I'm telling you, boss, they have the attention span of a gnat."

"Tell them: Three strikes and they're out." I pound my fist against the table. "No more excuses. They're costing us money because they refuse to pay attention."

Javi sighs and leans back in his chair. "You got it."

I turn to Benny, one of the other project managers, and prepare for the recap of his ongoing jobs while cursing the lack of sleep I got last night as the reason for my low patience today.

Who am I kidding? I never have any fucking patience, but it just seems to be very minimal today. I'm already about to snap, and it's not even noon.

When I started working for High Performance Construction at nineteen, I never imagined being the owner of the company someday. But after dropping out of college and finding an outlet in pounding nails into wood, I realized there was a lucrative future in this industry. The former owner, Nick, also saw that I had a knack and respect for the trade. And as he got to know me and I grew to respect him, his plan of passing down the company to me one day became an opportunity I couldn't pass up. Nick never had kids or married, so he didn't have a child to pass the fruits of his labor to. The honor he bestowed on me is not one I take lightly, and today I'm fighting to keep his company and legacy alive, not only for him but also for myself.

Nick retired five years ago, so at the ripe age of twenty-nine, I became the owner of a multimillion-dollar company and the stress that came with it. But I guess it beats sulking over the life I had planned that never panned out.

Don't get me wrong. I like what I do. I'm good at it. Hell, when I was in the field, I'd run circles around the men who'd been building houses for years. I worked my way up from the bottom, proving myself at every level, from running my own crew to being a construction manager, project manager, and then area manager. Now, the company has offices in five cities and is a household name in Texas.

But this also isn't what I saw myself doing back when I graduated from high school. Nope. I had an entirely different vision of running my parents' ranch, marrying the love of my life, and raising a gaggle of kids.

Funny how plans can change overnight, yet those dreams still haunt us years later.

After the meeting is over, I settle back into my office to catch up on emails that I had to neglect for the past three hours. But I haven't gotten very far when my assistant, Jill, comes waltzing into the room holding her iPad.

"You got a minute?" she asks, never meeting my line of sight.

"Nope. All out of those."

My sarcasm makes her roll her eyes as she finally lifts her head up to make eye contact. "Funny."

"You know better than to ask me a question like that, Jill. Just say what you need to say."

Shaking her head, she looks back down at her screen and mumbles, "You're lucky you pay me well."

I huff out a laugh and direct my attention back to my emails. Shortly after hiring her, we both realized that she wasn't going to put up with my shit, but I couldn't survive without her. So she does the job I pay her very well for, and I continue to give her a hard time just to make sure she earns every penny. In all honesty, she's a ball-buster, and I couldn't run this company without her organization and attention to detail. She keeps my life and business running smoothly, and the guys who work for me know not to mess with her.

"I got confirmation from the convention in Vegas," she starts, catching me off guard. Just the mention of anywhere in Nevada always gets my heart rate up.

"And?"

"I booked your flight and hotel. I have you staying at the MGM Grand since the convention is in their conference center. I had to pay an arm and a leg for the room, though, as well as the rooms for the rest of the guys. Vegas isn't cheap, even with the convention discount."

"Don't worry. I'll throw twenty grand down on a table and get the rooms comped."

"I figured. Also, I rented you a car so you don't have to worry about using an Uber or a taxi to get around."

"Probably won't need it, but I appreciate the thought."

"You never know. I hate being stranded somewhere without wheels, so I took the liberty of giving you the option."

"Anything else?"

She scrolls down on her screen. "Nothing else that's super pressing at the moment. You have several meetings lined up for the rest of the week, though. I've added them to your calendar."

"Any that Javi can go to in my place?"

Her hands find her hips instantly. "As the owner, I think you should show up to a meeting with someone wanting to pay you over ten million dollars to build their house."

Smugly, I lean back in my chair and smirk up at her. "Yeah, probably should."

She spins to leave my office, and I waste no time getting back to my computer. These emails aren't going to write themselves, and time is money. Better make the most of it.

∾

"I'll let you have that one, fucker," I mumble against my mouthguard as Javi lands a punch on my jaw. The truth is that I'm so fucking tired and antsy right now that my concentration as we spar is shit.

"Don't make this easy on me, boss. At least try to land a punch."

"Don't forget who signs your paychecks."

"Believe me, I don't. But this is the perfect way to get revenge for having to put up with your grumpy ass."

It's Friday night, and there's nothing like a good workout to burn off the stress of the day at the end of the week. Javi's brother-in-law owns Elite Gym, and I've been a member since Javi started working for me. He teaches self-defense classes here as well a few nights a week. That's actually how he met his wife, Sydney.

The timer buzzes on the wall, signaling the end of our match. We both take off our head pieces and yank out our mouth guards.

"Good battle," I offer to him through labored breaths.

"Sure. We both know who the winner was, though." Javi smiles knowingly.

"My focus is shit, but next time, I'll be more prepared."

"You stressed about that Anderson job?"

The Anderson Corporation signed a fifty-million-dollar contract with us this week for their latest high-rise in Dallas. It's one of the biggest accounts we've landed yet, and I'd be lying if I said I wasn't stressed about it. But that's not the only source of my mental fog.

"That, among other things."

"What's going on?" Javi asks, trailing me as I head toward the locker room, eager to shower and move on with my evening. If I don't get out of here soon, I'll be late for my gig.

"Same shit, different day."

"No, you're grumpier than normal. Woman problems?" he teases as I strip off my tank top.

"Not exactly." I'm not one for talking about my feelings and shit, but this convention in Vegas is rattling me more than it should. Honestly, I don't know why I'm worried about going to Nevada. Las Vegas is huge, and the likelihood that I'll run into Shauna is slim to none. But just knowing I'll be in the same city as her has me fucking spinning. At least I think she's still in Vegas. Who the hell knows anymore? I don't have social media, and she's the main reason. I don't need any reminders of the woman I thought would be the one.

After we broke up, I tried like hell to push her out of my mind. I packed away all memories of her and tried to pretend she never existed. But the memories I keep in my head never stay locked in the file I made just for her. The most minute details will spark a moment from our past that has me searching for distraction at the bottom of a bottle of whiskey or against a punching bag. And since I can't drink tonight, I chose the punching bag.

Regret is a fickle fucking bitch, and lately, she and I feel like best goddamn friends, especially as I've watched both of my younger brothers fall in love and get married in the last year and a half. There are so many moments from my past with Shauna that keep knocking the wind out of me that I feel like I can't stand up straight before I'm tackled out of nowhere with three-hundred pounds of feelings. The thing is, I've been hit by a man that size, and even that doesn't compare to the elephant sitting on my chest and the ever-present reminder of her in my brain.

But this convention is such an important fucking networking opportunity. If I don't go, I'll kick myself. The area managers from our other offices around the state are attending, too, so it's vital that I go to build camaraderie and help expand the business across Texas and hopefully the country one day. I just need to keep my head focused on work and forget about the woman who broke my fucking heart into fragments that can never be pieced back together.

"Man, you don't have to hold it all in," Javi continues as I glare at him over my shoulder, huffing out a grunt. He holds his hands up. "I know. Talking about feelings and shit sucks, but the only time I've ever been as surly as you was when shit was going wrong with Sydney. I'm just saying, I'm here if you need to vent."

Sighing, I plop onto the bench in front of the lockers and rest my forearms on my thighs, letting my head hang. I guess if there's anyone I feel even remotely comfortable opening up to, it'd be him. "My ex lives in Vegas where the convention is next week."

"Ah. Well, that makes more sense. I take it things didn't end well between you two?"

The last conversation we had plays back through my head at that fucking moment, and suddenly, I feel the urge to hit something or someone again.

I'm sorry you came all this way . . . truly. But this is the end, Forrest. I'm not going back.

"Yeah, you could say that."

"Well, you know the chances of seeing her are about the same as finding a needle in a haystack, right? Vegas is full of fucking people, man."

"I'm aware. Still, it just has me on edge."

"I get it. How long since you two were together?"

"Sophomore year of college," I reply, thinking back to how long ago it was that we were happy and how fucking pathetic it is that I'm still letting that woman affect me. I've tried to move on, I have. But no one has compared to Shauna, and I'm beginning to think no one ever will.

"Damn. That's a long time."

"I know. But I thought she was the one. We made plans . . ."

"Most of us do with young love," Javi counters as he shrugs. "But life rarely works out that way."

"This wasn't naïve young love, man." I shake my head as the anxiety kicks in like it always does when the subject of Shauna comes up. I know Javi wanted to let me vent, but I just can't go there right now. So I do what I do every time—deflect and change the subject.

Standing from the bench, I turn back to my locker and grab my towel. "Doesn't matter, though. It's in the past."

"Sure as hell doesn't sound like it," Javi says behind me. My hackles rise, ready to argue with him, but I don't have any more time to jog down memory lane. The band is waiting on me to arrive, and no one else can fill in for me.

"Just drop it, Javi."

"Whatever you say, Forrest. Got any plans for the weekend?"

"Nothing worth sharing," I toss over my shoulder as I head for the shower. "Enjoy your time with the family."

"Oh, I will," he calls after me. "See ya Monday, boss."

"See ya then."

By the time I exit the shower, Javi is gone. I change into the outfit I brought with me and then head for my truck, firing up the engine while hoping that the traffic into Perryton doesn't make me late. But it's Friday night, and there's no way to predict the future, so I take off for the highway, hoping the forty-five-minute drive is peaceful, though thoughts of Shauna are still on my mind.

∼

Leland finishes up the last chorus of "Last Night" by Morgan Wallen, and the crowd goes nuts. This bar is packed as usual, and more and more regulars gather each time we play.

Joining this band was a saving grace for me once I moved back home after dropping out of Texas A&M. Leland and I crossed paths working for High Performance Construction, and when he asked if I was interested in starting a band, I figured I had nothing to lose. Now, Leland works for a different company, but we've kept in touch and play a few gigs here and there with our drummer, Max. These performances are one of the only things that keep me sane.

Playing the guitar gives me relief in the strangest way. I can't explain it. Even though we sing songs about love and finding the one, I don't listen to the words. The only thing my mind focuses on is the melody, and it's one of the only times my mind is truly empty of any thoughts.

"We're gonna take a small break, and then we'll be back for our final set of the night," Leland announces into the microphone, and the crowd applauds. As soon as they stop, he turns to me and bends down so he doesn't have to yell. "You want something to drink?"

"Just water. Got a long drive later."

He nods. "Be right back then."

I watch him walk toward the bar, shaking hands with a few patrons as he ambles through the crowd. But then a voice behind me pulls my attention from him.

"Hey, there."

I twist my head over my shoulder and come face-to-face with a blonde smiling up at me from the bottom of the stage. "Hey."

"Nice job tonight," she says, her voice sultry and her eyes full of innuendo. I watch them pass all over my body, but the heat of her gaze does nothing for me. Truth be told, it's been a long time since I've indulged in a little flirtation or taken a woman up on her offer for sex, but sadly, even this beautiful woman isn't intriguing me enough to break that dry spell.

"Thanks," I simply reply.

"What's your name?" she asks, leaning forward now to give me a clear view down the front of her blouse, which isn't necessary since her entire chest is on display.

"Forrest. How about you?"

"Tina."

I reach across the space between us and extend my hand. "Nice to meet you, Tina."

"Likewise, Forrest. You aren't from around here, are you?"

"Nope."

"I knew it because I *know* I would have remembered you," she purrs suggestively.

"You think so?" I egg her on, enjoying the attention even though I have no intention to act on it. But hell, what's the harm in flirting? It has been a while, and it's not like I have anything else to do at the moment besides maybe take a piss.

"Oh, I know so. A man like you looks like he knows his way around a woman's body."

"How do you figure?" I lean forward on my thighs, still perched on my stool.

She draws a finger along her collarbone and tilts her head. "Any man who can play an instrument tends to be good with his hands. He understands the intricacies of touch—how to apply just the right amount of pressure, how to twist his fingers so he can hit the perfect note." She licks her lips now, and I'm not gonna lie, just listening to her suggestive words is making me more intrigued by the minute.

Unfortunately, my phone buzzes in my pocket right at that moment. I pull it out of my jeans and see Wyatt calling. "Fuck. I need to take this," I say, watching Tina's face fall in disappointment. The woman was doing a damn good job of reeling me in, but I know deep down I probably still wouldn't have taken her up on her offer.

"No problem." She places her hand on my thigh and gives it a squeeze then begins to retreat with backward steps. "Have a nice night, Forrest."

"You too."

Standing from my stool, I seek out a quieter part of the bar, dipping behind the stage where only murmurs out front can be heard. I swipe across the screen and answer, plugging my open ear with my finger. "What's up?"

"Forrest?" Wyatt speaks. "Where are you? Why's it so loud?"

"I'm just out. What do you need, Wyatt?"

"Jesus. Cranky, much? Did I interrupt you getting laid?"

The prospect of it, anyway. "No, fucker. But I can't talk for long. So speak."

"Calm down, Grumpy Gibson," he says, using that unfortunate nickname my brothers gave me when I returned home from college right after I threw one last Hail Mary trying to fix things with Shauna. "I'm at the brewery, and one of my back-of-the-house guys put a fucking hole in my drywall today. Plus, I have an expansion question for you."

"So you're calling me at ten o'clock at night to talk about it?"

"Like I said, I'm here and the night rush just died down, so I figured I'd let you know about it while it's fresh on my mind."

Pinching the bridge of my nose, I reply, "I can send someone out on Monday to fix the drywall, but the expansion question might have to wait until next week. I leave for Vegas on Thursday."

"Oh, shit, that's right. That convention you mentioned?"

"Yup. And I have a mountain of shit to take care of before I leave." Leland comes around the corner, snapping his fingers at me to get my attention, motioning for me to follow him. Guess our break's over. "Listen, I have to go. Call Jill, and she can put you on the calendar."

"The little brother gets handed off to the assistant. I see how it is."

"Yup, that's exactly how it is."

"Fine. Just do me a favor when you're out in Vegas next week, will ya?"

"What's that?"

"Get laid, Forrest."

"Hanging up now!" I shout, shaking my head and then ending the call before he can reply.

"Everything all right?" Leland asks as I head back on stage.

"Yup, just my little brother, or as I like to refer to him, Pain-in-the-Ass Number Two. He's a twin and was born second, so the other one is Number One."

Leland laughs. "Only have a younger sister myself, but damn, they can be needy sometimes, can't they?"

"Just imagine how they are when they're together, doing their twin thing, and you might understand my constant headaches." I grab my guitar and place the strap over my head, situating it around my neck and shoulder before taking my seat again.

"Can't say I envy you, then."

"You shouldn't," I reply, even though I know that life wouldn't be the same without those two assholes. Our six-year age difference has come with its challenges through the years, but I'd take a bullet for them, no question. Now they're both married and living the life I thought I'd always have, so perhaps—though I'm not ready to admit it—a bit of resentment is there as well.

Whatever. Having a woman comes with its own set of problems, and at least I don't have to deal with that on top of the demands of my business.

I don't have much time to ponder that thought further, though, as Leland steps back up to the mic, Max and I give each other a head nod, ready to get back to business, and my fingers strum the first few chords of "Friends in Low Places" by Garth Brooks. And for the rest of the night, I push all of my responsibilities out of my mind and just focus on the music, hoping I can make it through the next week without wanting to punch one of my brothers—and praying this mounting anxiety in my chest over going to Vegas doesn't eat me alive.

∽

There's nothing quite like Las Vegas heat, temperatures so scorching hot that you can see heat waves coming off the asphalt. It's the beginning of September and just after nine in the morning, but apparently Vegas is experiencing record-high temperatures for this time of year—*lucky me*.

At this moment, I'm grateful Jill took the liberty of renting a car for me, because walking anywhere in this heat is a surefire way to pass out from dehydration.

As I drive along the strip, I cast my eyes down both sides of the road, taking in the sights.

It's been fourteen years since I've been here, and even back then, I wasn't here for work or pleasure—I was here to get my girl back, to try to fix us before we crumbled apart completely.

I think we all know how that went.

Still, on my way to UNLV to talk to Shauna, I had to drive down the strip. And in some ways, nothing has changed. In others, everything is different.

I shake off those thoughts—which is tough since just being in the same city brings up all of the shit that makes me even more anxious—and focus on driving, arriving at the MGM Grand ten minutes after nine.

The cold air of the casino blasts me as I walk in and head for the check-in counter. Once I've secured the key to my room, I hightail it up there, toss my bag inside, and then head for the first session of the day since there's less than an hour before the convention starts.

I should have had Jill fly me in last night. The rest of the area managers from my company are already here, so we gather by the door to the welcome session, pick a row of seats, and settle in for the next hour.

The rest of the day is spent in more meetings, but damn, I learn a lot. Even though my brain is fried by the end of day one, I'm glad I came. I've learned about so many ideas and projects I think can take my company to the next level, and we all share what we took in when I take my boys out to a nice steak dinner on night one. At the end of the second and final day, they invite me to go out and gamble, but I'm beat. I decide to have a few drinks by myself before I head up to my room to pass out.

I know that Wyatt suggested finding some female company, but I think I'm too tired to even get it up at this point, and the thought of putting that kind of energy into someone I don't care about makes the idea that much less appealing.

"What'll it be?" The bartender slides a cardboard coaster in front of me as I take a seat in one of the stools at the hotel bar. At least I know I don't have a long way to go when I'm through.

Convinced I need to treat myself, I reply with, "Macallan. Neat, please."

"You've got it," he replies, pouring a few fingers and setting it in front of me. But before I can even take a sip, the woman next to me speaks.

"The boy I remember wouldn't drink anything but Coors Light or Jack Daniels," she murmurs, and I don't even have to turn to the side to know who it is.

Goosebumps break out all over my arms, and my shoulders clench and tighten around my neck. As I close my eyes and take a deep breath, trying to steady my heartbeat, I wonder why I thought I could let my guard down, even for a minute.

I knew the chances were slim. Hell, I'd probably have a

better chance of winning the jackpot on a slot machine at this point than crossing paths with this woman.

But the universe knew it couldn't pass up the chance to make my past collide with my present. And as I twist in my seat and brace myself against seeing her again, I only know one thing for certain when her blue eyes meet mine and her long, dark waves cascade down around her face like an angel: Nothing could have prepared me for what it would feel like to come face-to-face with the woman who broke my heart. Especially when I see she's wearing a dress that's a mix of pinks, oranges, and greens—just like rainbow sherbet.

"Hi, Forrest. Long time, no see."

CHAPTER TWO

Shauna

"Hi, Forrest. Long time, no see."

Seriously? That's what you decide to lead with? Insert face palm here.

"Shauna," he says gruffly, clearing his throat and then continuing, "What are the odds?" He stands from his chair, towering over me just like he used to, before reaching out and pulling me into a hug.

I'm not going to lie, the gesture takes me by surprise. But perhaps he's running on pure adrenaline right now, like me.

God, he feels good—solid, strong, and familiar. We both

breathe each other in simultaneously, but I don't get much time to dwell on that before he releases me, sits down once more, and leans back in his chair. I take a moment to appreciate him even though my heart is hammering frantically in my chest.

Damn, time has been good to him. Honestly, seeing him here stole the breath from my lungs and momentarily made me question if I was dreaming. The last person I expected to encounter in this restaurant was the boy who first stole my heart and still holds a piece of it. Although Forrest is far from being a boy anymore. No, this boy grew up into a man, the brawny and muscular kind that only seems to get more attractive with age.

When I confirmed with my eyes what my heart already knew, I had to come over and say something. It's been so long since I saw him last, and I knew I would have regretted not at least saying hello—not that I hadn't done a little social media stalking here and there to keep tabs on him in between, which was complicated given that he doesn't have any profiles himself. However, his two brothers post the occasional picture of him, granting me glimpses of the man I left behind all those years ago, a decision that seems to be poking at me more and more lately.

But I can't even begin to unpack that right now.

God, what the hell is he doing all the way here in Vegas?

"The odds of winning a jackpot in this casino are

probably better," I toss back at him, appreciating the way the corner of his mouth tips up from my response.

"Funny. I was just thinking the same thing." He lifts his glass and takes a sip of his whiskey—his very *expensive* whiskey. Seems he's doing rather well for himself, or he's trying to make himself appear more affluent by ordering a drink he really can't afford. I seriously doubt it's the latter, though. Forrest never gave a shit what people thought about him. He was true to who he was—always.

"So why on earth are you here, and why did it result in us crossing paths?"

"I'm here for the convention at this hotel," he replies simply.

"Ah. I didn't know you were in construction." I saw the signs up around the lobby earlier today about the convention. I'm here to help prepare for the wedding I'm coordinating that's being held here next week, only a week before my own. The mental reminder has me slipping my ring off my left hand behind my back and depositing it into the pocket of my dress, hoping Forrest didn't see it already.

Thank God for dresses that have pockets.

But why are you removing your ring, Shauna? It shouldn't matter if he sees it or not because you are engaged. Remember?

Yes, but I can tell him later. Not now. Not while he's still smiling at me. It's been a long time since I've seen that smile.

Ignoring my subconscious, I focus back on what

Forrest just said. Construction? My brain starts spinning with all sorts of unanswered questions.

"There's a lot you don't know about me now." His eyes drop down to the stool I'm resting my now ringless left hand on the back of. "Are you gonna sit down? Or do you need to be somewhere?"

I glance down at the time on my cell phone in my other hand. Brock was supposed to be here ten minutes ago to meet me for dinner, but it seems he's forgotten how to send a text message letting me know he's going to be late—*again*.

I guess there's no harm in catching up with an old friend in the meantime, right?

"I can sit." Sliding onto the stool and resting my back against the cushion behind me, I keep my eyes locked on his, remembering how it felt to have that chocolate-brown gaze focused solely on me. God, it seems like a lifetime ago. "I still can't believe you're here," I huff out through a laugh.

He scoffs and then takes another drink. "Believe me, no one is more surprised than me. I told myself I'd never step foot in this city again after my last visit."

His words slice right through my heart. The last time he was here is not a memory I like to revisit. But it's hard not to remember that night as I stare back at him and notice the pinch in his brow as if he's traveling down memory lane as well.

"Has the convention been worth it, though?" I ask, trying to steer clear of the previous topic.

"Absolutely. I brought the top guys from the company out with me, too. It was definitely worth the trip."

"Are you in charge or something?" I tease him.

He tilts his head to the side, a proud smile spreading across his lips. "I own the company, Shauna. High Performance Construction is mine."

My brows nearly hit my hairline. "Oh my God, Forrest. That's amazing. I had no idea." And truly, I didn't. Wyatt and Walker never post about Forrest's personal life, and since I don't have any connections back in Newberry Springs anymore, I wasn't sure what he'd been doing for work or with his life in general. An ex isn't privy to that information, anyway.

"I guess I thought you'd be running the Gibson Ranch by now. I had no idea you were in construction."

"Yeah, well lots of things didn't work out the way we thought they would now, did they?"

My shoulders fall. "Forrest . . ."

He holds a hand up. "Don't. I'm sorry. I should be over it by now, right?"

"That *was* a long time ago," I whisper, the sting of tears hitting my eyes. A flood of feelings comes rushing through me, the force so powerful I feel like I have no control over it. The last time I saw him we were nineteen, yet somehow, it feels like it was yesterday. And in the past few months particularly, this man has been an ever-present memory that pops back up in my mind. Perhaps because I'm getting married and it's not to *him*, the man I thought I'd eventually walk down the aisle toward even though life took us away from each other.

"I guess you never left Vegas then, huh?" he asks, moving past the awkward moment as the well of *what ifs* in my mind keeps filling up the longer we stare at each other.

What if I had left with him that night he came here for me? What if I had gone back to Newberry Springs when I thought about it after graduation? Would he be the man I married like we always planned?

Where would we be right now?

"The company I interned with right out of college offered me a job I couldn't refuse. And well, there are plenty of events to plan in Vegas, you know," I answer, keeping our conversation in safe territory. That job was the main reason I stayed and told myself it was better to keep moving forward than traveling back to the past. My mother agreed wholeheartedly, of course, even though my reason for coming out to Vegas in the first place rattled our relationship.

Thankfully, we've moved past that for the most part.

"Event planning, huh?"

"Mostly weddings," I say, discretely rubbing my now naked ring finger with my thumb. I know I need to tell him eventually, but there's no need to bring that up just yet. "But I'm not open to planning anything from conventions to company parties. The possibilities of what someone will hire me to coordinate are endless, and I'm one of the top associates in my firm."

"You always were the type to get shit done," he says, staring at me wistfully. The scrutiny of his gaze reminds me how much he appreciated who I was when we were younger. I was student body president in high school before I moved, captain of the cheer team at Newberry Springs High School, and could run circles around him and his brothers on the ranch sometimes. Getting shit done was ingrained in my blood, and Forrest never tried to change me, but he also never asked me what *I* wanted out of my life, either.

I think that was part of our problem.

It took me moving a few states away to meet my father to show me how little I understood about how the world worked and how naïve I was about love and relationships. I was too young to know what I wanted back then, what could have been possible if I only spoke up—and now, it's too late to go back.

"Well, some things never change." I smile at him and watch him drain the rest of his whiskey.

"Refill?" the bartender asks just as he sets his empty glass down.

Forrest looks over at me, arching a brow. "That depends on if my friend here is going to have a drink as well."

God, I really shouldn't, but Brock hasn't even

messaged me yet. I have no idea how much longer he may be, and I'd hate to waste an opportunity to visit with Forrest. Even though every nerve ending of my body is on high alert right now, that inkling of playing with fire keeps growing.

Is it dangerous for me to sit here with the one man who set the bar for all others? Or does it not truly matter, anyway, because I'm engaged to someone else?

As if my thoughts conjured him up, my phone dings with a text from my fiancé.

Brock: *I'm so sorry, babe. This meeting is running long, but I've secured the contract with Fredrickson. I can't wait to celebrate with you, but don't wait on me to eat. I'll be there as soon as I can. Love you.*

Guilt hits me like a wave, but Forrest's voice pulls me out from under the tide instantly. "Do you need to go?"

When I lift my head, our eyes meet, and my gut tells me what my brain has already decided. "Nope. Looks like I have time for that drink after all." His smirk is borderline lethal as I watch his eyes dip down my body. Goosebumps scatter all over my skin as the heat of his gaze reminds me what it was like to have that stare directed at me. And when his eyes land back on mine, I get the feeling that Forrest approves of how much I've grown up.

You shouldn't care what your ex thinks about how you look, Shauna.

"I'll have what he's having," I tell the bartender, much

to both of their surprise. "You're the one buying, right?" I cast a challenging look at the man sitting next to me.

Forrest dips his chin once. "Of course."

"Then I might as well see what kind of whiskey good money can buy."

The truth is that both my fiancé and I could afford this whiskey as well, but I've never chosen whiskey as my drink around Brock. I'm not sure why that is. But far too many memories of taking shots of Jack Daniels with the boy in front of me remind me that you can take the girl out of the country, but you can't take the country out of the girl.

Seems tonight I'm going back for a little reminder of my roots—and a reminder that sometimes those roots are still buried in the ground beneath us for a reason, waiting to reveal themselves until we least expect them to.

∽

"That was all your fault!" I shout, stifling my laughter behind my hand.

"Nope. That was all you, woman. You knew Mrs. Williams's schedule and told me it would be safe!"

"How was I supposed to know she'd come home early from work that day due to the stomach flu? Normally, that woman was a creature of habit. You're the one who crawled out of the window that faces her house!"

"That was the only window that wasn't locked! I didn't have any other choice!"

Holding my stomach from laughing so hard, I forget that we're in a crowded restaurant and just bask in the familiarity of talking to this man again. Forrest and I have been reminiscing for the past hour and a half, grabbing a table and eating dinner in between since I was starving, and the stories just keep getting wilder and wilder.

We recalled all the nights we'd sit down and watch movies with Walker and Wyatt while we made out on the couch behind them.

We recounted horseback riding together on his parents' ranch.

Forrest brought up playing football and how he had to do extra drills after he was late to practice—shocker, I was the one who made him late.

But our latest trip down memory lane was the time my neighbor, Mrs. Williams, caught Forrest sneaking out of my bedroom window after we snuck over to my house after school to have sex. Football season had just ended, so he didn't have practice right after school for the first time in months. And after only being able to sneak away to the shack on his parents' property to partake in a few shared orgasms, we were both eager to take full advantage of my bed.

Unfortunately, my neighbor came home early that day from work and ratted us out to my mom.

"I'm convinced that's why your mother didn't like me. She knew I deflowered her little girl."

"It wouldn't have mattered if it were you or any other boy, Forrest. She didn't want me to follow in her footsteps." Falling for my high school sweetheart would have ended my life, according to her, since her own young romance didn't work out. Unfortunately, years down the road, we both realized how wrong we'd been about my father.

And now I'm set to marry a man she adores, a man who supports me in a career and life that I'm proud of. But something about sitting here with Forrest right now has me questioning all of that.

"How is your mom?" he asks, avoiding pushing me to answer the question I'm sure he's asking himself as well: *Would we still be together if I hadn't left?*

"She's good. Remarried about ten years ago to a man named Frank. He adores her."

"Is she still in Newberry Springs?"

I'm surprised he doesn't know the answer to that, but perhaps he's chosen to completely ignore my existence since I left and denied his offer of reconciliation, unlike me, who's been keeping tabs on him the best I could.

"Nope. She actually lives in North Las Vegas. She moved out here during the summer between my sophomore and junior year since she didn't want to live in a different state than me anymore. And then when I realized I was staying here after college, she decided to put down some roots here herself and escape that small-town life. We just both decided to stay, even after my dad died."

He stares down into his whiskey, deep in contemplation. And I hate that I can't read him as well as I used to.

There are a million thoughts that could be going through his head, and as much as I know our time together will come to an end eventually, I'm not ready for it to just yet.

"I'm sorry about your dad," he finally mutters. And as painful as it is to be reminded of how my father's presence played a role in our relationship, it means a lot to hear him say that.

"Thank you." I hold back my tears because the last thing I want to do is take a trip down that memory lane. "How are your parents?" I ask instead, steering the attention back to him.

Forrest huffs out a laugh, shaking his head and leaning back further in his chair, spreading his legs even wider. I have to fight the urge to stare down at the bulge in his jeans because I remember distinctly how big he is, and his entire body is even bigger now—his arms, his laugh, his presence.

God, he still makes my body come alive.

"They're good. The ranch is booming. Mom's dream has surpassed what anyone could have imagined it could become. Dad had a health scare almost two years ago, but he's good as new. And now they're enjoying being grandparents, even though the thought of Walker with a kid still boggles my mind."

I nearly spit my drink all over the floor. "Walker has a kid?"

Forrest shakes his head. "Yup. He's married, too. The kid is Schmitty's, actually. He, uh . . . John passed away at the end of last year while Evelyn was pregnant with his kid, and then Walker and Evelyn fell in love and got hitched without telling anyone. Crazy fucker. Momma was pissed."

"Oh, I bet. Momma G loves her boys." I think back to the love I could feel pouring off that woman by just being in the same room as her, and it instantly makes my heart ache. "What about Wyatt?"

"Wyatt and Kelsea are married now, actually," he explains, the same tone of shock laced through his words.

"Why do you sound so surprised by that? They always were inseparable. Honestly, they were the only two people who probably couldn't see that they loved each other."

"It's not that," he says, his eyes darting off to the side.

"Then what is it?"

"It's that both of my younger brothers are already married. I don't understand what the fucking rush is."

Nerves race through me. There once was a time when he was in a rush to do the same with me. "How about that they're in love?"

"Are you in love with anyone, Shauna?" he asks,

avoiding my question with his own, his voice low as he leans forward in his chair, clutching his whiskey between his hands. A lump lodges itself in my throat as he reaches out with one of his hands and strokes his fingers down my cheek. "Fuck. You're even more gorgeous than before. How is that possible?"

Now's when you tell him that you're engaged, Shauna. Now is when you admit that you agreed to marry another man.

"Forrest..."

"Tell me I'm not the only one who still feels this thing between us," he grits out, framing my face with his hand now, inching even closer to me.

"I..."

Speak up, Shauna.

But I don't say a word as my body starts falling forward, closer to Forrest, so close that I can see every fleck of gold in his otherwise brown eyes. Our eyes bounce back and forth, my pulse is lightning fast, and when his eyes dip to my lips, I brace myself for the feeling of his mouth on mine again.

No, don't lean forward, you nincompoop! What are you doing? Remember Brock? Your fiancé?

"There you are."

Someone could have just thrown a bucket of water on me with the way I shoot up in my chair, nearly falling over and colliding my head with Forrest's. But Brock, *my fiancé*, reaches out to steady me so I don't fall.

"Uh, hi!" I say, far too enthusiastically. I feel Forrest

move back in his chair, but I don't dare turn my attention to him at this moment.

Brock leans forward, wraps an arm around my waist, and plants a possessive kiss on my lips. It's sweet, but I don't angle into it like I should—kinda hard to when my ex is sitting in the chair to my right, watching the whole thing unfold.

When we part, Brock stares down at me and then flicks his eyes over to Forrest, straightening his spine when he sees the man I was just speaking to. Slowly, I face him as well, and if looks could kill, Forrest would be shooting literal daggers at the man holding me to his chest.

"Hello, there. I'm Brock, Shauna's fiancé." Brock reaches his hand out to shake Forrest's, and begrudgingly, Forrest complies. But not before shooting me a look that makes me want to curl up in a ball.

Fuck. This is not how I wanted him to find out.

"And you are?" Brock continues, glancing between Forrest and me now.

Forrest rises from his chair, standing eye to eye with my fiancé. "Forrest Gibson. I'm an old friend of Shauna's in town on business. We crossed paths and were just catching up."

His voice sounds calm, but I can read his body just as well as I used to. Forrest is pissed, but he's doing a pretty good job of staying composed. I'm surprised, honestly, because the man I knew had a temper that sometimes would get the best of him.

"Oh. How fortunate. Well, thank you for keeping my fiancé company," Brock says, reaching down for my left hand to kiss the top of it. But his brow scrunches when he sees my naked finger. "Shauna, where's your ring?"

"Oh. I, uh . . . took it off earlier when I washed my hands in the restroom and forgot to put it back on," I stutter, reaching into the pocket of my dress and sliding my ring back on the appropriate finger. I can feel Forrest slicing through me with his eyes, but I don't dare look at him right now.

"We need to get it properly sized," Brock explains. "It keeps sliding off, and she's afraid she's going to lose it."

"Right," Forrest chokes out. His jaw is so tight, he looks like he might crack a tooth. And his nostrils are flaring as he tries to breathe and remain calm.

Luckily, Brock's phone rings at that moment, breaking through the tension. "Crap. I have to answer this," he tells me. "I promise, I'll be five minutes, and then we can go."

"Okay. I'll just say goodbye to Forrest, then."

He kisses my cheek and then looks at Forrest. "Nice to meet you. Thanks for keeping her company. Work never stops, am I right?" he jokes, wiggling his phone in the air and then answering the call as he walks away from the crowded bar area.

Nervously, I turn to Forrest now.

"You're engaged?" he asks, his face still stoic.

"I was going to tell you . . ."

"When? After I kissed you?" he hisses, keeping his voice down, thank God.

"I'm sorry. I should have told you earlier, but—"

"I thought—" He shakes his head, sliding his jaw back and forth. "Forget it."

"Forrest . . ." I reach out to him, but he takes a step back.

"Does your mom like your fiancé?" he asks as his eyes flicker down to my ring.

My stomach bottoms out. It was only a matter of time before one of us brought it up. Forrest was always convinced my mother hated him and that's why we're not together. If only he understood that her issues with him were more about her. But I answer him, anyway. "She does."

"Even though he stood you up for dinner?" He flicks his eyes up to mine.

"Brock got caught up in a meeting," I reply, hating how it feels to discuss the man I'm about to marry with the one I used to picture waiting at the altar. "He let me know he wouldn't make it."

"Jesus, I can't fucking believe I'm standing here right now," he says, running his hand through his hair, looking around the bar. "Guess I was stupid to think we'd ever have a shot again, huh?" He follows up his last question with one that changes the entire tone of the conversation.

"You weren't stupid, Forrest. I just think we were naïve," I say, spinning my ring around my finger without looking at it. "And young. We were *so* young. And life happened—"

"I knew what I wanted, Shauna . . . what I *still* wonder about." He tips his chin toward my left hand, my pulse getting faster with each passing second. "Are you happy?"

Staring down at my ring now, I twist it back into place so the diamond faces up. "I am . . ."

"That didn't sound very convincing."

I slowly lift my eyes to meet his, reluctant to see the challenge in his gaze. My heart hammers as I try to persuade him when I say, "I don't need to convince you of anything."

He scoffs and drains the rest of his glass, slamming it down on the bar. "You're right. You don't." I watch him dig into the back pocket of his jeans, extracting his wallet and pulling out a wad of cash before slapping it on the bar, and signal to the bartender that he's ready to pay his tab.

"Forrest . . ." I almost reach out to him, but I stop myself before I get too close. His entire body is tense, and suddenly I'm regretting coming over here in the first place.

I thought it would be nice to catch up, to prove that we've both moved on and could act like civilized adults even though both of us own a piece of the other's heart, and deep down, I know that fact may never change.

But I also withheld an important piece of information from him all those years ago, shattering what was left of us by the time I came clean, and now I'm responsible for hurting this man yet again.

"When's the big day?" he asks, never meeting my eyes.

Reluctantly, I say, "In two weeks. On the fourteenth." But the sting of tears in my eyes follows my reply.

"Jesus," he mutters.

"Forrest..."

"Don't, Shauna," he says through clenched teeth as I retract my hand. "I-I gotta go."

"I'm glad we got to catch up," I offer, trying to end things on good terms.

"Yeah. It was... eye-opening."

"I'm proud of you," I tell him. "I always knew you'd be successful, even after your injury. You should be proud."

That was the injury that prompted him to drop out of college because he couldn't play football anymore, the one that pushed him to fly to Las Vegas just a week later and ask me to go back to Texas with him.

"I didn't really have a choice, did I? This isn't the life I envisioned for myself, but it's the one I have now, and I *am* proud. I've worked my ass off to make something of myself. I just hope you're happy in your life, too." He darts his eyes down to my ring once again and stares at it. "Just for the record, I never would have kept you waiting." And with one final lift of the corner of his mouth, giving me just a glimpse of a smile that could only be described as sad, he turns and stalks toward the exit, and once again, I'm left watching him walk away.

Only this time, the overwhelming urge to go after him is even stronger than before.

∽

Age Nineteen

"So What" by Pink blasts through my iPod dock as I chew on the end of my pen cap and stare at the same page I've been reading for the past ten minutes. This psychology class is kicking my butt, but I've been studying for the past two hours, and I think my brain is finally fried. I'm never going to make the material stick like this, so I might as well take a break and try one last cram session in the morning.

I glance over at the clock and see it's after ten. I never ate dinner, and my stomach decides to grumble at just that moment, signaling that it's time for food.

I hop off my bed in my studio apartment and take three steps, crossing over into my kitchen just as a knock sounds at my door. My best friend since last year, Willow, said she might stop over tonight since I ditched her for my textbooks. But when I open the door, nothing could have prepared me for the person standing on the other side.

Dressed in dark denim jeans and a plain white tee, his hair in utter disarray, is Forrest. But he's supposed to be back in Texas—not here.

"Shauna," he breathes out, clearly distressed with bags under his eyes. He looks like he hasn't slept in days.

"Forrest? What the hell are you doing here?"

"I had to come see you. I can't . . . I can't do this anymore."

He and I haven't spoken in a few days, but he wasn't set to come out to Vegas for another three weeks. So why on earth is he here now?

"Is everything okay? Did something happen?" I hold the door open further for him, and he rushes inside, yanking on his hair and breathing heavily. He honestly looks like he's about to have a panic attack or try to climb the walls.

"Yes, something happened," he finally replies, standing tall now and looking me dead in the eye. "I left Texas A&M."

My stomach drops. "What? Why?"

"I got injured. I can't play football anymore, so I said fuck classes. I don't need a degree. But you know what? I don't even care about school anymore. I don't care about any of that because the only thing that has mattered and will ever matter in my life is you."

My mouth falls open. "Forrest . . ." I bring my hands together, placing them in front of my lips as my body threatens to collapse.

He shouldn't be here. I can't do this again. Saying goodbye to him the first time was hard enough, but things have changed even more now. My dad's health has taken a turn. My mother is set to come out here in a few days so I can tell her everything.

I can't have Forrest here, too. It's just too much.

"I'm miserable without you, Shauna." He closes the distance between us, standing right before me now but not touching me. I feel locked in place by the intensity of his eyes, and I can't look away as the reality of him being here hasn't registered yet. "I know you ultimately came here because of your scholarship, and you assured me that long distance wouldn't be that big of a deal, but I know what *I* want. I've always known. It's you. I want you to come home with me."

Sighing, I drop my hands and take a step back, needing space between us again. His showing up like this is throwing me for a loop worse than my psychology textbook was just moments ago. "Forrest, I'm not sure what you thought was going to happen with you coming here, but nothing has changed for me. I'm a year and a half into my degree. If I leave now, I have to pay back the scholarship money, and . . . I've made a life here."

He winces like he just got stabbed in the ribs. "How has nothing changed? I feel like everything has. What about our life together? The plans that we made? I *love* you, Shauna. I've been a mess without you. Nothing matters if I don't have you next to me. Do you hear me?"

"And don't you think that's a problem, Forrest? That so much of your happiness is dependent on me?" I shout, throwing my hands in the air. I'm honored that he loves me, but sometimes it feels suffocating. He makes it hard for me to think rationally, and right now, my thoughts are on so many other things.

Perhaps that's unfair to him as well.

"No!" he yells back. "I think that means I love you and know that you are the woman I'm supposed to be with! Being apart is too hard!"

"I don't know what you want me to say. We're knee deep in the decisions we made a year and a half ago, Forrest. I can't just leave."

"Then what if I came here?" he asks, throwing me for a loop.

"What?"

Reaching for my hands, he clasps them between his own and lowers his voice. "What if I moved to Vegas? I can get a job, wait for you to finish your degree, and then we can move back together."

"I can't ask you to do that!"

"You're not asking, I'm offering. I'll stay, wait for you—"

"My dad has Parkinson's disease!" I shout loud enough for the whole building to hear. But it's out there, the secret I've been keeping from Forrest and my mother—the reason I'm not going anywhere.

Forrest's mouth drops open, and then his brows draw together. "What the hell are you talking about?"

"That's why I came out here, Forrest. My dad . . . he lives here now. I reconnected with him just before we graduated, and he wanted a chance to get to know me. He's not the man my mother painted him to be," I start, but Forrest's scowl is growing by the second.

"You've been talking to your dad . . . and you didn't tell me?" The hurt that laces his words is worse than I feared it would be. He drops my hands and then says, "Why? Why wouldn't you tell me something like that?"

"Because I didn't want you to feel like I chose him over you," I admit.

"But you did." He rears back. "Instead of being with me, you chose a man who left when you were three, a man who showed no interest in being a part of your life."

"But he did. My mother never told me, but he tried to reach out to her once he realized his mistakes." I shake my head as tears build. "I can't expect you to understand, Forrest, which is why I didn't tell you about it. But he didn't cheat on my mom like she said. He found out about his diagnosis and lied to her. He didn't want us to watch him deteriorate, to become a shadow of the man he was. But now he's deteriorating quickly, and . . . he has cancer."

Forrest blows out a breath and runs a hand through his hair. "I'm sorry, Shauna. I'm sorry that his health is so shitty. But I can't believe you lied to me, that you kept something like this from me." He points a finger at his chest. "I'm supposed to be the person you tell everything to. And instead of letting me be there for you, you pushed me away, lied, and moved hundreds of miles away from me without telling me the real reason why."

Tears fall freely down my cheeks now. I hate that I've hurt him, but it was inevitable. At least now he knows the truth. "I'm sorry, but I knew you'd follow me. You deserved to play football, to bask in what you earned. You deserved to stay close to your family. I wasn't about to take you away from that when I had no idea what was going to happen when I got out here."

He glares at me and then says, "Well, you took me away from it all, anyway." And then he follows up with "Does your mom know why you're here?"

"She's coming out here in a few days. I'm going to tell her everything then," I reply. "I'm mad at her, too, for keeping him from me. We . . . we have a lot of things to work out."

He nods, staring down at the floor. "Yeah, you do."

"And as hard as it is for me to say this, I need to focus on my family right now, Forrest. I want to know that I'm making the right decision for *my* life so I don't live with regrets and resentment. I love you, I still do. But I tried to tell you I needed this space, this time, and it seems to me like you still aren't listening."

"Because I'm aching, Shauna." His voice cracks as he pounds his chest with his fist. "My heart is fucking bleeding and broken, and you're the only one who can fix it."

Tears build in my eyes as I watch the boy I love break apart in front of me all over again. God, the last thing I wanted to do was hurt him, but I can't go back now. I have to keep moving forward, even if that means hurting us both.

"I'm sorry, Forrest," I say, the vision of him standing before me growing more fuzzy as tears fill my eyes and flow down my cheeks. "But I can't be the one to fix you, not when I'm broken right now, too. I have to focus on me, my dad and my mom, my family, what *I* want, what *I* need . . . and I need *you* to respect that."

"So what *do* you want, Shauna?" he asks desperately. "Just say the word, and I'll give it to you."

"That's the thing, Forrest," I whisper because I don't want this next part to hurt him even more. But he needs to hear it, and it's the truth. "I don't know yet, but I don't think that you're the person who can give that to me. It's unfair of me to ask you to."

He takes in a trembling breath, shaking his head from side to side. "So that's it?" His hands fly up in the air as a tear trails down his face.

"I'm sorry you came all this way . . . truly." I clasp my hands over my heart. "But this is the end, Forrest. I'm not going back."

"Fuck!" he shouts, staring up at the ceiling, yanking on his hair again. "God, I can't fucking do this," he mumbles now as I stand there, wondering if he's truly going to be okay. I hate that I've caused him pain, but I have to stay strong. I don't want to resent him down the line. I don't want to resent myself.

"Are you going to be okay?"

His eyes slice right through me as he brushes away another tear. "I guess I don't have a fucking choice, do I?" He stalks toward the door, and my heart lurches like I want to go after him. The tug of war going on between my heart and my head right now is giving me whiplash.

I love this man. Ever since he looked at me that first day, I knew he'd own a piece of my heart. And he still does. But right now I need to own the rest. I need to find out who I am and what I want without worrying about his feelings as well.

And I refuse to sacrifice this time with my dad when every moment is precious.

"I'm sorry, Forrest."

"Yeah, me, too, Shauna. I'm sorry you felt like you had to choose . . . because I never would have asked you to," he says, yanking the door open and slamming it shut behind him as I drop to my knees and begin to sob—because I want to go after him, but I can't.

I hope one day he can learn to forgive me for giving us what we both need: a chance to live without me being the center of his universe and him being the center of mine. Even if mine doesn't feel like it's spinning anymore.

CHAPTER THREE

Forrest

Present Day, Two Weeks Later

"Stupid fucking desk!" My voice echoes off the walls of my office as I shove the hunk of wood out of my way after stubbing my toe on it for the third time today.

"Do I need to put you in a timeout?" Jill asks from behind me. I close my eyes, take in a few deep breaths, and then slowly twist to face her.

"Yes. I need a timeout from work, life, and my mind. Can you do that for me?"

"I mean . . . it might cost you," she teases, winking at me for good measure.

"Name it, and it's yours." I cast my arms out to the sides, wishing that this woman really could shut off my brain for me right now. There's not a price I wouldn't pay for some mental peace, but sadly, I know no one else can fix my thoughts but me.

"What's going on, Forrest? You've been on edge all week." She moves like she's going to shut the door behind her, but then my phone rings.

"Fuck." I stare down at the screen, watching Walker's name flash across it. He rarely calls me because he knows I end up hanging up on him half the time, but he's had a rough few weeks, so who knows what he might need right now. And hey, maybe he has some job for me that will be just the distraction I need to keep my mind off the fact that Shauna is getting married this weekend. "I've got to take this, Jill."

"Okay. But if you want to leave early, I can cover for you. You don't have any more meetings today, either. Maybe hit the gym and take your shitty mood out on a punching bag, yeah?" she suggests.

"I'm giving you a raise." I call out to her. She gives me a thumbs up over her shoulder as she walks out of my office, and then I answer Walker's call before it stops ringing and I have to call him back. "What's up?"

"Hey. You busy?"

"Not really. I was actually planning on getting out of here early."

"You? Leave work early? Are you running a fever?"

"Fuck off. Now I suggest you tell me why you called before I hang up on you."

His laugh filters through the line. "Easy, big brother. Take a chill pill." I roll my eyes. "I was just calling to remind you about dinner tomorrow at the ranch. John's parents are coming by for their first visitation with Kaydence, and Mom wants to make sure the whole family is there."

I pinch the bridge of my nose. Fuck. The last thing I want to do is put on a face in front of people. My anger is practically wafting off of me right now. I'm not in the right headspace to smile and pretend like everything is fucking okay. But after the custody battle Walker and Evelyn have been through with Schmitty's parents, I know he needs everyone there to support them.

Jesus, why did my brothers have to go and get married and become all domesticated and shit?

Shauna's words from our reunion in Vegas ring out in my mind at that moment. *Maybe they're in love...*

Shit. Like I needed another reminder of her, let alone one in which she's absolutely right. Hell, before she and I broke up, I was exactly how my brothers are now—obsessed with the woman who let me call her mine.

But now she's about to be someone else's.

"Hello? Forrest? Did you have a coronary embolism over there? Or did you finally take a vow of silence?"

"Shut up, fuckface. I'll be there." Begrudgingly, but I'll go because that's what I've signed up for.

"Are you gonna pull the stick out of your ass before you show up?"

"Nope. I'm gonna leave it there and ask you to pull it out for me."

"Hate to inform you, but I wouldn't touch your ass with a ten-foot pole, even if you're my brother."

"Good to know."

"Dinner is at six, but Mom wants everyone there by four."

"Fine."

"Nice talk. I can feel all the love through the phone," he snipes back, sighing. "Just don't forget, please."

"I won't, Walker. I'll be there."

"Thanks. See you tomorrow."

When we hang up, I shove my phone in my pocket, grab my keys, and race out of the office like my ass is on fire. I know Jill suggested taking out my aggression on a punching bag, but I'm pretty sure my good friend, Jack Daniels, will offer an even better type of reprieve from my anguish, which is what I need right now—numbness and the ability to stop thinking.

So I stop at my favorite watering hole on the edge of town, The Tipsy Cow, and drown my feelings in a few glasses of whiskey—and by a few, I mean enough to not remember how the fuck I got home that night.

∼

"Dumbass." Groaning, I drain the last part of the Gatorade I picked up at the gas station on the way to my parents' ranch and toss the empty bottle on the floorboard as I curse myself.

Nothing like a little self-loathing to make me feel better about myself.

Jack Daniels reminded me last night that although he likes to help me forget, he also doesn't leave my system until a day or two after our rendezvous, and right now, I desperately want to go back to bed and sleep the rest of this hangover off.

Morty, one of the bartenders, apparently called me an Uber to take me home last night since I was way beyond able to drive, so I had to take one back this morning to pick up my truck from the parking lot. Even after a shower and some greasy food, I can still smell the alcohol coming out of my pores, but it's too late to do anything about it now. Though I'm not sure the smell I'm picking up is the remnants of my hangover or my pathetic desperation.

After I woke up this morning, I made the idiotic mistake of creating a Facebook profile to stalk my ex. I went fifteen years without doing such a thing, but knowing that she's getting married tomorrow is fucking with my head. I wanted to see if she's shared the impending nuptials with the world. Honestly, I don't know how any other social media bullshit works because I never got into any of that. I knew if I did, I'd be tempted to keep tabs on her, and I didn't want that temptation—even though I know that avoiding stalking her online never kept her from ruling my mind.

I couldn't see much since her profile is private, whatever the fuck that means. But she had some information on her page about where she works, so I started my detective work there. Shauna has been working at Ember & Stone Events for the past five years as one of their top-tier wedding planners. Her bio on their website boasted about her accomplishments, but that was all I could gather from there.

Her profile picture on Facebook, though, was of her and her fiancé, *Brock*. What a fucking douchebag. I wouldn't have believed she was engaged to the man if I hadn't met him myself. They were at some company picnic in the photo, which I figured out from the banner in the background of the picture, and her face was red from crying, I'm assuming. She was holding her hand out to the camera, showing off her ring.

I wonder if that's where he fucking proposed to her, at his company picnic.

Dickhead.

The Shauna I knew would have hated a fucking public

proposal. Even though she was the center of attention in high school because of everything she was involved in, the girl I grew up with loved meaningful moments and privacy when it came to showing her emotions. She loved being alone and free from people's scrutiny and keeping the people close to her in her own little bubble.

She pushed you out of that bubble, though, didn't she?

Perhaps that's why she left me to begin with—because she didn't need me in her life to be whole. That woman was the entire sun on her own in my world, but I guess I wasn't the same for her.

She's fucking marrying someone else.

When I walk through the front door of the ranch, I open it so forcefully that the screen slams against the outside of the house, startling everyone as I enter the living room.

I should feel bad, but I'm here and I don't want to be, so everyone is gonna get me in all of my grumpy glory today.

I notice Evelyn looking through a photo album while sitting on the couch, Walker balancing himself on the arm of it right next to her. John's mom is holding Kaydence on the cushioned chair to their right, smiling from ear to ear, bouncing the child up and down. And I don't blame her. That little girl is really fucking cute.

I bet mine and Shauna's kids would have been adorable, too.

"Jesus. You're going to scare Kaydence," Walker chastises me as I trod across the carpet like a hunchback who just came out of his cave. Kaydence's lip trembles as she fights off her desire to cry, but luckily, Margaret soothes her and prevents her from letting a wail out.

So much for favorite uncle status.

Walker's eyes trail me as I stomp along. I'm sure I look like a Neanderthal, but at this moment, I just don't give a fuck.

"Sorry," I mutter, heading for the fridge to grab a beer. Alcohol is the last thing I want right now, but perhaps a little hair of the dog will make my body feel better and help me get through the evening being surrounded by happy couples. I don't say anything to anyone in the house before opening the back door and heading toward the barn, just wanting to be alone.

I mean, at least I showed up like I said I would, right?

Arriving at the horse pen, I lean against the metal, resting my arms over the top rung and holding my beer between my hands, enjoying the silence. I'm only going to stay for dinner, and then I'm out of here.

Hyacinth, one of our most intelligent mares, walks over to me as soon as she becomes aware of my presence. But I don't get a chance to give her any attention before my twin brothers come waltzing over, determination etched into their faces.

Fuck. Here we go.

"This can either go great or horribly wrong," Wyatt mutters as they get closer to me.

"I agree, but I'm fucking tired of his surly ass. He's pissed about something, and it's time he fucking talks."

"Agreed."

As soon as they reach me, Wyatt and Walker take a spot on each side of me, flanking me and caging me in.

"All right, Grumpy Gibson," Wyatt starts, pissing me off even further with that stupid nickname. The thing is, these two have no idea what it's like to lose what I did.

"Fuck off, Wyatt."

"No can do, big brother. Enough is enough." Wyatt crosses his arms over his chest, facing me dead-on now. "What the fuck is going on with you? You've been an asshole more than normal since you got back from Vegas, and you're scaring everyone."

"You frightened my kid," Walker adds. "I'm not gonna pretend like that's okay."

Fury begins to race through me. Growling, I drain my beer and toss the bottle into one of the cans stationed next to the horse pen. "I don't have to tell you two anything."

Walker shoves me, which catches me off guard. I bounce into Wyatt's chest behind me, which thankfully he's prepared for, but all it does is piss me off even more. I feel like a human ping pong ball, and I'm not in the fucking mood for this shit.

Once the initial shock has worn off, I shove Walker back, knocking him off-balance this time. But then he swings at me, which I luckily dodge before trying to return the favor. This isn't the first time one of my brothers and I have come to blows, but maybe that's what I need right now, to let out this anger on someone else. Maybe that will make me feel better.

My fist grazes his cheek when I swing back, sparking Walker's fight response. I don't have time to prepare before he bends low, rushes me, and tackles me to the ground, the loud crack of my ass hitting the dirt echoing out around us.

"Am I supposed to just stand by and let this happen?" Wyatt asks as Walker and I wrestle on the ground. Normally, this would be no contest. I have about thirty more pounds of muscle than both of my brothers. But with the hangover currently taking over my body, I don't have as much strength to fight back.

Walker ends up on top of me, pinning me beneath him as we both struggle to breathe.

"That depends on when Forrest starts talking," Walker says, holding my arms down.

"Get the fuck off me, Walker!"

"Not until you tell us what the fuck is going on!"

"Shauna is getting married tomorrow!" I finally scream, catching both of my brothers off guard. But fuck. I can't hold this in anymore. I don't have any fight left in me to take my anger out on my brother. And bottom line —he doesn't fucking deserve it.

"So you *did* see her in Vegas?" Wyatt asks to clarify, and part of me wonders if he found out from Javi or someone else. But in all honesty, it really doesn't fucking matter at this point. The truth is, that trip fucked me up beyond reason, and I'm drowning while trying to recover.

"Yes, and it was . . ." I close my eyes, huffing out air through my nose. "She's still . . ."

". . . the love of your life," Walker finishes for me.

All I can do is nod with my eyes still closed.

"What did she say when you saw each other?" Walker asks, still holding me to the ground.

I breathe in deeply before finally opening my eyes again. "She hugged me, said it was good to see me. We shared an entire meal and several drinks, and I swear I was sixteen falling in love with her all over again." Not wanting to continue this conversation on my back, I shove Walker off, and he doesn't push to keep fighting. Now, we're both sitting on the ground, our asses covered in dirt as Wyatt hovers over us with his arms crossed over his chest.

Walker pushes me to keep going. "So then . . ."

"I went to kiss her, just wanting one more taste of her, and that's when her fiancé showed up. She wasn't wearing a ring, so I didn't know."

"Fuck," Wyatt mutters, staring off into the distance. "So she's getting married tomorrow?"

"Yeah." I hang my head, trying to hold back my tears. Jeez, I don't want to cry. "She's going to be someone else's wife—"

"Not if you stop her from marrying him," Walker says, cutting me off.

I snap my head over to him, my heart hammering at his suggestion. "What?"

"Well, she's not married yet, right? Haven't you ever seen the episode of *Friends* where Rachel decides to crash Ross's wedding? I believe her words were, 'it's not over until somebody says I do.'"

"What the fuck are you saying?" *He's joking, right?*

"He's saying you go fight for her. You don't let her go without telling her that you're still in love with her," Wyatt clarifies for me.

"I can't fucking do that."

"Why not?" Walker shoves my shoulder again, but this time, I just glare at him instead of shoving him back. "If it were Evelyn, I'd be there on my fucking knees, begging her to see reason, to remember how good we were together."

"If it were Kelsea, I'd tattoo her name on my ass and drop my pants in front of her to show her that she's branded on me forever."

Walker rolls his eyes, laughing at Wyatt. "That actually sounds like something I would do, asshat."

"Well, we both already have tattoos for our girls, so . . ." Wyatt shrugs. "Point made."

"You two have fucking tattoos for Kelsea and Evelyn?" I ask, glancing between the two of them. How the hell did I never know this?

"Yup." Walker lifts up his shirt and shows off the moon and owl on his pec.

"I got mine before Kelsea and I were ever together," Wyatt says as he lifts his shirt and shows me the camera he has on his ribs for Kelsea.

"Jesus," I mutter while realizing that perhaps my brothers and I have far more in common than I thought—we all fall hard.

I've never shared my tattoo with them, but there's no time like the present. I drag my hand down my face and then start unbuckling my jeans.

"Uh, what the fuck are you doing?" Walker says as he begins to scoot away from me while I start shoving my pants down. I'm sure he thinks I'm fucking crazy right now, which is definitely how I've been feeling lately. But then I pull the leg of my briefs up far enough that Wyatt and Walker can both see the tattoo on my upper thigh of a girl on a horse, charging forward, her hair flung back as if she's racing against the wind.

"Holy shit," Walker says, leaning forward to get a closer look. "That looks like Shauna! When did you get that?"

"During college," I reply, pulling my underwear and jeans back in place before straightening my legs out in front of me. It was two weeks before I went to Vegas and we broke up for good. She never saw it. "She's always been the one."

"We know," my brothers say in unison.

"But now the question is: Are you going to let her get away, Forrest?" Wyatt pushes, kicking me in the ass while I'm still on the ground.

"You'll always live with regrets if you don't try to tell her how you feel, how you've always felt," Walker adds.

Jesus, are they right? Are my younger brothers seriously giving me relationship advice right now?

I know what I felt that night in Vegas, and it was even stronger than what I felt for that woman fifteen years ago.

I love her. I've always loved her. And if I didn't know any better, I'd think she was about to kiss me back when I tried.

She didn't tell me she was getting married until her fiancé showed up. Would she have ever told me? Is she honestly happy with him? With the life she's created out there?

Would I be a complete selfish ass by going all the way back there to ask her if she's sure about marrying Brock, the douchebag? Is that fair of me to do that to her?

And even if it's not, is it fair to myself to never find out if there's still a chance she could want me?

It's a risky move, one I told myself I would never make again. She turned me down once. I'm not sure I could handle a second time.

But I can't live with regrets. I can't just sit around tomorrow and wonder what time she's going to become some other man's wife when I know, deep down in my bones, that she's always been meant to be mine.

I have to fight for her one last time.

Launching from the ground, I don't even bother to wipe the dirt off my body before I stalk away from my brothers. I have to get to Vegas as soon as possible.

Do I fly? Drive? Would it be faster than waiting around for a flight?

I hear footsteps behind me, so I know my brothers are fighting to catch up as I head for the house to tell Momma I need some food to go.

I may be in a rush, but her cooking will give me the fuel I'll need to get through the rest of the night into tomorrow. Who knows how long it will take to find her or where the wedding actually is? I might not even make it in time, but I have to at least try.

"Forrest?" Walker calls out to me, but I don't reply. "Forrest!"

Finally, I spin around, forcing Wyatt and Walker to both stop dead in their tracks. I look between my two brothers, knowing I have to tell them where I'm headed, and then declare, "I have a fucking wedding to stop, boys. Wish me luck."

But I don't wait for their reply before turning back to the house and racing up the steps. I hear them high-five behind me, though, and Walker calls out to me, "Hell, yeah! Go get her, man!"

Hiding my smile and shoring up the determination I feel running through my veins, I reach the door and rip it open, startling everyone inside once again.

"Forrest?" Momma calls out to me as I enter the kitchen.

"Sorry, Momma, but I have to go. I haven't eaten much today, though. Is anything ready yet?" I ask as my eyes scour the countertops full of food.

"Uh, yes. I can fix you a plate." She starts to move while studying me with a pinch in her brow. "But what's the rush? Where are you headed?"

Walker and Wyatt barrel into my back as they enter the house right behind me. I twist to them, arch a brow in warning, and then turn back to Momma. "I had an emergency come up. I'm sorry I can't stay."

"Oh. Is everything okay?"

"Hopefully, it will be," Walker answers for me as Wyatt elbows him in the ribs. "Ow."

"Shut up, dipshit," Wyatt whispers, but he's not very quiet about it.

Momma plants her hands on her hips. "Okay. What's going on, boys?"

I take a step toward her and press a kiss to her cheek. "Everything is fine right now, but I have to leave or I might be late."

"Late for what?"

"I can't say." I don't want to tell her right now and listen to a lecture, or worse, get her hopes up, too. My mother loved Shauna and always assumed she'd be her daughter-in-law one day. I don't want her to know what I'm up to in case this doesn't go the way I hope.

"Well, that's cryptic." Rolling her eyes, she grabs a Tupperware container and prepares to fill it. "I guess you'll tell me when you're ready, then?"

"I promise."

Glaring at me, she puts a few pieces of barbecue chicken, fresh fruit, and potato wedges in the dish before handing it to me. "Here. I hope everything turns out okay." Framing my jaw with her hand, she stares up at me. "Be safe, Forrest."

Nothing about what I'm going to do is safe, but I'm tired of sitting around and playing by the rules. It's time to take a risk. "I will, Momma. Thank you."

I say my hurried goodbyes and hop in my truck, calling Jill on my Bluetooth while I speed toward my house to pack a suitcase.

She greets me as soon as the call connects. "You feeling okay? Heard you tied one on last night at The Tipsy Cow."

"I'm fine. I need you to find me the next flight to Vegas, hopefully leaving tonight. And if there isn't one, I'll just drive."

"Wait, what?" I hear noise in the background, and then she says, "What the hell is going on, Forrest?"

Shoving a hand through my hair, I glance in my mirror before I change lanes. "I have to get to Vegas as soon as possible, Jill."

"Does this have something to do with why you've been so pissy lately?" I can hear her clicking around on a keyboard in the background, so I know she's already getting to work.

"Yes, but I can't say more. Do you have anything yet?"

She's silent for a minute, but then she finally says, "There's one more flight leaving at eleven. It's a red eye, so you'll be there around two in the morning. Do you need a hotel room, too?"

"Yes, please."

"Anywhere specific?"

"I don't care. Probably off the strip but not too far."

"You got it. It's gonna be close for you to get to the airport in time."

"I can manage." I press my foot down on the gas pedal, speeding even faster toward my house. The drive to Dallas from here is about five hours, but I can make it with time to spare as long as I don't stop.

"When will you be back?"

"I want to say Monday, but I honestly don't know." I won't know anything until after I speak to Shauna. If she tells me to get the hell out of her life again, I know I'll want to leave as soon as possible. But if she doesn't—if she wants to be with me and give us another chance—then I'm not sure what it will take for her to leave, or even if she'll want to.

I honestly can't answer that question right now.

"Hold down the fort for me in the meantime?" I ask Jill, so fucking grateful for her in this moment.

"Don't I always?"

"You do. Thank you, Jill. Seriously, I don't know what I would do without you."

"Go get your girl, Forrest," she whispers.

"How did you—"

"The only reason any man gets his briefs in a bunch like you have lately is a woman," she replies, cutting me off. "I hope she's worth the fight."

Smiling, I glance at myself in the rearview mirror and nod. "She is. Believe me."

CHAPTER FOUR

Shauna

"I'm still surprised you went with that dress." Willow, my best friend from college and maid of honor, studies me with a tilt of her head as I stare at my reflection in the mirror.

It wasn't my first choice, but it was the one my mother loved the best, and she was paying for it, so I appeased her —yet again.

Repairing our relationship since I came out here for my father has been a work in progress, but ultimately, I still have this innate desire to please her. She's only human and did the best that she could with the knowledge she had at the time.

"It's timeless. There's nothing wrong with a princess-style ballgown," I counter, even though the bottom of this dress makes me feel like I'm wearing a cupcake.

"Oh, I know. It just doesn't seem very . . . you." She steps closer and adjusts my veil from the back. "Doesn't matter, though. I'm sure Brock will be in tears as you walk down the aisle toward him."

"Uh-huh," I mutter as that dread fills my stomach again. I keep telling myself it's normal to feel jittery, but the closer I get to walking down the aisle of the church—not my choice, either—the more I find myself asking for a sign that I'm making the right decision.

Here I am, in my freaking wedding dress for crying out loud, about to marry a man who loves me, and I can't stop thinking about Forrest.

It's been two weeks, and with each passing day, memories of our past rush in like a hurricane—feeling so consumed by him that I never wanted us to be apart, helping his mother cook in the kitchen after a long day of riding horses on the ranch, watching movies with his brothers in the living room, and daydreaming of the family I always thought I would marry into.

Why do these thoughts have to be so strong right now?

Our conversation from the other night has also been

on constant replay in my head—reminiscing about how crazy we were about each other, the look on his face when he realized I was engaged, the ache in my heart when I watched him walk away for a second time, although I'm the one who pushed him to walk away in the first place.

"Shauna?" my mother calls out as she knocks but doesn't wait for permission to enter, not that she hasn't seen me already. "The church is filling up. I talked to the coordinator, and she said we are right on schedule to start just fifteen minutes late, like you wanted."

Erin is one of the associates I work with at Ember & Stone Events, and I knew I could trust no one else to make sure my own wedding ran smoothly since I wouldn't be able to do that myself.

"Oh. Okay. Good." I hold my hand over my stomach, wondering if I should try to use the bathroom one more time. Or maybe I need to go outside and get some fresh air.

My mother places her clasped hands over her lips as tears well in her eyes. "I still can't believe my little girl is getting married." She drops her hands and walks toward me, reaching out to grasp mine. "I'm so proud of you, so honored to be your mother."

"Oh, Mom . . ."

"It's true. You've grown into such a successful woman, so confident, so headstrong, so sure of what she wants. That's all I've ever wanted for you, for you to prove that you could have everything you've ever wanted in life."

But do I really have that?

"And to think, you could have ended up in that small town..."

With Forrest.

"I love you, Mom." I lean forward and kiss her on the cheek as she swipes a tear out from under her eye.

"I love you, too, Shauna. And I love Brock. He's a good man. He accepts you, appreciates you, and he wants the same things you do."

He does accept me, shows me love and affection, and treats me with respect. But is that enough? He doesn't get my blood pumping, he doesn't challenge me, he doesn't make me feel alive like someone else once did.

"He is a good man," I reply instead, knowing there's no way I can voice my concerns now. It's too late. The dress is on, the church is filling up, and in a few moments, I'm going to be Mrs. Brock Robertson. That's what I wanted, right?

My mother waves her hands in front of her face, trying to dry her tears and prevent more from falling. "Okay. I'm going to go out there one more time and make sure everything is ready."

"Okay, Mom."

I watch her leave and then turn back to the mirror, adjusting my veil behind my head over my bun. I wanted to wear my hair down, but my mother insisted an updo would be more appropriate.

"You ready for this?" Willow asks as she takes a step

toward me now. She stood by in the corner, allowing my mother and me our moment, but now she's back in maid-of-honor mode. It's the same look she has when she's running her million-dollar business.

"Yes," I reply on a shaky breath.

"I still can't believe you're getting married," she teases, bumping her shoulder against mine.

"I know."

"You swore off men for so long in college, I just assumed you'd become a workaholic like me. But then along came Brock." Willow moved back to Washington, D.C. after college to start her own advertising agency and be closer to her godparents. Over the past twelve years, she's fostered the growth of her firm, Marshall Advertising, and is now a multi-millionaire who dedicates most of her time to her job. I've rarely seen her date, either, so we naturally gravitated toward each other while we were in college. After she moved, every few months, we'd take turns visiting one another, basking in our single-girl lives until I met Brock shortly after my father died.

No one was as shocked as Willow that I began dating him since I avoided relationships for years—because how does a girl move on from a man like Forrest? But she was actually the one who encouraged me to give Brock a shot when I told her about him, and now here we are.

"You guys will be happy together," she continues, rubbing my shoulder. But when she sees my face in the mirror, her brow furrows. "Hey, you okay?"

"Yeah, I'm fine," I lie.

"You sure? You look kinda pale."

"I'm just hot. This dress has a lot of layers." I fluff the fabric of the skirt, knowing it won't help because that's not the problem. But I don't dare cast doubt thoughtlessly.

"Want me to get you some water?"

"Yeah. I think that's a good idea." The room was only stocked with champagne today, and one glass was enough for me. Not sure more alcohol is the best decision right now.

She pats my arm. "Okay. I'll be right back."

I hear the door shut and then move to the window, staring out at the grounds as I watch people slowly stride toward the church, most of whom I don't even know. Brock's family is well-known around Vegas, so our guest list grew by the hundreds rather quickly once our engagement was announced.

I always imagined a small wedding, just family and a few close friends, outside, in a field . . .

Or a barn . . .

The door opens behind me as I continue to gaze out the window thinking about a life that could have been. But when I hear the voice of the person who enters, my knees nearly buckle as I try to convince myself I'm dreaming.

"Shauna . . ."

Spinning so fast I almost fall over, I brace myself on

the window frame behind me as I face the man I haven't been able to get out of my head for weeks—years, really.

"Forrest? What . . . what are you doing here?"

He's dressed in jeans, a plain black t-shirt, and Ariat boots—the same outfit he was wearing in Vegas that still doesn't fail to make my entire body warm up just at the sight of him. He's the quintessential cowboy and always has been.

All he's missing right now is the hat.

His hair is a mess, and there are bags under his eyes, but his presence is still as overpowering as ever. I'm frozen in place by his stare.

His eyes drop down my body as he takes in my dress, the pinch in his brow almost alarming. But when our eyes meet again, he takes a step closer to me, and suddenly all of the oxygen is sucked out of the room. "I need to speak with you."

"Now? I'm, uh . . . I'm kind of busy."

"I know, and I know that the timing of this isn't ideal, but if I don't say something right now before it's too late, I'll regret it for the rest of my life, and I'm tired of regretting shit. I'm tired of missing you, too, Shauna." His voice sounds much steadier after that speech.

"Oh my God . . ." My heart is pounding so violently, I definitely feel like I might pass out. But I can't deny that I want to hear what he has to say.

"Running into you two weeks ago was fate. I have to believe that." He takes a step closer, the smell of his cologne hitting me with a force that is borderline hypnotizing. "Did you feel what I felt that night? Did you feel like part of your heart snapped back into place when we spoke?" He reaches for my hand and begins to rub the top of it with his thumb.

Heat blooms in my veins.

Yes, I felt it. "I'm . . . I'm about to get married, Forrest."

"But you're not *yet*, Shauna. You haven't said 'I do.'"

Shit. I can't handle this. I can't stand here and let him make my mind spin.

Your mind was already spinning, Shauna. And this man and how you feel about him were the main cause of that.

"And I know I told you all those years ago that I would never ask you to choose between me and another man, but I guess I lied—because that's what I'm doing right now. I'm asking you to choose me."

I'm going to pass out.

He said that.

He actually just told me not to marry Brock.

"Forrest . . . you—you need to go." I pull my hand back, much to his dismay, but he stays right where he's standing.

Swallowing roughly, he nods once but then bends his knees so we're looking at each other eye to eye. "I will, but only if you can tell me that *he's* the love of your life, that when he touches you, you feel like your body comes alive and the adrenaline that courses through you is powerful enough to catapult you off a cliff because it makes you believe you can fly. That's what my love for you made me feel—and still does, Shauna. And I know we can find that again if you just give us a chance." He trails a finger down my cheek. "Tell me you don't still have feelings for me."

"I . . ." Our eyes are locked on each other's, but I don't get a chance to finish that sentence because Willow returns at that very moment, interrupting his declaration and reminding me of my impending nuptials, of where I am.

I'm here in the present, on my wedding day, not back in the past—even though my past is standing right in front of me.

"Oh. Sorry. I, uh . . . didn't realize you had company." Her eyes jump back and forth between me and Forrest, and I can almost see the wheels turning in her head.

Forrest turns around and smiles at Willow. "It's okay. I said what I needed to say." With one more glance at me, he says, "Think about it, Shauna." And then he leaves, tugging on my heart strings as he does.

Willow softly shuts the door behind her and then hands me the glass of water she went to find. I down it in one fell swoop. "Um, who the hell was that?"

I smack my lips together when I'm done drinking and stare at the door before replying, "That was Forrest."

Willow's eyes double in size. "Holy shit. *The* Forrest?"

Of course I told Willow about the boy from my past I pushed away to establish a relationship with my father.

But she's never seen him in real life, so I understand her shock right now.

"Uh, yup."

"Oh my God. What the hell is he doing here?"

"I . . . uh . . ."

A knock on the door interrupts me. "It's time!" my mother croons as she prances inside the room, oblivious to the emotional turmoil I'm currently going through.

Willow's eyes dart to me as if asking me what happens next. But I don't answer her. I can't even find any words to speak at the moment.

This is what shock must feel like.

Mom grabs my bouquet, adjusts the roses, and hands it to me. "Let's go make you Mrs. Brock Robertson, baby."

Pasting on a smile, I take the bouquet from her and weave my hand through hers, even though my gut is telling me this is all wrong.

I miss my dad. I wish he were here to walk me down the aisle.

But part of me feels like the man I'm walking toward is all wrong, too.

Willow fluffs out the back of my dress as Erin holds the door to the bridal suite open wide enough that I can fit through. "You look gorgeous, Shauna," Erin says as I plaster on the best smile I can manage at the moment.

"Thank you," I whisper, trying not to open my mouth too wide for fear of throwing up.

I can't believe Forrest came all this way to say those

words to me—although, this isn't the first time he's done that, so I shouldn't be so surprised, should I?

You're the one who asked for a sign, Shauna. And well, I think you just got it.

I follow my mother's lead to the chapel doors as my pulse grows louder in my ears.

"Mom?" I whisper, trying to get her attention, but she's listening to the directions that Erin is giving her, oblivious to me.

The bridal march starts, and suddenly, the heavy wooden doors float open and a sea of people greets my eyes. I don't have time to look for Forrest and see if he's still there because my mother takes a step forward. My feet follow her on instinct.

Hundreds of people smile and nod at me as I walk past, but I don't even know if I'm smiling in return. My body is vibrating with nerves, there's a lump in my throat that feels like a softball, and when my eyes land on Brock at the end of the aisle, the look he's giving me tells me what my heart already knew.

I can't do this.

He doesn't deserve a woman who has any doubts about marrying him. And right now, I have plenty.

Unfortunately, I end up right before him far too quickly, taking his hand as my mother gives me away. I have no idea what to say, what to do, and then the preacher starts speaking.

"We are gathered here today to join these two in holy

matrimony," he starts just as the sound of a side door closing rings out. Everyone turns toward the sound, myself included, but there's no one there. Whoever left did so in a hurry.

Murmurs echo through the space, but the preacher redirects everyone's attention to us once again.

"Now, where were we? Ah, yes." He points down at the book in front of him as my stomach twists in knots. And then he says the words that have me leaning forward, anxious to know what happens next, as if I'm not the one in control of the moment I'm standing in.

"Marriage is not a vow that should be taken lightly, but with love and support, these two can make it through. However, if anyone here has just cause why these two should not be married, please speak now, or forever hold your peace."

Little did I know, the voice that would speak up would be mine.

CHAPTER FIVE

Forrest

Six Weeks Later

"I can't believe it's already November," Kelsea says as she moves around Momma in the kitchen. The two of them are doing their normal dance like a well-oiled machine, and I'm watching them from my seat on the other side of the counter, wishing there was whiskey in my coffee.

"I know. And Kaydence is going to be one next month," Evelyn adds, bouncing her daughter in her arms as she stands to the right of me.

"Are you gonna plan a party?" my mother asks, and I instantly groan. A kids' birthday party? Just what I want to do with my life right now.

Better than what you've been doing for the past month and a half... which is a whole lot of sulking.

Evelyn grabs a biscuit from the basket on the counter and starts feeding small chucks of it to her daughter. "I'm not sure yet."

The three of them start sounding like the teacher in the Charlie Brown cartoon as I remind myself why I'm even less enthusiastic about life than normal.

Leaving Vegas empty-handed six weeks ago was the definition of rock bottom for me. I really thought that by showing up at Shauna's wedding, I'd convince her that what I felt that night two months ago wasn't all in my head and that she was still in love with me like I still am with her.

But I guess that kind of shit only happens in the movies and books, right? The guy pleads with the girl for one last chance just as she's about to marry someone else, and then she runs off with him and they live happily ever after...

Fuck. Is it too early to start drinking?

Since it's nine o'clock on a Sunday morning, I'm going to say yes. However, given my life lately, I think God might understand and give me a hall pass.

"You have to throw her a party," Kelsea continues. "The poor girl has a birthday close to Christmas and will have to deal with that fact for the rest of her life. She deserves her own day."

"She's one," I mutter, but my mother catches it.

"Doesn't matter. My first grandbaby is having a birthday, and we're going to celebrate it." She glares across the counter at me, sliding the basket of freshly made biscuits in my direction. "Sounds like you didn't eat this morning. Take one."

"I'm not hungry."

"Take a biscuit, Forrest. Maybe some food will turn that frown of yours upside down," she says through clenched teeth, her words laced with that southern drawl that makes her sound a lot sweeter than she intends to be.

And since I respect my mother and she makes the best biscuits this side of the Mississippi, I oblige her and bite off a huge hunk of one.

"That's better." She winks at me and goes back to stirring the pot of jam on the counter as Kelsea lines up the jars to be filled.

Each week, the two of them make batches of homemade jam to sell at the farmers market along with spice blends and homemade sauces fresh from my mother's kitchen. It's part of the Gibson Ranch brand, and presenting our ranch and bed and breakfast in town each week helps to cement our name in the community and draw in new customers.

"Now, back to the holidays. Thanksgiving and Christmas are coming up, and you girls know how I wanted to put on a Winter Wonderland Festival this year?" Momma says, lifting the pot as she begins to fill jars. Kelsea holds a funnel in each one, seamlessly proceeding down the line with my mom.

"But what about Sheila? I thought she quit?" Evelyn asks as she watches Kelsea and Momma. Sheila was the event coordinator who's worked at the ranch for the past ten years, but she recently moved to Florida to be closer to her mother whose health has been declining over the last year.

I keep shoving biscuits in my mouth, listening to the conversation but avoiding being an active participant. I'm also killing time until I have to go outside and do my duty around the land. Each week, my brothers and I show up on Sundays to help out, and over the years, I've just grown bitter about it. This ranch was supposed to be mine one day, but that idea didn't sound so appealing without Shauna by my side to help.

Shauna.

Fuck. I think I lasted an entire five minutes without thinking about her this time.

She's probably deeply entranced in marital bliss right now, laughing about how her high school ex thought he could stop her from marrying her now husband.

"Ugh." I slap myself on the forehead as all three women turn toward me.

"You okay?" Kelsea asks.

"Yeah, I'm just tired," I lie, standing from my stool but

not before grabbing one more biscuit from the basket on the counter.

Kelsea flashes me a small smile, one that seems more out of pity than concern, but doesn't say anything. I'm pretty sure she and Evelyn know what's bothering me these days since my brothers can't keep anything to themselves, and they wouldn't stop bothering me when I returned from Vegas, wondering how things went with Shauna.

Hey. That was only thirty seconds this time. It's getting worse.

"Yeah, well, so am I, which is why I hired a new event coordinator," my mother chimes in, directing all of our attention back to her.

"Huh?" I ask, wondering what the hell she's talking about since I was barely listening to begin with.

"I've been trying to tell you three that the Winter Wonderland event is still going to happen, but I just can't do it all on my own. And I found the perfect person to take it over."

"We could have helped you, Momma G," Kelsea declares. Evelyn nods in agreement.

"That's sweet, you two, but between your photography business and the brewery, Kelsea, and your shop and this sweet little girl," she says to Evelyn, pinching Kaydence's chubby cheeks before she continues, "we're all too busy to take on a task this big. If I hadn't already opened my mouth about it to everyone around town, I'd just say to hell with it and cancel. But I can't do that now, and honestly, I don't want to. I think it will be a fun thing for families, bring new people out to the ranch who wouldn't normally visit around the holidays, and maybe start a new tradition that my kids can carry on one day when your father and I finally retire. Plus, it's time to bring some fresh blood in here, someone more up-to-date with current trends, and someone who understands how special this place can be."

"Well, that's great, then. So who's taking over for Sheila?" Kelsea asks.

"I found someone with great experience, someone who is looking for the perks of small-town life after living in a bigger city for years, and I think she'll fit in just perfectly around here," my mother says just as my father and brothers walk through the back door.

"Hey. You gonna sit in here and gossip, or are you gonna come outside and help?" Walker asks me, slapping my shoulder before reaching around me to grab a biscuit. He then moves to my right to kiss his wife brazenly in front of all of us.

"Biscuit before me; I see how it is," Evelyn teases as he offers her a bite, and she takes one.

"The biscuit was closer. I was just trying to be efficient."

"Sure."

"And it looks like my little owl is enjoying her biscuit as well?" He leans forward and nuzzles his nose against

Kaydence's, making her squeal, and everyone laughs with her.

Everyone but me, that is.

My brother has taken his new title as a father seriously, and I'm damn proud of him for that. But seeing him happy, and Wyatt and Kelsea as well? It just reminds me of what I don't have—what I'll never have now that Shauna is gone.

Will I move on someday? Can I now knowing that she's married and that the chance of us getting back together is zero? I'm not sure. But all I know is that the idea of dating again is the last thing on my fucking mind.

The doorbell rings at that moment, startling everyone.

"Are you expecting someone, honey?" my father asks my mom as he starts walking toward the door.

"Yes. The new event coordinator is coming by today to get settled and start taking over the haphazard plans I already have in place." She unties her apron and follows my father. "I can get it."

"It's okay, honey. You're busy," my dad replies as my brothers and I watch them battle over something as simple as answering the door. The truth is, this is what they do—try to do more and be involved in every little thing that goes on at this house.

My mom jokes about the day that the two of them will retire, but honestly, I don't know if that will ever happen. Both of them are each too much of a control freak to let anyone else be in charge.

"Randy. Let me get the door," she grates out between her teeth, pulling him back by the shoulder before reaching for the door knob. The glare she gives him is one I'm very familiar with myself.

"Jesus, Elaine. I don't understand what the big deal is, honey. It's just—"

But his words get cut off as my mother opens the door and a collective gasp fills the room. Everyone gasps except for me, that is, because I'm pretty sure I'm asleep and dreaming right now.

It fucking can't be.

"Shauna?" my father asks as Momma unlocks the screen door and reaches for Shauna's hand, pulling her inside.

"Oh. Hi, Mr. Gibson." Shauna doesn't look beyond my parents, but I'm sure she can feel everyone's eyes on her. Hell, I can't take mine off of her because I don't understand how she's fucking here right now. "Momma G," she says when she turns to my mom who yanks her into her chest, hugging her tightly just like she does to all of us kids. I swear, I'm being transported back in time, the image of my mother hugging my high school girlfriend shining right in front of my eyes.

Momma cups the side of her face. "Shauna, girl. I am so happy to see you."

"What the fuck is going on here?" Walker mumbles in my ear, breaking me out of my stupor.

"That *is* Shauna, right?" Wyatt asks on the other side of me.

"*Shauna*? Shauna is in the house right now?" Kelsea's eyes go wide as she stands right in front of my face. "Did you know she was coming?"

That question snaps me out of my shock. "What? No. I had no fucking clue."

"But if she's not here for you, then . . ." But Kelsea doesn't get to finish because my mother begins leading Shauna over to where we're standing, my father trailing closely behind.

"Kids, meet our new event coordinator. I believe you all remember Shauna Collins." The proud smile on my mother's face has me snapping my eyes to her in a flash. But the gleam in hers has me questioning my sanity right now and everything I've ever believed to be true about my mother.

Seems Momma G has been up to no good, and the thing is, she probably has no idea the emotional turmoil she's causing her oldest son right now, either.

"Shauna! Long time, no see!" Walker says, stepping forward first and wrapping her up in a hug.

"God, you two are all grown up," she says through a laugh as he releases her and her eyes shift over to Wyatt.

"That's what happens," Wyatt says, giving her a hug next. "I guess we can say the same for you, too, though." When he lets her go, he turns his back so she can't see his face and then mouths to me, *What the hell is going on?*

My teeth are clenched together so tight right now that I don't even attempt to answer. What the hell is she doing here?

She took a job at my parents' ranch?

And then it happens. Our eyes lock, and she flashes me an unsure smile, a look that says she knows she shouldn't be here but it's too late to back out now.

"Hi, Forrest."

A grunt. That's my reply.

"Now, Forrest," my mother admonishes as I feel everyone's eyes on us, like our interaction is a fucking science experiment and they are all taking notes on how we'll interact—two exes in the wild, one who put their heart on the line and the other who shattered it not once, but twice. "Where are your manners? I taught you better than that." She smacks my shoulder and then pulls Shauna behind her, further into the kitchen. "Shauna, are you hungry, honey?"

"Oh, uh . . . I'm good, but thank you."

"You sure? I made biscuits," my mother croons, holding the basket out to her in offering.

"You know you want one," Walker whispers behind her, making everyone laugh, including Shauna. He hands her one like a slimy salesman, bouncing his eyebrows as he does.

"God, it's been years. Are they still as good as I remember?" She smiles right before she takes a bite and then closes her eyes and lets out a moan of approval, one that goes straight to my dick. "Yup. Still fabulous."

Momma laughs and moves to the sink to wash her hands. "In my opinion, they've gotten better."

"I think I'd have to agree," Shauna mumbles around her last bite.

"So how was your flight? Not too terrible, I hope."

Her eyes dart over to me, but only for a second. "Uh, it was fine. Felt like it took forever. I haven't been on a plane in a long time."

"I hate flying," Kelsea interjects, visibly shuttering. "Granted, I've only done it four times when I went to New York and back twice, but I was terrified the entire time."

"I guess for me it was the anticipation that made it hard to get through, but I'm here now," Shauna declares enthusiastically, "and I'm ready to get to work."

"Now, now . . . there will be time for that in a minute. I want to make sure you have a few other things in place first before we go there." Mom moves over to the pot of jam as Kelsea jumps back into place and they begin filling the jars again. I swear, these two could do this in their sleep. "Did you find a place to stay yet? You know you can always stay here."

"Oh, not yet. I think for tonight that will be fine, but I'd like to get my own place."

Walker clears his throat behind me. "Uh, I might have a place." Everyone turns toward him, including me.

"You do?" Shauna asks.

"Yeah. I was renting out my townhouse to a coworker of mine, but he ended up buying his own place. So if you want, it's yours for the time being. Rent free," he adds.

"That's a great idea!" Evelyn interjects, still holding Kaydence on her hip. "It's perfect. Saves us from having to find someone new to move in."

"If you're sure . . ." I can hear the hesitation in Shauna's voice, but my brain feels drunk from how hard it's spinning right now as this is all unfolding in front of me.

"Of course."

Note to self: Beat Walker's ass later for being a fucking traitor.

"Okay, but I will pay you. I don't want a handout."

"It's not a handout, Shauna. Hell, you're practically family," Walker says, and those words are enough to pull me out of this mindfuck. I need space from all of this as fast as possible.

"Jesus," I mutter, spinning on my heel and heading for the back door.

I have to get the fuck out of here.

"Forrest?" my father calls out as I scramble to exit the house.

Keeping my back to everyone, I say, "I'll be outside." And then I stomp down the stairs of the back porch, heading straight for the barn.

Fuck.

Shauna is here.

My mother hired her.

She's going to be living in my brother's old place.

And she looks so fucking good.

"Did I do something in a past life to deserve this kind of torture?" I call out, looking up at the sky. I swear, God must be fucking with me right now, and I'm not finding the humor or lesson in this at all.

When I step into the barn, I locate a bale of hay and plop down, bracing my arms on my thighs before I take a few deep breaths. I need to get my head on straight, but that's really fucking hard to do when I have so many questions going through my mind right now.

Lucky for me, I barely get a chance to start sorting through them before I'm interrupted by the last person I want to look at right now.

"Forrest," Shauna calls out as she steps into the barn, her eyes landing on mine as I lift my head and take her in from head to toe.

She's wearing dark denim jeans, black boots, and a red paisley printed top with soft sleeves, her hair hanging down in waves around her face, just like she had it that night in Vegas.

She looks like the girl I fell in love with at sixteen. She looks like she belongs here.

But she doesn't. She's married.

And that's when my eyes drift to her left hand and I notice that her ring is missing.

Oh, hell no, she's not going to pull this shit again with me.

I rise from my seat and stalk over to her, intent on hashing out whatever it is that led her here. I don't know what the hell is going through her head, why she thought it would be a smart idea to come work for my parents after what happened six weeks ago, but I sure as hell don't want her to think that this means anything, that we're going to be cordial or something.

I can't do that with her.

She needs to leave.

When we come to a halt in the middle of the barn, just a few inches of space between us, we end up in a stare off —me towering over her, her staring up at me with caution in her eyes but sureness in her stance.

"What are you doing here, Shauna?" I finally grate out, glancing down at her left hand again. I lift it and hold it in front of her face. "No ring? Did you wash your hands and forget to put it back on again?"

But the answer she gives me takes me by surprise, making my head spin even more than it already is as she pulls her hand out of my own.

"I . . . I didn't marry Brock, Forrest. I came back here . . . for *you*."

CHAPTER SIX

Shauna

Forrest looks like I just asked him to send a rocket to the moon. "What?"

"I didn't get married, Forrest. I couldn't go through with it."

His brow pinches further, and his eyes dance back and forth between my own as he contemplates his next words. "And you waited six weeks to tell me that?"

Shaking my head, I draw in a shaky breath. "I couldn't just chase after you, Forrest. I made a mess of my life back in Vegas, and I had to clean it up."

It's been weeks of dealing with the aftermath of

leaving Brock at the altar, and I know all of the loose ends aren't tied up yet. But when I quit the firm I was working for and started talking to a headhunter, looking for another job on a much smaller scale, I'll never forget what she said to me that told me what I needed to hear—even though my heart already knew.

"Anything new this week?" I ask Sasha, the headhunter I contacted a few weeks ago when I decided I needed a change. I already ended an engagement and left a man standing at the front of a church, thinking he was about to marry me—what's a new job on top of that?

"There was one posting, but the job will probably move at a much slower pace than you're used to."

"Maybe less pressure and responsibility would be a good thing. Where is it?"

"A small town called Newberry Springs in Texas. It's for an Event Coordinator at a bed and breakfast."

And that was my sign.

"So why are you here now? And working for my mom? Is this some sick way for you to worm your way back into my life?" Forrest says, anger and confusion lacing through his words.

I have to say, I was expecting a slightly different reaction from him. But if he's going to be pissed, then I can be, too. He's definitely not innocent in everything that has happened. "*Your* life? You mean the one you were begging me to be a part of six weeks ago?" I throw back at him.

He scoffs and scrubs a hand through his hair. "That was different. That was before you left me looking like an idiot as I watched you walk down the aisle to that guy."

My stomach drops. "You were there? I couldn't find you after I left."

"I walked out as soon as the preacher started talking. I went out a side door."

"Why didn't you stay?"

"Because I thought you chose him, Shauna! I couldn't stand there and watch you get married!" he yells, causing a few horses in nearby stalls to neigh their complaints.

So the sound of the door slamming was him? He didn't see me leave Brock all alone in front of all those people? No wonder he's so pissed.

"But I . . . I didn't. I left him at the altar, Forrest—which was a horrible thing to do, but you were right. I didn't love him the way I loved you once, the way I wish I could again."

He shakes his head, staring down at the ground. "This is a lot. I was completely blindsided by you walking into that house a few minutes ago, Shauna," he says, pointing back up at the farmhouse that holds so many memories for us. "And even though every fiber of my being wants to kiss you and claim you . . . I can't."

"Why not?"

Did you really think it was going to be this simple, Shauna? That he'd scoop you up in his arms and you two would live happily ever after? Maybe I'm far more delusional than I thought.

"Because too much has happened, Shauna." His brow is furrowed so deep, I'm afraid it might get stuck that way. But his words are the truth, as much as I don't want to accept them.

"You're right. A lot has happened, but I'm here now. I'm not going anywhere."

"Until the Winter Wonderland event is done, correct?"

"What do you mean?"

"I mean, the only reason my mom hired you was to take over that event for her, right?"

Do I tell him that she's offered me the position full-time if I want it? Do I tell him that I hadn't decided to take it yet, depending on how things went with us? I was highly optimistic things would be simple, but this conversation is proving to me once again that I underestimated the stubbornness of this man.

As much as being away from him all this time has hurt, I think having to see him every day and him *not* reciprocating these suffocating feelings in a tangible way would be worse.

But I have to try, right? That's why I'm here—to find out if there really is something still between us.

Six weeks ago, he was eager to tell me that there was, at least for him.

Now, I have no idea where we stand, but the attitude he has about my reappearance isn't a promising one. Who knows, though? Six weeks is long enough to get back into someone's good graces, to show this man that although time and double-edged decisions have kept us apart, he's still the person I see myself spending my life with.

He always has been, even if I lost sight of that for a while.

All I know is that if I don't try, I'll regret it. And I'm tired of having regrets with this man. I made them once at eighteen, again at nineteen, and I refuse to do it again at thirty-four.

"Yes. I'm here to plan the event for her," I reply, not showing all of my cards yet.

"So you left your other job?"

"I did. A lot has changed in my life in the past six weeks, but my heart brought me back here, and I'm ready to listen to it."

Forrest shakes his head at me, his eyes narrowed while he contemplates his next words. And I hate that the way he's looking at me right now is making my doubts about finding our way back to each other grow exponentially.

"Yeah, well, things have changed for me, too," he finally says.

"What do you mean?"

"I mean, I don't want you here, Shauna. I can't . . ." He stares at the ground but doesn't finish his thought.

Instead, he says, "I have to go," and spins on his heels, giving me his back as I watch him retreat.

"Forrest!" I call after him, but he doesn't acknowledge me. His feet carry him away from me so fast you'd think his pants were on fire. "Well, that went well," I mutter to myself, pushing my hair off my face and breathing in the fresh air as I exit the barn, willing my emotions to stay in check.

There's only so much I can do right now, and until Forrest sees that I'm not leaving and I'm here to remind him of what we had, I have to accept where the cards lie right now—in a fucking mess on the floor.

When the sun hits my eyes, I lift my hand to shade them from the rays. Fall in Texas is so beautiful, the morning air crisp yet still warm enough that I don't need a jacket, but I definitely wish I had some sunglasses right now.

As I bask in the sunshine, I take a moment to stroll around the property, eager to see all of the changes but also feel the familiarity that has always made this place feel like home.

A few horses are stationed in their stalls to my right, chomping on hay and neighing to one another. The trees all around the house and the property have multiplied in size since the last time I was here. And the fields in front of me stretch out for miles, leading to a rustic building on my left, a barn that looks far more polished than the one Forrest and I were just arguing in.

I wander over to that building, stepping inside to see what they've done with the space.

"Wow." My head cranes back as I stare up at the high-beamed ceiling, the whitewashed wood walls, and the dark-brown wood floors. Strings of bulb lights hang from a pole in the center of the room over a flat space that is perfect for a dance floor. That's probably what they use it for.

"It's beautiful, isn't it?" Momma G's voice makes me jump, and I spin to face her.

"It's gorgeous."

She beams with pride, her eyes darting above her and all around. "I remember when we finished this building. It came out just as I imagined it would, and then all I kept seeing was you and Forrest getting married in here."

My smile drops from her reminder of what could have been. "Momma..."

We lock eyes, and then she says, "There's something you're not telling me." With an arch of her brow, she continues, "My son just stormed through the house like a lion let out of a cage, muttering to himself about something. Now, I'm not saying he hasn't carried around some anger about the way things ended between you two, but I feel like his reaction to seeing you again was exaggerated."

"I take it he hasn't told you much about the past few months."

Momma G scoffs. "This is Forrest we're talking about, Shauna. He's locked up tighter than a bank safe."

Nodding, I follow her to a set of chairs stationed against one wall. They're the simple white ones with cushions commonly used at weddings.

We take a seat, and then I let out a deep sigh. "Well, to make a long story short, I saw Forrest two months ago in Vegas when he was out there for a convention. We had dinner and a few drinks, but then my fiancé showed up. I—I wasn't exactly forthcoming with the detail that I was engaged," I admit, twiddling my thumbs and avoiding her eyes.

"I see."

"Seeing him again caught me off guard. I'd been thinking about him so much leading up to the wedding, considering all of the *what ifs*, which only amplified the doubts I was already feeling." I turn to her and grab her hand. "But when I tell you this next part, please don't hold a grudge against your son. He may have shown up to stop my wedding, but I already knew I shouldn't marry Brock. Hearing what he said just helped me see the truth and take action on it."

Her brows hit her forehead. "He went to Vegas and tried to stop your wedding? *My* Forrest?"

I huff out a laugh. "Yeah. He told me he still loved me, that if I still felt any sort of feelings toward him, I should give us another chance."

Momma G shakes her head slowly as she takes in all the information I just shared. "I'm not gonna lie. Part of hiring you was with the hope that you two would find your way back to each other. You have no idea how miserable that man has been since he came home after his injury and you two split up. But I had no idea you'd been in contact. I thought this would be a much friendlier reunion, even though I know you two have a past."

"Well, I imagine the past few weeks have been worse because he saw me walking down the aisle toward Brock and thought I chose him. If he had stayed just a few minutes more, he would have seen me leave him at the altar."

Momma G gives me a tight-lipped smile and squeezes my hand. "That must have been hard to do."

A tear slips down my cheek. "It was. It was awful, hurting him like that. But it was the right decision. It wasn't fair to marry a man when another one still resided in my heart. But in the process, I hurt Forrest, too." I swipe the tear away and then look up at the woman I've always considered a second mom. "I came back here to see if we could find our way back to each other, too, Momma. But if Forrest can't forgive me, if we can't move past the past, I don't see that happening."

She pats my hand and shimmies her hips, getting more comfortable in her chair. "Oh, Shauna. You underestimate the power of a mother who knows her children better than they know themselves. And guess what," she leans forward, whispering, "I now have two other daughters-in-law who enjoy a little meddling as well."

I let out a laugh, and God, it feels good. "I'm sorry that

I wasn't totally honest with you, that you didn't know about everything."

She waves a hand in the air dismissively. "It's all right. I kind of had a feeling there was more to you coming back than just needing a new job or wanting to visit temporarily." She winks at me. "But just know that the job is yours permanently if that's what you want."

"I appreciate that, but I haven't decided yet." Honestly, it depends on Forrest, and I don't want to get her hopes up if things don't pan out.

"Give him some time, Shauna. That man might try to pretend that he doesn't care about feelings, but the truth is, he feels them too much sometimes, and it's overwhelming for him."

He always did love hard. "I feel like we've lost so much time . . ." My words trail off because I don't want to think of what the consequences of that could be.

"You did, but it wasn't lost. It was time spent figuring out who you two were, working toward goals and careers, building relationships with other people. It wasn't wasted, but all you can focus on now is the future. You're still young. There's still time to get everything you want."

"You think?"

"I *know*." Standing from her chair, she grabs my hand for me to follow her. "Things with Forrest will work themselves out, I'm sure of it. But right now, I say we talk Winter Wonderland business because this momma has a vision, and you only have six weeks to make it come alive."

Laughing, we walk hand in hand back toward the house. "That's what I'm here for. Put me to work, Momma G."

"Oh, honey. You definitely have your work cut out for you in more ways than one. But if there's anyone who is up for the challenge, it'd be you, sweetheart. Now, let's get down to business."

CHAPTER SEVEN

Forrest

"The Anderson high-rise is coming along really well," Javi tells me as we walk through the yard of High Performance headquarters. The temperatures have dropped considerably in the last week which makes being outside much more tolerable.

"Good. It's a big job. We can't lose money on it."

"I don't think that will be an issue," he replies. "We're actually ahead of schedule right now."

I groan, looking up at the sky and then glaring at him when I drop my chin. "Why did you say that? You should know by now that uttering those words in the construction world is just asking for bad juju."

"Did you just use the word 'juju'?" he asks, frowning at me.

The truth is, I've never used that word in my life, but my world is just full of surprises right now.

"Fuck, Javi." I run my hand through my hair, blowing out a breath. "I just don't need any more shit to stir the pot right now, all right?"

"Well, what's going on?"

What's going on? My ex showed up at my parents' house yesterday after taking a job working for them, and I acted like an ass.

I told her I didn't want her here, but I think we all know that's not the truth.

"Shauna's here." I groan again, pinching the bridge of my nose.

His eyes double in size, and then his head starts to swivel. "Holy shit. Where?"

"Not here in the yard." I shove him. "In Newberry Springs, man."

He rolls his eyes, widens his stance, and crosses his arms over his chest. "Jesus, Forrest. Why is she here? I feel like I need more information."

"I swear, you're worse than my brothers sometimes."

"That's fine." He shrugs. "You can wallow in your own turmoil if that's what you want, or you can fucking tell me what's going on in your head and I can help you work through it. Your call."

I glare at him once again. "Fucker."

He puckers his lips and makes kissing noises. "You love me. Now, talk."

"Remember when I went to Vegas to try to stop her wedding?"

"Yup. It was badass, even though it didn't turn out the way you wanted." Javi pushed me to tell him where I went when I up and disappeared for a few days and came back pissed off at the world. And even though I won't admit it out loud, I'm glad he did. I slipped into a dark place there for a while, and he was the one who helped pull me out of it. Of course, that consisted of him kicking my ass in the boxing ring numerous times, but it helped. And I know that sharing what's going on with me is the right thing to do, even though I hate talking about my fucking feelings.

"Well, that's the thing . . ." I stare out across the yard. "I guess she never married the guy."

"Oh, shit. You didn't know?"

"Nope. I left when I saw her walking down the aisle. She said she left him there, but I missed that part."

"So now she's here?"

"Yup, and she also took a job working for my parents at their ranch."

Javi stifles a laugh with his hand. "Oh, fuck. That's convenient."

"Right? She says she came back for me, but then why

go behind my back like that? And my mother hired her, knowing who she is. I feel like this was all a big scheme."

Javi purses his lips as he ponders my dilemma. "Well, let me ask you this. If your mother hadn't gotten involved, and Shauna had just knocked on your door and told you that she wanted you back, would you look past all of that and give her a shot?"

My heart says yes, but my head says too much shit has happened. "I don't know, Javi. My mind is a fucking mess. And the worst part is, I told her I didn't want her here."

He blows out a breath. "Damn. You really have a way with words, don't you?"

I shove his shoulder. "Don't fucking rub it in."

"Well, is that how you really feel?"

"No. But I was caught off guard. I wasn't prepared for her to be there and say all that shit."

"Kind of like what you did to her when she was about to marry another man," he counters, crooking his eyebrow at me.

"You know what? Maybe talking this out with you isn't the best idea."

"Hey, I'm just telling it like it is. You did the same shit to her. It sounds like you both have a lot you need to discuss. But the question is, Forrest, do you want to? Is it worth going through all of that? Do you think you'll be able to work past everything you've been through if it means having her at the end of it?"

"I think so . . . I'm just so fucking angry right now. I

mean, did she leave her fiancé because she actually wants to be with me? Or was she just unhappy, and I gave her an out? Does she even know what she really wants? It's only been six weeks. Can she really have her head on straight that soon? Because I know I don't. I haven't had my head on straight for months, especially where it concerns her. One day I hate her and regret ever falling in love with her, and the next, I feel like I would give every last organ in my body for another chance with her."

"You're so eloquent with words," he snipes.

"Well, it's the truth." I let out a sigh as my phone buzzes in my pocket. "Fuck. I need to get back to the office."

"I know, me too, but we're not done. Look, here's what I suggest. Instead of worrying about all of the romantic bullshit right now, what if you just focus on trying to be friends again?"

"Friends?"

"Yeah. I mean, when Sydney and I started our little arrangement back in the day, I was hell bent on keeping feelings out of it. But then we started spending more time together outside of the bedroom and developed a friendship, which led to more." He holds his hands up. "I mean, I don't have much other experience to go off of, but getting to know her made those feelings develop naturally on their own."

He drops his hands and grabs his own phone out of

his pocket as it begins to vibrate, checking the screen before glancing back up at me.

"You know you already have feelings for her, but just focus on getting to know the woman she is now instead of holding shit against her from before, and maybe the rest will fall into place." With a slap on my shoulder, he strolls off, answering his phone and leaving me pondering his suggestion.

Can I just be friends with Shauna?

I think a resounding *no* was the answer that got me into this mess in the first place.

The first time I saw that woman, I knew I had to make her mine, and I was a naïve boy back then. But now, as a man, it feels like taking a step backward. But what if that's what we need?

She's here. She will be for at least six weeks.

Don't I owe it to myself to at least give us one last shot?

Before I can answer that clearly, my phone rings again. But this time, it's my mother. "Hey, Momma. Any more scheming you've been up to that I should be aware of?"

"Oh, you stop that sass, Forrest Eli, before I show you just how wicked I can be."

Groaning, I head for the main building so I can get back to my office. "I'm fully aware. It's just been a while since I've been the victim of it."

"Well, I'm not sorry, but I *do* have some chicken fried

steak for dinner tonight that might get me on your good side again. If you'll come over for dinner, that is."

My stomach rumbles on command at the mention of my mother's chicken fried steak and gravy. It was my favorite meal growing up, and I've tried cooking it for myself, but it never comes out the same.

She must add something special to it since she knows I'll never turn it down.

"I guess I can do that."

"Wonderful. And bring a bottle of wine. I feel like I need a glass after today. It's been wild, and it's only noon."

"You got it, Momma."

"Thank you. See you later, Forrest. Love you!"

"Love you, too." I end the call just as I plop down in my chair and wake up my computer.

A few hours go by as I answer emails, talk to suppliers, and check in on a few of our biggest jobs right now. But when my phone rings right before I'm about to leave, I fucking grin as soon as I see who it is.

"Maddox Taylor!"

"Forrest Gibson! How are you, man?"

Maddox Taylor is one of my best friends from high school. We grew up playing football together and both went to college on athletic scholarships. While my career ended in an injury, his went on to blossom, and now he's one of the top quarterbacks in the NFL. He's currently living in sunny California, playing for the Los Angeles Bolts.

"Oh, I'm hanging in there. Work's good, fucking busy, but that's not a bad thing."

"Yeah, I hear ya. This season is already kicking my ass, but I feel strong. Here's hoping we make it to the Super Bowl this year."

"You can always use another ring, right?"

He laughs. "Of course. I gotta beat Tom Brady's record, you know?"

"A noble goal. How's Penelope?" Maddox fell in love with his PR rep when he got traded to the Bolts a few years ago. Pen is a force to be reckoned with—strong-minded, confident, and bold. No wonder he fell hard for her.

Huh. Sounds like someone else you know, doesn't it, Forrest?

"Oh, keeping me in line like always. But I finally got her to marry me and have my babies, so now she's stuck with me."

"Lucky for her."

"How about you? You seeing anyone?"

Maddox knew me and Shauna back in high school, and he was one of the only people I leaned on when we broke up. In fact, he's the only one who knows the real truth behind why I left Texas A&M.

"Uh, no. But Shauna's back in town."

"Holy shit. Really?"

"It's a fucking long story, man."

"Shit. I wish I had more time so you could tell me all

the juicy details," he jokes, "but I have hours of film to watch before we play the Buccaneers on Sunday."

"Don't worry about it. I'll fucking figure it out."

"I hope you do, man. I know what she meant to you. But listen, the reason I called was to ask if you still wanted tickets to the game after Thanksgiving?"

The Bolts will be playing the Dallas Cowboys in Arlington the Sunday after Thanksgiving. Maddox usually gives me three tickets, one for me and each of my brothers.

"Hell yeah, man. I always look forward to that game."

"Awesome. I'll have Pen email you the details."

"Sounds good."

"I hope you work stuff out with Shauna, Forrest. I'm telling you from experience, when you find a woman worth fighting for, it's worth the effort."

We hang up, but his words don't leave my mind as I drive home to shower before going to my parents' place.

I *have* fought for Shauna, not once but twice.

But is that enough?

Do I have any more fight in me to do it a third time?

Lucky for me, the shower and drive to my parents' house are quick, and listening to my favorite band on max volume the whole time drowns out any thoughts.

But when I turn off my truck and the silence of the country invades as I saunter up the walk to the farmhouse, my mind starts swirling again. Fortunately, I don't even have a moment of peace to contemplate it, because when I step into my parents' house, guess who's sitting on the couch, laughing with my mom?

The woman they should name a hurricane after given the way she just stormed right back into my life and knocked the pillars of what I thought I knew to the ground.

∼

"Gosh, I missed your cooking, Momma G," Shauna says as we sit around the dinner table. It's just me, her, and my parents—talk about awkward. She leans back in her chair and pats her stomach. "I'm stuffed."

"Well, if you want me to pay you in food, I could." My mother winks across the table at her.

"It's tempting, but I hate to think what it would do to my waistline."

Her waistline? Does she mean the one that dips in and highlights the curves of her hips? The one I haven't stopped staring at every time she walks around in those tight-ass jeans that look painted on?

Fuck, I'd love to grab onto those curves again. She has much more to grip onto now than she did the last time I had permission to touch her like that.

"Having a little meat on your bones isn't the end of the world, is it, Randy?" My mother turns to my father with a mischievous grin on her lips.

"Not at all, honey," my father replies, smirking right back at her.

I drop my fork and wipe my mouth with my napkin. "Please, you two. I don't want to throw up that delicious dinner."

My mother leans forward in her chair. "You do realize that the only reason you're alive is because your father and I had sex, right, Forrest?"

"Okay. That's taking it too far." I stand from my chair and grab my plate to clear it while my parents and Shauna share a laugh.

"Well, that was amazing, but I'd better be going," Shauna declares from her seat at the table.

"Oh, nonsense. There's no rush. We did a lot of work today, so you should enjoy the evening out here. You even said it's been so long since you've gone for a ride. Perhaps Forrest can take you?" My mother turns to me as I face her from behind the island.

Done scheming, my ass. Is that why she invited me out here for dinner? To try to get me to spend time with Shauna?

I'd bet my left kidney that the answer is yes.

Shauna turns to me, meeting my eyes for only the fifth time since I've arrived. And yes, I've counted. "I'm sure Forrest wants to leave, too."

Momma stands from the table, bringing her plate to the sink. "He doesn't have anything going on or someone to rush home to. I'm sure he wouldn't mind."

"I didn't know you kept tabs on my schedule, Momma."

She eyes me over her shoulder, arching her brow. "I know more than you think I do, young man. Now, go saddle up Farbi and Karma. Those two are in desperate need of a ride, and I know Shauna would enjoy the company."

"Fine." Without looking over at her, I exit the house and trod down to the stables, irritated with my mother and nervous to be alone with Shauna again. Yesterday, when we spoke, things were heated. Can I trust myself to keep my anger in check this time?

After about ten minutes, I hear the sound of footsteps crushing dirt and hay beneath them. I glance over my shoulder as I secure the harness on Farbi, finding Shauna striding toward me, her hair flowing behind her, her lips pursed in thought.

God, she's so fucking beautiful.

I can't be friends with this woman, not when I want to fuck her into next week and show her everything she's been missing—what we've both missed out on for fifteen years.

"Sorry about this. I tried telling your mother I didn't need to ride, but you know how she is," she says when she arrives right next to me.

"It's fine."

"Forrest..."

I twist my head to face her, fighting to keep my voice

friendly. "The horses are ready, so we might as well go, Shauna. You remember how to ride?"

She narrows her eyes at me and then smiles. "That's not what you should be worried about, Forrest. You should be worried about being able to keep up." She flicks her hair over her shoulders, puts her boot in the stirrup, and launches herself up and over Farbi, settling into the saddle.

And I'm instantly hard.

Fuck. Now I have to ride a horse with a fucking hard-on. Not ideal.

Shaking off my desire for this woman that hasn't dwindled over time, I walk over to Karma, one of the few mares big enough to hold me, and mount her, getting as comfortable as I can given the tightness in the crotch of my pants now.

"Where are we headed?" Shauna asks as I adjust the reins in my hands.

"Doesn't matter to me. You remember your way around?"

She chuckles. "Yeah, if anything, I remember too much." And then she digs her heels in Farbi's sides and gallops past the barn we use for events, her hair blowing in the wind, twisting up my insides. I take off after her like we're young and in love all over again.

The tall grass whooshes beside us as Karma and Farbi find their stride, heading out toward the northern part of the land. My parents have just over five square miles of property, so there's plenty to explore.

And even though I've seen most of it so many times I've lost count, it feels like I'm seeing it for the first time again because I'm focused on the woman in front of me.

Shauna's laughter carries as I catch up to her. She shouts over at me, "God, I missed this!"

I smile back at her, but it catches me off guard, and then I remember that I can't just slip back into old habits with this woman. That's just asking for more heartache.

When Shauna makes a turn to the left, I instantly know where she's headed—to the old shack we used to escape to when we wanted to be alone. I haven't been out here in years because why go back to a place that holds memories of a happier time, one that's too painful to remember? Those memories just haunted me more and more until I avoided this place altogether.

Shauna pushes Farbi to her limit as we close in on the shack, but the moment we arrive, I feel like I've run a marathon. I forgot how much strength it takes to ride a horse.

"Looks like I can still beat you," Shauna states proudly as she catches her breath. Guess I'm not the only one winded from that ride.

"Give me a break, will you? I haven't ridden a horse in years." I dismount Karma and walk her over to the hitching post as Shauna follows my lead.

"Years?"

"Yeah. Kinda didn't appeal to me after we broke up." I shrug, but I'm not going to lie to her. She deserves to know how hard it was for me and why it's not easy to just let her back in again. And that's the unfortunate part—I naïvely thought it would have been.

"I kept riding out in Vegas," she says, pulling my attention to her.

"Really? How?"

When Farbi is secured, she turns and says, "I volunteered at a horse rescue out there. I missed being around them too much, so I found a way to fill that missing piece." She rubs Farbi's nose. "You can take the girl out of the country, but you can't take the country out of the girl, I guess."

As I take her in—her jeans, cowboy boots, and pink top—I think about how differently she looked when I saw her in Vegas. I barely recognized her with the way she presented herself there. But this—this is how I remember the girl I knew—*the girl I loved.*

"So of all the places to go on the ranch, you chose this spot?"

Shauna walks away from me toward the door, jiggling the lock. "Can you blame me? This was our place, Forrest."

"Yeah, back when things were good."

She spins and says, "They could be good again, you know."

"Shauna . . ." I shake my head and stare at the ground.

But she doesn't allow me much time to think before she closes the distance between us and lifts my chin so our eyes meet.

"Talk to me, Forrest. Tell me what you're thinking after our conversation yesterday."

Even though I see the moment her smile drops when I take a step back, I do it because I can't think right when she's this close to me. She smells like some kind of citrus and berries and a mixture of flour. I wonder if she made biscuits with my mom today like she used to.

"I don't know what I'm thinking, Shauna." I hold my hands out to the side. "My head's a fucking mess, if I'm being honest."

"I'm sorry. I didn't mean to make things difficult for you, but I had to come back here, Forrest. You get that, right?"

"I guess, but here's where I'm struggling. My feelings have never wavered, Shauna. I've loved you since I was sixteen. I spent years trying to convince myself that I could move on, but I never did. But you were about to marry another man. I know I'm the one who wanted to stop you, but it's like you said, the whole thing was messy, and you were in a relationship with this guy for years. So I guess I need you to tell me what you need. Do you need space to figure out what you want? Do you need time to make sure that you made the right choice? Or do you think you might leave again when this is all over, when you've finished this job my mom hired you to do?

Because I can't handle having my heart ripped in two again. Just because you're here doesn't mean everything is fine."

She takes a step toward me again. "I ran away and came here when I felt like I had my head on straight. Doesn't that answer your question?"

"No, because even though you ran away from *him*, that doesn't necessarily mean you want *me* right now." God, it sucks to say it, but there's no sense in keeping this in. "You made a decision that impacted a lot of people, and as much as I want you wholeheartedly, in every way, and I want to pick up where we left off all those years ago, it would be unfair to you and me to pretend like we don't have a lot of shit to work through."

She looks at the ground for a moment before meeting my eyes again. "You're right. We do. But here's what I'm afraid of. I'm afraid that you're going to hold all of my mistakes and past choices against me, that you'll never forgive me or try to understand why I did what I did back then, Forrest."

Her words give me pause. Can I let go of the past? That's one of the questions Javi asked me that I still don't have an answer for.

But she doesn't let me reply before continuing. "Look. I made mistakes, okay? I should never have kept the information about my dad from you. I was scared about what you'd think, how'd you react, and I was terrified that you would tell my mom. But that was my mistake. I was wrong, and I'm the one who's owned it." She closes a few more inches between us, reaching up to brush my hair from my face. "Here's the thing about mistakes, though, Forrest. Our greatest mistakes are also our greatest opportunities. I might be fifteen years late, but I was given the opportunity to try to repair what we had. And you helped me do that. I have to believe that you showing up that day was a sign. Our story is messy, but together, I think we can clean it up and create something even more beautiful than it was before."

Her eyes dip down to my lips as she darts her tongue out. "Don't you feel this? You asked me that question first, and I knew the answer to it, even though I couldn't say it at the time. It's always been you, Forrest, no matter how hard I tried to move on."

"Shauna . . ." I close my eyes as I feel her move in, her lips just a breath from my own. But fuck, I can't just give in this soon. I need time.

When I step away from her, she almost falls forward, but I grab her biceps and catch her before she does. Her eyes widen as she steadies herself. I know I caught her off guard, but this isn't the right time for that yet.

Instead, I suggest, "What if we try to be friends again while we figure everything out?"

"Friends?" she asks, her voice emotionless.

"Yeah. I think we should go slow, get to know each other again because jumping right back into the physical? We know how to do that, Shauna, but you and I aren't the same people we were back then. I think we owe it to ourselves to make sure this is what we both want."

Are you listening to yourself right now? Can you feel your dick weeping at this moment, Forrest?

Shauna clears her throat and then plasters on a smile. "Okay. Friends." She reaches out to shake my hand, and I intercept it, grateful for the relief this agreement gives me.

She's here. It's what I wanted, so the fact that I'm hesitating tells me there's more we need to figure out. And if I'm not burying myself in her to cover up our mess, perhaps I can think clearly.

Yeah, good luck with that while she walks around wearing those tight fucking jeans for the next six weeks.

"Good. Glad that's settled."

Shauna walks backward toward Farbi, loosening the rope and preparing to climb back on her. Once she does and settles in, she peers down at me where I'm still standing on the ground. "I have to warn you, though, Forrest. Just because we're friends doesn't mean I'm going to let you beat me back to the ranch. I hate to lose. Remember that?"

I hoist myself back up on Karma and look at my high school sweetheart over my shoulder. "Oh, I remember vividly, Shauna. But do *you* remember that I'm not actually losing when I get to watch your ass as you ride in front of me?"

Her laughter fills the air as she takes off. "You haven't changed all that much, Forrest Gibson."

Maybe she's right. In a lot of ways, I'm still the same guy, and she's the only woman I've ever loved.

And that's when I realize: If it's not her, then it's no one. But I can't go through that kind of heartache again.

So we either figure this out and find our way back to each other, or I accept the fact that I had one great love in my life at the age of sixteen, and that's all I get.

Here's hoping we can figure it out together.

CHAPTER EIGHT

Shauna

"I'm not so sure about this," I tell Momma G through the phone.

"Nonsense. You deserve a place to work out just like anyone else, and Elite Gym is the best."

"But what if Forrest sees me and gets all pissed again?"

"You have as much of a right to be there as he does. It's a public establishment. And if that boy gives you any trouble, you tell me, and I'll set him straight."

I blow out a breath. "Fine."

"Now, go enjoy your workout. I'll see you tomorrow."

"See ya then."

I place my cell phone back in my purse as I stare up at Elite Gym, convincing myself to walk inside.

When I mentioned to Momma G the other day about finding a place to work out, she immediately recommended this place, making sure to tell me that this is where Forrest works out, too. And she just so happened to know his gym schedule, alluding to the fact that I could "accidentally" bump into him here if I wanted to—which I did, until about five minutes ago when I pulled into the parking lot.

After our ride last night, I'm not sure if trying to cross paths with him so soon is a good idea, but I'm on a limited time frame. I can't just stand around and hope that he lets me back in on his own. That man can be as stubborn as a bull, so I have to keep pushing, give our second chance my all. Because if I don't, I'll regret it.

Mustering up every ounce of courage I can find, I take a deep breath and open the door to the gym. I'm instantly hit with the smell of rubber, metal, and sweat.

"Hi, there. How can I help you?" The hostess behind the counter greets me.

"I'm interested in a membership."

"Great. We have a one-week trial pass if you'd like to try it out first, or you can sign up monthly right out of the gate?"

Not wanting to be presumptuous, I decide on the week pass, and after signing my paperwork, I head toward the locker room. Once I secure my belongings, I grab my water bottle and head toward the stair stepper, needing a good sweat to help burn off my nerves.

I program the workout I want and begin, glancing around the gym as I climb.

Multiple weight machines are scattered all over the floor. A set of free weights stand in a corner in front of full-length mirrors. Classes are being held in several rooms in the back, and toward the front is a boxing ring and an MMA cage.

In fact, two men are in the cage right now, circling each other. And as I study them a few seconds longer, I realize one of them is Forrest.

God, he looks good.

His arms are bulging as he throws punches, blocking some from the guy he's fighting as well. Unfortunately, he has a tank top on so I can't see his entire torso, but that's probably a good thing so I don't drool—or worse, fall off this damn stair stepper.

They end their match and bump gloves, and then he steps down from the cage, headed in my direction.

I hold my breath as he walks past, but he recognizes me instantly. "Shauna?"

"Hey, Forrest." I wave like an idiot then focus back on the machine.

"What are you doing here?"

"What does it look like? Working out."

He narrows his eyes at me. "Did my mom tell you this is my gym?"

"Last time I checked, this gym was open to the public, so . . ."

He rolls his eyes. "I know, I mean—"

"I just came to work out, Forrest. You know, like you did? It's good for my mental health," I say, adjusting my sports bra and drawing his line of sight to my chest.

And it works like a charm.

Forrest nearly burns a hole through my outfit as he takes me in. The teal sports bra and shorts set I chose may have been with the intention of giving him a glimpse of what he's missing by suggesting we be friends. By the clench in his jaw, I'm guessing it's working.

"And that's what you work out in?" he growls.

"Is that a problem?"

He pinches the bridge of his nose. "Nope."

Silently celebrating my victory, I watch him walk toward the locker room and I finish up my time before moving on to do some arm exercises.

About fifteen minutes later, Forrest comes out of the locker room freshly showered and changed. He searches the room before his eyes land on me.

A wave of heat rushes through me, and it has nothing to do with the sweat I'm working up.

He stalks to where I'm standing in front of the free weights and mirror and watches me finish up my set. "Arm day?"

"Yeah."

"Mind if I offer you a pointer on your form?"

I stand up and spin around to face him so I'm not looking at him in the mirror. "Sure."

This is good, Shauna. He's talking to you. Granted, he's going to critique your form, but at least he's not avoiding you. He's trying to be your friend like you agreed, right?

"You need to bend over more," he says, putting his hand on my waist as he pushes my torso down. My nipples harden from the contact.

He clears his throat and then continues. "Hinge at the hips and then push your chest out more before you do your reverse chest flies. This will help target your chest more."

"Like this?" I do a few repetitions, watching for his approval.

"Yeah, like that . . ." His voice turns huskier as he watches me, but once he realizes what he's doing, he snaps out of it. "I've got to get going."

I stand up tall again and meet his eyes. "Oh. Okay. Well, maybe I'll see you around here again. I got a free week pass just to try it out, but who knows if I'll have as much time as the event gets closer?"

"Yeah." He takes a step toward me as if he were going to lean down and kiss my forehead, but then he catches himself. "Uh, have a good night, Shauna."

"You, too, Forrest."

He takes two steps away from me but then freezes, turning back to face me dead on. "You know, you didn't have to wear that little outfit to get my attention."

My heart is racing. "What do you mean?"

"I mean, you could be wearing a wet paper bag, and I'd still recognize your ass, Shauna." With a smirk on his face, he walks away for real this time, leaving me yearning to go after him to find out how fast he could strip this little outfit off of me.

Instead, I turn back to the mirror, take a deep breath, and finish my workout, intent on making the drive into town worth it in more ways than one.

∽

"Hey, Kelsea."

The little girl I watched grow up spins on her heels and flashes me her contagious smile when she sees me. Only, she's not that little girl anymore, and I'm not the same person from back then, either. Kelsea was twelve when I left and coming back to see how much she's changed since I was in Newberry Springs last is just another reminder that I can't go back in time.

Forrest reminded me of that distinctly the other night.

"Shauna! Hi! What are you doing here?" She walks over to the front of the Gibson Ranch booth, greeting me with a twinkle in her eyes. It's Thursday, which means the Newberry Springs Farmers Market is in full swing.

"Well, I needed to come down and grab a few things for Momma G today, and I wanted to scope out some vendors to see if they'd be interested in participating in the Winter Wonderland event."

After talking with Momma G all week, we decided that the event would run for seven days straight, leading up to Christmas Eve. Her vision is to create her own Santa's Village, including photos with Santa himself—who Mr. Gibson reluctantly agreed to portray—crafts for kids, a reindeer petting zoo, a snowman-building contest using artificial snow, and hayrides around the ranch to see the light displays that Randy and the boys will be constructing. We just need people to donate supplies, businesses that might want to make some money on last-minute shoppers, and food vendors to come in so people can eat while they shop and partake in the festivities.

It's going to be a lot of work, especially given the short timeline. But I'm grateful for the distraction right now, especially after the ride with Forrest the other night didn't go the way I wanted it to, and seeing him at the gym on Tuesday left me lusting after him even more.

I take a moment to look around the street, overwhelmed by how much the farmers market has grown since I lived here, and then direct my attention back to Kelsea. "I came here to work, but now I'm thinking I could spend all day here just buying stuff for myself."

Kelsea laughs. "I understand, but this is the last week of the market until next spring. The market shuts down for the winter because it's just too cold."

"Makes sense."

"When Walker or Wyatt are here to help, I'll take off sometimes to grab a cup of coffee and browse different booths. Lord knows that's the only time I have to do that sort of thing now between working at the brewery and managing my photography business." She catches me staring at the racks of clothes in the booth next to hers. "Are you looking for anything in particular?"

My eyes land on a sweater dress hanging on a rack. I take a few steps over to it and reach for the dress, rubbing my hand across the soft, ribbed, burnt-orange fabric. "I could use some new clothes, actually. I only packed so much when I flew out here, and I don't have much besides jeans and tops that I don't care about getting dirty."

Evelyn strides up to us with Kaydence on her hip. "Well, you've come to the right place." She smiles, and then Kelsea nods, reaching out to grab Kaydence's hand, pretending to eat it.

"You remember Evelyn from last weekend, right?" Kelsea asks me.

"Yes. It's good to see you again."

"Oh, I'm sure we're going to be seeing a lot more of each other now." Evelyn winks at me. "But just so you know, these pieces are from my clothing boutique, Luna. I'm down on Main Street, and I'd be happy to help you find anything you're looking for. If I don't have it in stock, I can order something from one of my suppliers, too."

"I appreciate that. Thanks. I don't have a lot of time

right now since I'm here on another mission, really, but when does your store close? Maybe I could swing by later."

Kelsea and Evelyn share a look, and then Evelyn faces me again. "How about you come by tomorrow night after I close? You can have your own personal shopping experience, complete with wine and girl talk."

"Really? I don't want to impose."

"You aren't. I'm offering. Besides, I feel like the three of us have plenty to discuss when it comes to those Gibson boys."

Kelsea snickers. "I'm dying to know what's going on with Forrest, Shauna." She leans forward and whispers, "Are you two getting back together?"

That is the million-dollar question at the moment.

"Ha. I can't even answer that right now. It's . . . complicated."

"I'm sure it is, because Forrest is complicated himself."

"Isn't that the truth," I mutter.

When he suggested we be friends the other night, I questioned who I was talking to. Forrest—*my Forrest*—would have been hell bent *against* just being my friend fifteen years ago. But when he explained that we have a lot to work through and that he was struggling with my reappearance, I saw his perspective and understood where he was coming from. And when I realized he was right, that it would be wise to start off slow, my desire for this to be fixed quickly dissipated. But that doesn't mean

I'm still not eager to get back to us and what we had, if that's even possible at this point.

"I have so many questions," Kelsea continues. "All I keep thinking about is how you two used to be back in high school."

"Yeah, things were much simpler then, that's for sure."

"But besides Forrest, you look like you could use a friend." Kelsea tilts her head at me, her soft smile reminding me of the pure sunshine she is. This girl was always a beacon of light, willing to give so much of herself to others back then—and apparently still now.

And the truth is, I could use someone to talk to who isn't Momma G. I've been in touch with Willow, but she's busy and lives on the East Coast. It's hard to coordinate phone calls with the time difference. However, I wouldn't have gotten through the last six weeks without her.

When I ran out on the wedding, she was the one who spoke to the guests and made sure the vendors were taken care of. She was the one who picked me up at a nearby coffee shop that I was hiding in after running down the street looking for Forrest. And when all of the dust settled, she helped me figure out how to put my life back together.

I'll always consider her my best friend, but she's not here and doesn't have the insight into the workings of this family and this small town.

But Kelsea and Evelyn do.

Trying not to cry from her suggestion because I don't

want to seem that desperate, I fold my lips in and nod. "That would be nice," I manage to squeak out.

Evelyn tips her chin. "Perfect, then it's settled. See you around five?"

"I'll be there." Inhaling deeply, I turn back to Kelsea. "All right. I'd better get going. I have a lot of people to talk to."

"Good luck, and have fun. We'll see you tomorrow."

~

It's just after five when I pull up to one of the parking spaces in front of Luna. The boutique sits between two other small shops on Main Street, but those don't have the same pizzaz as Evelyn's storefront. The store name sparkles as the sunlight catches it where it's positioned just above the door, and the windows in the front are covered by glittered curtains hanging from the inside.

It's adorable, but even the welcoming atmosphere isn't quelling my nerves.

Despite the anxiousness flowing through my veins, I exit my car and step up to the door, knocking since it's after hours. A few minutes pass before Evelyn unlocks the door from the inside and pushes it open to greet me.

"Shauna! Come in!"

"Thanks."

She locks the door behind me as I step in and glance around the space.

Racks of clothing—dresses, shirts, pants, and sweaters—are situated along both walls and displayed on the walls themselves. Down the center of the room are tables with folded items and several displays of purses, jewelry, and shoes as well. A girl could get lost in here for hours and never bat an eye.

"Kelsea's in the back changing Kaydence for me. Walker will be here any minute to pick her up, but feel free to start browsing. Anything you like and want to try on you can hang on the outside of dressing room one." She points it out.

I turn to face her head on. "Thanks again, Evelyn. This is really sweet of you."

She reaches out and grabs my hand. "Nonsense. I know what it's like to be alone in a small town. If it weren't for Kelsea, I still would be." With a smile, she heads toward the back of the store, leaving me wondering more about her story.

And that's the reality of the situation I'm in, isn't it? We all have a story, and mine and Forrest's can't be over yet. I refuse to accept it.

Taking a deep breath, I begin to look through the clothes, finding a few sweaters that look as comfortable as they are soft and the sweater dress I was eyeing yesterday at the farmers market. Only a few minutes pass during my perusal before there's a knock on the door.

"I've got it," Evelyn calls out behind me, unlocking the door again to let Walker in. And as soon as he steps inside, he yanks her to him by the waist, possessively planting his mouth on hers.

It's so wild to see the little boy I knew back then now married and in love. But I can clearly tell by the way they stare at each other when they part that Walker and Evelyn are desperately in love with each other. And I know that without hesitation because Forrest used to look at me the same way.

Walker finally turns his head in my direction, his smile meeting his eyes when he sees me. "Shauna!"

"Hey, Walker."

He ambles over and pulls me in for a hug. "How's it going?"

He releases me, and I readjust my shirt. "It's going. Your wife here is helping me find some clothes."

"Well, you've come to the right place. I just need to pick up my little owl, and then I'll leave you ladies to your girls' night. Please tell me you're going to gossip heavily about my grumpy ass brother?"

"Oh, we definitely will," Kelsea announces as she joins us in the front of the store now with Kaydence in her arms.

Kaydence makes a sound like an owl when she sees Walker, and suddenly his nickname for her makes perfect sense.

"There's my little owl," he says, taking her from Kelsea and tossing her up in the air, causing her to squeal in excitement.

A pang of jealousy rushes through me. There was a time when I imagined Forrest doing the same thing with our child.

Can we still have that?

"I gave her a snack an hour ago, so she'll be ready for dinner once you get home," Evelyn says to Walker as Kelsea hands him her diaper bag.

"Don't worry, I've got it handled." He leans forward to kiss Evelyn's lips once more. "You girls have fun. If you have a little too much wine, you call me, and I'll come get you, all right?"

"Don't worry. I have Wyatt on standby," Kelsea interjects.

"That works, too." Then he turns to me and says, "Nice to see you again, Shauna. Let me know if you need any extra help with wearing my big brother down."

"Ha. Thanks."

"I'm serious. I'm glad you came back here after he tried to stop your wedding. You have no idea how fucking miserable he's been, but he's a stubborn ass, and I know that you know that. So like I said—if you need me to nudge him a bit, just say the word, and I'll gladly offer my time." He gives Evelyn one more kiss and then exits the store, leaving the three of us alone.

"Well, I guess now would be the time to tell you we know all about Vegas," Kelsea says with a shrug.

I sigh. "I'm actually surprised. Knowing how private Forrest is, I wasn't sure that he'd tell anyone."

"He was with Walker and Wyatt when he decided to fly back to stop your wedding. And well, since we're married to them, you know they had to tell us."

Chuckling, I pick up another top from a rack nearby and add it to the stack hanging over my arm. "I understand. But just so you know, Momma G had no idea about that when she hired me."

Kelsea's and Evelyn's eyebrows raise. "Really?"

"She knows now because I told her, but I think she assumed that my coming back would help push us back together anyway."

Kelsea sighs. "All right. We have way too much to discuss, but we definitely need some wine before we continue. Shauna, go start trying on clothes. Evelyn, lock the door and shut the drapes, and I'll get the wine." She claps her hands together. "This is gonna be so much fun."

Two bottles of wine later between the three of us, I come out of the dressing room wearing the sweater dress I was drawn to yesterday.

"Oh, shit," Evelyn says, nearly spitting out her wine. "Girl, that dress was made for you!"

"You think?" I turn around to see myself in the mirror and nearly face-plant because my equilibrium is off. Yup, the wine is definitely doing its job.

"Heck yes," Kelsea says. "You have to get it. Forrest will just die when he sees you in that."

"I don't know. We're trying to be just friends, remember?"

Over the past hour and a half, I've filled the girls in on what's happened with Forrest since I returned and what happened between us in the past. It felt good to talk it out, help me remember everything that transpired, leading us up to this point. It also reminded me that Forrest was right to push pause on moving forward too fast. We do have a lot of shit to work through.

However, they were practically salivating when I told them how Momma G convinced him to take me for a ride the other night and how I tried to make a move, but he wouldn't reciprocate. I also told them about the gym on Tuesday—they were dying at the comment he made.

"That man could never be just friends with you, Shauna." Kelsea rolls her eyes at the idea. "I've been around him the entire time you've been gone, all right? And I'm telling you, he's always been hung up on you. I'm not sure he's even dated in the past fifteen years, and if he has, he's been very discreet about it."

The idea of Forrest with another woman makes my insides twist, but I was engaged to another man until two months ago, so I have no right to be jealous. The reality is, we've both been with other people since we broke up, so neither of us can hold that fact against the other. The only thing I can focus on is the connection between us that hasn't wavered no matter how much time has passed.

"Well, I can't blame him for moving on, but I came out here to see if there's something still there between us, you know?" I run my hands down the front of the dress, smoothing out the lines. The soft, rust-colored fabric hugs my hips and highlights my hourglass figure. I have to admit, I think Forrest *will* have a hard time keeping his hands off me when he sees me in this.

"Trust me. His willpower won't last long. Just don't give up."

I twist around to face the girls as a hiccup escapes my lips. "I'm not, but how do I get him to change his mind? Without stalking the man, I need a reason for us to spend time together, to get to know each other again."

Evelyn stares up at the ceiling, pondering her reply for a moment. When the idea hits her, she nearly launches herself off the couch she and Kelsea are sitting on, spilling her wine on the hardwood floor beneath her. "I've got it!"

Kelsea giggles and then pulls her back down to the cushions. "You're making a mess!"

"It's okay. I can clean it up in a minute." She waves off her best friend, and I can't help but laugh as well. "Shauna, ask Forrest to help you with the Winter Wonderland event."

"How?"

"Well, you're going to need things to be built, right? Ask him if he'd be willing to do that. The man knows his way around a hammer, some wood, and nails."

"What if he just assigns one of his employees instead?" I counter.

"He won't," Evelyn declares smugly.

"How do you know?"

"Because he won't be able to stand the thought of some other man being near you, talking to you, laughing with you. It will drive him nuts."

Kelsea nods in agreement. "Totally."

Groaning, I take another drink of my wine. "I can already see his reaction, you guys. He's going to close his eyes, pinch the bridge of his nose, and act like getting a root canal would be easier than helping me."

"Damn." Kelsea snickers. "That was perfect. Forrest to a T."

"I know." I let out a wistful sigh. "But God, that man..."

Evelyn wiggles her eyebrows. "Oh, yeah. The grumpy thing just does it for you, doesn't it?"

I take a seat on the chair opposite them, sipping on my wine again. "I never thought it would because that's not who he was back then, you know? But when we reconnected, I could see that change in him, and I hate to say it, but... it really is hot."

All three of us giggle simultaneously.

"Wyatt gets that way sometimes, too, and I just want to jump his bones and hope he takes that aggression out on me," Kelsea says.

"Walker is so hot when he's grumpy," Evelyn adds. "And when it's because of me? Like he's protecting me from something or I did something to piss him off... it's even hotter."

I cover my mouth to stifle my laugh. "Lucky girls. But

I don't think pissing off Forrest any more is going to help me here. He's already mad enough."

"Have you guys spoken about the past yet?" Kelsea asks. "I mean, I know it sucks to bring that stuff up, but like he said, it was a lot."

I stare down at my wine. "I know that we need to, but I'm not sure if it's the right time for that." I shake my head and gaze out the window. "Sometimes I wonder where we would be right now if I had just been honest with him. And if I hadn't let my mom get in my head about young love . . ."

To say my mother wasn't pleased with me when I ran out of my wedding is an understatement. In fact, our conversations lately have been very one-sided—that side being her telling me how big a mistake I've made.

"Oh, Evelyn and I know all about mommy issues," Kelsea says, slurring her words slightly.

"My mother is a piece of work, Shauna. Believe me, I'm sure yours is a saint compared to mine." Evelyn raises a brow.

"I don't blame her, not anymore. It took a long time, but once I told her about my dad and the real reason he left, she started to see the error of her ways, how talking badly about him ruined our relationship, too. Believe me, it took several years for us to work past all of that, but I know that her influence affected my relationship with Forrest, too. She was so convinced that my being with him would ruin my life, that I would be stuck in a small town like she was, and that Forrest wouldn't stick around—because that was her experience." She made sure to remind me of that when I told her I was going back to Newberry Springs. "But the thing we really have to work past is that when Forrest found out I kept all that stuff from him, it hurt him deeply. I don't want to bring that up out of the blue and catch him off guard again, you know?"

Evelyn nods. "No, I agree. The right time will present itself naturally. That's what happened for me and Walker, and I'm glad that I waited to share the tough stuff with him when I did."

"Well, I didn't speak up soon enough, and it caused a lot of heartache for me and Wyatt, so don't wait too long," Kelsea adds.

"I know. I just—"

"I'm telling you, Shauna. Ask him for his help. Make him feel like you need him." Evelyn shrugs. "It's the perfect starting point."

"I *do* need him . . ." I whisper, draining my glass and then setting it on the table beside me. "It took me fifteen years to realize it, but it's the truth."

Kelsea stands and comes over to me, pulling me from the chair. "Just don't give up. And Evelyn and I are here to help in any way we can."

That familiar sting of tears builds behind my eyes. "Thank you. And thank you for tonight. I really needed this."

Evelyn comes over to join us now. "You're welcome.

Kelsea and I are best friends and now sisters-in-law, but you're practically one, too. And if we're going to survive being married to those Gibson boys, we're going to need to lean on one another."

A laugh escapes my lips. "I appreciate the optimistic thinking, but Forrest and I have a long way to go before anyone hears wedding bells."

Kelsea smirks. "I don't know about that. I think you're right on track."

Evelyn juts her thumb toward Kelsea. "This one with the romantic side, always rooting for true love. I'll have you know, she meddled in my relationship with Walker, too."

Kelsea playfully shoves her. "Yeah, I did. Because you were too stubborn to figure out yourself that he was meant for you."

"Hey, I got there. It just took me a minute."

"More like an hour," Kelsea mutters under her breath and then turns back to me. "Anyway, I'm not above helping if you need it too, okay?"

"Thanks." I stare down at my empty glass. "Ugh. I think I've had enough wine for the night."

Evelyn nods. "Agreed. And you still have more clothes to try on, so get that ass back in the dressing room." She smacks said ass as I turn around. "We need to make Forrest's mouth water when he sees you, so we have a lot more work to do."

CHAPTER NINE

Forrest

"Hey, boss. You mind signing these papers for me?"

I look up from my computer to find Javi standing in front of my desk, clutching a stack of inventory sheets in his hand.

"Yeah, sure." I blow out a breath as he hands them to me, scribble my signature across the bottom, and pass them right back. "There you go."

"Thanks. We still on for the gym tonight?"

"Hell yeah. I need to work off some aggression," I

reply, leaning back in my chair and running a hand through my hair.

"Why don't you let Shauna help with that?" Javi smirks, crossing his arms over his chest.

"Well, since she's the reason I'm fucking on edge right now, I'm not sure that's the best idea."

Javi shakes his head. "Hmm, I disagree. When I'm pissed at Sydney, the best way to let her know about it is to fuck her into next week. She doesn't seem to mind, either."

"Charming."

"I take it being friends isn't going well, then?"

"It's hard to do that when I feel like she's avoiding me."

Yesterday was Sunday, the day my brothers and I stop by the ranch to help out. I anticipated seeing Shauna there, even though I felt a sense of dread at the idea. It's not that I didn't want to see her, it's that being near her makes me feel a lack of control, like I don't know how I might react, and I hate that. Being in control for the latter part of my life is the only thing that's saved me from going insane, and the only time I feel out of it is around her.

But when Momma told me that Shauna took the day off to relax and catch up on a few things at her townhouse—the one Walker so graciously offered up to her—I felt something I wasn't expecting: disappointment.

And now I'm wondering if she's changed her mind about staying here—or at the very least, trying to get back on solid ground with me. It sure as hell didn't feel that way after our ride last Monday and her showing up at my gym on Tuesday.

"Forrest?" Jill pops her head into my open office door, halting the conversation between Javi and me.

"Yeah?"

"You have a visitor." The smirk on her face tells me this probably isn't a visitor I'm going to be happy about. But then Shauna appears behind her, and I eat my own thought.

What the hell is she doing here?

"Hi," she says softly, smiling down at me before I stand from behind my desk. Then her eyes dart to Javi standing on the side of the room, basking in the awkwardness and my turmoil. *Fucker.* "I'm Shauna," she says, reaching out to shake Javi's hand.

"Javier, but you can call me Javi. Nice to meet you, Shauna. It's good to put a face to the name."

"So you've heard my name, then?" she teases.

"Oh, yeah." Javi grins over at me, and I've never wanted to strangle the man so much in my life. Guess who's going to be dodging punches left and right later?

"Javi was just leaving," I say, willing him to leave. I don't need him to witness whatever Shauna came all the way to my office to say.

"I was?"

"Yeah, you were. You have crew evaluations to

complete before five today, and lord knows you love to procrastinate with those."

Javi shakes his head, an amused smile on his lips. "Okay, okay. I can take a hint. No need to ride my ass, boss." He walks past Shauna and then glances back at me. "Good luck, Shauna. But if anyone can wear that man down, I think it might be you." And then he leaves just as Jill walks back in.

"I'm so sorry to interrupt again, but I need you to look over these really quick before I send them off to the Houston office." She walks over to my desk and hands me three sheets of paper, invoices and paperwork for crews who will be traveling out to the coast to help on a project.

I glance up at Shauna. "I'm sorry. Give me just a minute."

"No problem."

I gesture to the chairs on the other side of my desk. "You can take a seat, if you want."

She smiles and moves to one of the chairs, sitting down while watching me and Jill.

Jill places her hand on my shoulder as I take my seat again and she leans over the papers with me. "Here's what I want you to approve," she says, pointing down at one of the totals. "It seems like a bit much, but I know you'd rather not skimp on items like that."

I nod. "Yeah, you're right. It is a bit high but not astronomically so."

Jill squeezes my shoulder, and then I hear Shauna clear her throat.

"Sorry," she says when I glance up at her.

Jill chuckles under her breath. "One last thing." She slides one of the other papers in front of me and points to the item she wants me to review, leaning over my desk even more, making our faces uncomfortably close. But I try not to focus on that and do some mental math before replying, "Yeah, that looks good, too."

"Excellent." Jill gathers the papers, hands me a pen, and I sign the bottom of each one. She ruffles my hair and then says, "Thanks, boss. I'll be at my desk if you need anything."

When Jill leaves, I look back at Shauna and notice that the soft smile she had on her face before is nowhere to be found. In its place is a look of annoyance.

"You okay?"

"Your assistant seems nice. A little unaware of personal space but efficient, nonetheless."

The corner of my mouth tips up as I lean back in my chair and fold my hands over my chest. "Jill is the best. I couldn't run this company without her."

Shauna pops her eyebrows and then looks over to the side of the room, avoiding my eyes. "Seems like she wants to be more than your assistant, at least from where I'm sitting."

I fight like hell not to laugh. If I didn't know any better, I'd say that Shauna is jealous.

And I'm not gonna lie, that little fact makes me feel all warm and fuzzy inside.

I could let her believe that Jill is a threat, but I think we have enough obstacles in our way without adding that one to the list. So I decide to put Shauna out of her misery sooner than I probably should.

"Well, I think Jill's wife, Becca, would be strongly opposed to that idea."

Shauna's head snaps back to me. "Her what?"

Leaning over my desk, I let my pleasant smile show. And the second I do, I can tell it catches Shauna off guard. "Jill is gay, sweetheart."

Shauna's lips part slightly, forming a little *o*. And fuck, does it make me want to leap over this desk and smash my own mouth to hers, but I already know that getting physical with this woman isn't going to solve anything.

"Oh," she says. "Uh, well . . ."

"Glad to know you're jealous, though, Shauna. I'll be sure to share that with Jill later."

Shauna glares at me. "You will do no such thing, Forrest."

"Can't tell me what to do, sweetheart. This is my company, after all."

She rolls her eyes but doesn't say anything else. And suddenly, I'm wondering if her eyes still roll back when she comes too.

My dick twitches under my desk, and I try like hell

not to focus on that fact, instead focusing on why Shauna is really here.

"So how can I help you, Shauna? I gotta say, I'm surprised to see you show up at my company's office today."

She sits up taller in her chair and focuses her attention back on me. "I know, but because I need your help in a professional sense, I thought this would be best."

"You could have asked me yesterday if you would have shown up at my parents' house."

"I had some things to do." Her eyes dart away for a second but then return to mine. "But that's why I'm here now."

"Okay. So what is it?"

"Well, since you have experience building things, I was wondering if you'd be willing to help construct a few items for the Winter Wonderland event at the ranch?"

"Such as?" I lean forward, grab a pen and notepad from the corner of my desk, and hold the pen over the paper, ready to jot down her ideas.

"I need a backdrop for photos with Santa. Something that looks like his house or a toy shop."

"Okay..."

"I need a display for Pin the Nose on Rudolph."

I huff out a laugh. "Cute."

She smiles proudly. "I thought so."

"Anything else?"

"A couple of signs to direct customers to different areas, probably, and maybe a pen for the reindeer."

I glance up at her. "Reindeer?"

"Yes. They're coming from Colorado, actually. I read a book where this girl dared the guy she was dating to let a reindeer kiss him at a Christmas festival. It's what gave me the idea."

"I doubt you're going to have men lined up to prove their manhood by kissing a reindeer, but building a pen for you to keep the little fuckers under control shouldn't be a problem."

She smirks at me. "Great. So when can you get started?"

"Me? You want *me* to build these things? In case you haven't noticed, I'm running a multi-million dollar company these days," I say, fanning my hands out to the sides.

She bites on her bottom lip. "Well, that's true. I guess if you have to send one of your employees out to help me, that's not the end of the world." She fiddles with the hem of her sweater before glancing up at me beneath her dark lashes. "But these things might take a while, so he'll be spending a *ton* of time with me on the ranch, getting dirty and sweaty you know, as we make everything perfect."

The little minx. She knows exactly what she's doing. The thought of any other man spending time with her sends me spiraling, and suddenly I'm envisioning ripping limbs off of one of my workers.

"I can do it," I grit out, not happy that she played her cards perfectly but impressed by her determination, nonetheless.

The smile she flashes me is one of success and triumph. "Perfect. Does Thursday night work for you?"

I think about my schedule momentarily and then nod. "Yeah, that should be fine."

Tonight and tomorrow I usually spend at the gym in the evenings, on Wednesday I have band practice, and Friday night is my next gig with the band, so Thursday is the only afternoon I have free, actually. I might have to get a morning workout in that day so I don't miss out on that at least.

"Thanks, Forrest. I appreciate this." Shauna stands from her chair, and I follow suit. "I guess I'll let you get back to work, then."

She heads for the door, but I reach out and grab her wrist before she turns the knob, pulling her into my chest. Her breath hitches, and being this close to her gives me the chance to draw in her scent again, that sweet citrus smell that always reminds me of summer and her.

"Good to know you aren't going to make being friends with you easy, Shauna," I whisper in her ear.

"What do you mean?" she asks coyly.

"Don't. Don't act like you don't know exactly how you reeled me in just now, not to mention that little stunt you pulled at the gym."

She pushes her ass back into me, making me groan. I

have half a mind to rip that brown sweater off her body right now, yank her jeans down, push her up against the door, and fuck her into the wood for that little maneuver.

"Desperate times call for desperate measures, Forrest."

"Are you that desperate for me?"

"Yes, but not in the way you think." She turns around and faces me, her brow furrowed. "I don't want to play games, Forrest. I just wanted an excuse for us to spend time together."

When I hear the way her voice changes, my shoulders drop. "I guess I can respect that."

"And I know it would mean a lot to your mom for you to be a part of this, too."

"My mom has nothing to do with our relationship, Shauna, even though she likes to think she does."

"I'm not talking about our relationship. I'm talking about the event. She made a comment the other day about how you distance yourself from the ranch, how you have for years."

I blow out a breath and run a hand through my hair—it's already a fucking wreck, anyway. "Well, when I thought I was going to take over the place with you one day and I realized that wasn't going to happen, it made being there for too long too painful."

Shauna frowns. "I'm sorry, but the ranch is part of your family, it's part of who you are. Running from it has increased your resentment toward your family instead of allowing you to remember what an amazing thing you get to be a part of. I'd give anything to have something like that . . . again."

I stare down at her lips, wanting to kiss that frown away but knowing I can't. Instead, I take a step back and put distance between us. Distance allows me to think with a level head—at least, a fairly more stable level head.

Turning my back to her now, I head toward my desk again as my heart rate skyrockets. "I'll see you Thursday, Shauna," I say, not wanting to get into a debate with her right now about the ranch and my family dynamics.

"See you Thursday," she replies after a moment and then leaves me alone in my office, ruminating on our conversation.

Is she right? By avoiding the place that held so many memories and dreams, have I in turn made myself miserable? Would it have helped if I moved forward with the plan to take ownership over the place that made me who I am today? Hardworking, strong, a savvy business man, a family man. Have I not shown my appreciation to my parents for who they've raised me to be?

And why does that question have me feeling like a bigger piece of shit than I did when I came back from Vegas?

I guess there's no time like the present to try to repair the past, though, right? With Shauna *and* my family?

Are the two intertwined, and I've never realized it?

Or did I just need her to show me that?

"Hey, Dad." I walk up behind him as he hangs one of his tools back up on the wall in his shed. It's Thursday night, and I drove straight over to the ranch from the office.

"Forrest? What are you doing here on a Thursday?" I notice that the pinch in his brow is more pronounced as he stares at me, perhaps due to the deep lines and wrinkles that have formed on his skin over the years.

My dad is getting up there in age, a reality of time passing that I have chosen to ignore but suddenly slammed into me after Shauna stopped by my office on Monday and gave me a tongue lashing about how I take my family for granted. I'm still coming to grips with her words.

"I'm here to help Shauna build some stuff for the Winter Wonderland event."

"Ah." He smiles and then proceeds to clean up his mess on the workbench in front of him. "Funny how those women can rope you into doing pretty much anything, huh?"

"Don't I know it."

He turns around to face me again. "Forrest, I'm married to the queen bee. Surely you understand she's training Evelyn, Kelsea, and Shauna, too."

I huff out a laugh. "After she pulled the stunt she did to get Shauna back here in the first place, I'm scared to see what else she's capable of."

"Your mother means well. You know that."

"I do."

"And she just wants you to be happy. So when she saw Shauna's name on the application, she took it as a sign. She didn't know you two had been in contact recently, I swear."

"Good to know, even though I don't think that would have stopped her."

"But it was clear to us both there's still a lot of pain you two are harboring."

"That's to be expected, Dad."

He shakes his head. "You know, pain has deep roots, thick vines that bury themselves in our souls if we let them. The only way to dig them up is to forgive each other."

I stare at him, wondering where this philosophical side of him came from.

He must hear my thoughts because he starts laughing. "Don't look at me like that, son. I'm sixty years old. You think I don't know a little about love and pain?"

"I guess so."

"All I'm saying is, you both have wounds that have never healed. You've been living with them so long, you probably don't even know they're there anymore."

"Oh, I'm aware of them, Dad."

He looks me dead in the eye and says, "Then make the decision to let them take over or dig them out, Forrest. It's your call."

He turns back to the workbench as I grind my teeth together. The last thing I expected coming out here was a lecture or a heart-to-heart with my dad, but hearing the truth he just dropped hits me square in the chest.

I almost contemplate leaving because it feels too real, but then he says, "How have things been between the two of you in the past two weeks, though?" He keeps his back to me, organizing some screws and nails into storage containers in front of him.

"Well, I'm here to build shit for this event after she asked me. Does that answer your question?"

My father narrows his eyes at me over his shoulder. "I suppose."

"It's just complicated, Dad. We're trying to get to know each other again, I guess. Just friends."

"Well, friendship is the foundation of any relationship. Your mother and I were friends first before I finally convinced her to go on a date with me."

"I know, but being friends with Shauna feels so strange, especially given all that's happened."

"You just gotta dig out the weeds, son," he says, like it's so simple.

Forgiveness—how the hell do I do that?

Forgive Shauna for pushing me away, forgive myself for faking an injury to run after her? Forgive us both for not communicating like grown-ass adults since Vegas?

"So what does the woman have you building?" my father asks, breaking me from my thoughts.

"A bunch of shit."

He chuckles. "Sounds about right. Well, you know where all of the tools are," he says, gesturing to the shed around us.

"Yeah. Thanks."

I turn to walk away but then twist back to him. "Hey, Dad?"

"Yes, Forrest?"

"Thanks for the talk. I appreciate it, I hope you know that."

I swear I see tears form in his eyes, but then he turns back to his task. "I'm always here, son. And when you're ready to commit to her, Forrest, one way or another, I'll tell you the secret to making it last."

Stepping out of the shed, I stare off toward the sunset. It's almost dark, so whatever I start building, I will need to be in one of the warehouse buildings to have light and protect it from the fall weather that is changing with each passing day.

We have two oversized sheds where we store chairs, tables, and pretty much anything else we need for events just behind the newer barn, and one is pretty empty, so the space can be used for projects like this. As I stride over there, I see Shauna standing outside, talking to one of the ranch hands.

She has her tight-ass jeans on again, a kelly-green sweater that hugs every curve of her upper body, and her long brown hair is pulled back into a high ponytail. Fuck, she looks gorgeous.

"Hey," I say as I get closer to where she's standing.

Her smile is instant. "Hey there."

"I'm ready to be put to work."

"Great. Gary was just helping me load the lumber inside the shed here for you. Your dad said this would be the best one to use to keep the projects out of the elements."

My dad? So he already knew why I was here, the sneaky ass.

"Sounds good." I step inside, noticing the chill that fills the space. It's actually not too bad, and I know it will warm up once I start working, but in a few weeks, I might need to bring a portable heater.

I hear Shauna thank Gary for his help, and then she follows me inside. "Thanks again for helping, Forrest." When I glance over my shoulder at her, she tilts her head at me, smiling.

"Well, you were right. I should help more."

"I was right? Gosh, I can't hear that enough."

"Don't push your luck, woman."

She laughs and then pulls a few folded papers from her pocket. "Here are some sketches of the designs I was thinking. The paint, of course, will be done once they're built, but this can at least give you an idea of what I'm looking for."

Taking the papers from her, I study her drawings.

"These shouldn't be too bad. I need to write out some measurements so I have a blueprint to go off of, unless you know exactly how big you want everything."

"The measurements are on the other side." She gestures for me to turn the paper over.

"You did all this yourself?"

"This is what I was working on over the weekend. I wanted to have a plan in place in case you said no," she says, shrugging.

So this is why she wasn't at the ranch on Sunday...

"Well, I appreciate your forward thinking. This will make things go a lot faster."

Her smile is nearly blinding. "Good. Now, I don't want to get in your way, but I've set up a painting station in the corner so I can work on things as you finish. Obviously, you haven't started yet, so I'm going to paint a few small things I've already made while you work, if that's okay?"

I swallow down the awkwardness brewing and nod. "Shouldn't be a problem."

"Okay. Perfect." She shoves her hands in her back pockets and begins to walk backward. "I'll just let you get to work."

But before she gets too far, she trips over a board lying on the cement behind her. On instinct, I reach out and grab her arm before she tumbles onto her back on the concrete, yanking her into my chest. "Whoa! Shit." My eyes search hers. "Are you okay?"

Her hand rests on my pec, her eyes are wide, and both

of us are breathing heavily as she collects herself. "Yeah . . . I'm good. That would have been extremely embarrassing." I stifle my laugh, but my grin gives me away. "Hey, it's not funny!"

"I'm not saying it was, but a simple 'thank you' would be fine."

She swats my chest as I release her. "Thank you, you big meanie."

"You could have called me a meanie if I let you fall. But if you've already forgotten, I didn't."

"Yeah, yeah. Hold it over my head, why don't you?" she says, but I yank her back into my chest, catching her off guard again.

"I don't want to hold anything over your head anymore, Shauna. I'm working on that, okay?"

Her eyes bounce back and forth between mine. "Okay . . ."

"Just be patient with me. Please."

She blows out a big breath and nods. "I can do that."

"Thank you." Leaning forward, I plant my lips on her forehead without even thinking. It just felt natural because that's what I always did when I wanted to feel close to her without making it about sex.

And even though getting this woman naked again is always in the back of my mind, right now, it just feels really fucking good to be close to her again.

Focus on being friends, right?

When I let her go, the flush of her cheeks tells me that

our proximity affected her, too. But then she straightens her sweater, brushes a few flyaway hairs from her face, and heads toward the corner where her painting supplies are set up.

I grab a pair of safety glasses and slide them on before moving toward the lumber stacked in the corner and gathering what I need to start on the backdrop for photos with Santa. This project will take the longest, so it makes sense to get it going first.

I grab my phone from my back pocket, put on a playlist that I know Shauna will enjoy, and get to work, humming my way through the songs as I measure pieces and cut them with the electric saw.

When I stop to take a break, wiping sweat from my forehead and wishing I'd brought a bandana to wear, I catch Shauna staring at me from her seat in the corner.

"Is something wrong?"

She bites her bottom lip and shakes her head. "No. I'm just sitting here wondering how the hell you got into construction and why watching you work is so hot?" Her eyes widen when she realizes what she says, but then she shrugs off her comment.

"Hot, huh?"

"I mean . . ." She waves her hand up and down as I stand there. "Yeah."

Laughing, I take a drink of my water and then place it on the table beside me. "Well, after we broke up, I came back home and didn't really have any direction for my life anymore. Nixon, our friend from high school, was working for High Performance Construction at the time and encouraged me to apply. He was making more per hour than I would working minimum wage, so I figured what the hell? Turns out hammering nails into wood is really therapeutic."

"I can imagine."

"So I started at the bottom working on a small crew and then worked my way up into management. Got really close with the owner, and when he retired, he left me in charge. Now, I own the company outright and am focusing on expanding as much as I can."

"That's amazing, Forrest. You always were good with your hands."

Fuck. Don't go there right now, Shauna. I can't cut wood with a hard-on.

"And what do you do for fun when you're not running your company?"

That question makes my spine stiffen. Do I share my other passion with Shauna this soon? Part of the reason I found music was because of the heartbreak I went through.

But she's the reason for that, too.

Avoiding her eyes, I stare down at the ground. "Would you believe me if I said I play in a band?"

When I glance up at her, her mouth falls open. "What? No way..."

"Guess you don't believe me, then."

She chuckles and then says, "It's not that I don't. I guess I'd just have to see it to let that sink in. You? Playing an instrument? I just never thought that'd be something you'd get in to."

"Well, it was another way for me to shut off my mind, Shauna. Working out helps me do that, too."

She visibly swallows. "Then I'm happy you found those things."

"Does *this* make you happy? Planning a small-town event instead of the corporate shindigs and million-dollar weddings you're used to?" I ask, tossing my hand out to the side.

"I enjoyed working in Vegas, but everything out there was much more about pomp and circumstance. This event on the ranch . . ." She gestures to the wood around us. "This is way more fun. This means something, it has sentiment behind it, and I think that's something that's been missing from my job for years, especially after I no longer had my dad to take care of." She looks me dead in the eye. "Taking this job wasn't just about you, Forrest. It was about me, too. I haven't felt purposeful in a long time, but that's slowly changing with each day that I'm here."

I clear my throat. "I'm glad you found what you were looking for, then."

"I haven't found everything yet, but I think I'm getting close." She winks at me and then turns back to her project, ending the conversation.

I get back to work, cutting a few more pieces before I glance at the time on my phone. "Shit, it's getting late."

Shauna checks her watch. "Oh my God, I had no idea. Sorry."

"It's all right. I just need to get going. I have a long day tomorrow." I toss the safety glasses on the table and use the bottom of my shirt to wipe away the sweat from my brow. Shauna's eyes dance all over my abs as I expose them to her, and I don't miss the way they light up with appreciation.

My body's changed a lot since we were last together, but so has hers. I'm desperate to grab onto those hips of hers while I pound into her from behind and wrap my hand up in her hair that travels halfway down her back now.

But I can't go there just yet.

Why is it that when I struggle to make any sort of decision with my head and my heart, my dick chooses to interject his opinion at every turn as if he's the real one with brains?

"Is it hot in here, or is it just me?" she asks, waving her hand in front of her face.

"It's a little warm," I reply, gulping down my desire to cross the space and smash my lips to hers.

"Makes me want some ice cream."

"Ice cream or that crap you call ice cream that really isn't?" I tease her.

The corner of her mouth tips up. "Rainbow sherbet is

the best ice cream flavor, Forrest. I'm surprised you forgot that."

"I never forgot that you liked that shit, Shauna."

She giggles and then sighs. "Well, I won't keep you any longer. I hope you have a good weekend."

Not sure what else to say, I head for the door but then stop in my tracks. Turning back to her, I say, "My band is playing tomorrow night. You should come."

Shauna looks like she just saw a ghost. "Really?"

"Yeah. It's in Perryton, so it's kind of far, but I can pick you up if you want."

"Are you sure?" She bites her lip.

"I wouldn't have asked if I wasn't."

"Okay. Then I'd love to." She releases her lip from her teeth and then licks both of them.

"I'll pick you up at six."

"See you then."

I head for the door again, not bothering to look back because I'm getting kind of tired of doing that, anyway. So instead, I focus on moving forward—out to my truck, back to my house, and closer to letting Shauna back in—and I think showing her this other side of me is the perfect way to start doing just that.

CHAPTER TEN

Shauna

"Thank you. Please stop by again." Evelyn finishes up with the customer at her counter just as I walk through the door of Luna. As soon as the young lady heads for the exit, Evelyn's eyes meet mine. "Shauna!"

"Hey!"

"What are you doing here?"

"Well, I just realized the other day that I don't have any leggings to wear under that dress I bought, and I need some since I'm wearing it tonight."

She moves out from behind the register and heads

toward a display table full of leggings in every color of the rainbow. "Not a problem. Headed somewhere in particular?"

I have to bite my lip to fight my smile. "Forrest is taking me out."

She nearly falls over but catches herself before she does. "Oh my God! Seriously?"

"Yes." I try to contain my elation, but I can't. A squeal escapes my lips, and then I blow out a harsh breath. "Sorry."

"Girl, do not apologize for being excited. This is huge. How did this happen? I need all of the details."

Kelsea comes out from the back, snacking on an apple. "Hey, Shauna. What's going on?"

"Forrest asked her out on a date," Evelyn answers for me.

"Holy crap!" Kelsea nearly chokes on her mouthful but quickly recovers.

"It's not a date. I mean, I don't think it is. He didn't call it that." Suddenly, my anticipation dwindles. "Does that mean he doesn't think it's a date?"

"Well, where is he taking you?" Evelyn asks.

"To see him play in his band. He has a gig tonight."

Kelsea's and Evelyn's heads whip around, their wide eyes comically finding each other's before Kelsea turns back to me slowly. "Um, *what* did you just say? Forrest is in a *band?*"

"Yeah, he has been for a while, I guess."

Kelsea catches her best friend's gaze again. "How the hell did we never know that?"

"Uh, come on. This is Forrest we're talking about. The man is locked up as tight as Fort Knox," Evelyn replies.

"Believe me, I was just as shocked as you. But last night, before he left the ranch, he asked if I wanted to go with him, and of course, I said yes."

"What was he doing at the ranch on a Thursday?"

I bounce my eyebrows, smirking from ear to ear. "Helping me build some things for the Winter Wonderland event."

Evelyn slow claps. "Nicely done, Shauna."

I pretend to curtsy, which makes us all laugh. "Thank you. I went to his office on Monday to ask for his help like you suggested. And then, last night, we worked side by side in one of the warehouse buildings and just talked, you know? That led to him telling me about his band, and when he asked me to go with him, I swear I felt like I was sixteen all over again with the nerves and anticipation."

I had such a hard time falling asleep last night after I got home. My mind was buzzing with how monumental his invitation was. He's the one who initiated us spending time together, and he wants to share something very personal with me. This has to be a good sign, right?

"Obviously. But he didn't call it a date . . ." Kelsea taps her finger to her chin.

"He doesn't have to. They're going to be alone, driving

in the same car, and spending the entire night together. Sounds like a date to me," Evelyn declares.

I let out a big sigh. "I'm just so anxious about it because I feel like this is my chance to prove myself and my intentions to him."

Kelsea shakes her head. "Don't put too much pressure on it, Shauna. Just let it be what it is. Take his invitation as a huge step forward, but this is Forrest we're talking about. Who knows where his head is through all of this."

"I know. I just . . . it feels like things are finally moving in the right direction with us, and I don't want to screw it up."

Evelyn nods. "You won't because you two are meant to be together."

Kelsea agrees with a bob of her chin. "And please, do us a favor and take lots of pictures and videos." She laughs.

"Oh, I will."

Evelyn turns to Kelsea. "I wonder if Wyatt and Walker know?"

"I'm sure they will once the two of us get home," she says.

I shake my head. "Do me a favor, and keep this to yourselves for a while, please? I don't want Forrest to think I didn't value his privacy by telling you guys. If he's kept this to himself, there has to be a reason, right?"

Kelsea's shoulders fall. "Fine. I won't tell my husband," she says, pouting.

"Same," Evelyn echoes.

"Thanks. Okay, I need those leggings, and then I had best be going. I still need to shower and get ready."

Evelyn picks up a pair of dark-brown leggings that look softer than butter and hands them to me. "Here. These will match that dress perfectly, especially with the boots you got last week."

"Thank you. How much do I owe you?"

She waves me off. "They're on me."

"Are you sure? I can pay for them, Evelyn."

"I'm sure. Just promise if you get the chance to climb that man like a tree, you take it. I mean, his name is *Forrest*, right?"

Kelsea and I nearly fall over with laughter as I shout, "Oh my God, Evelyn!"

She smiles proudly. "What can I say? Subtlety has never been my strong suit. And tonight, Shauna . . . it needs to not be yours, either."

It's just past six when Forrest pulls up to my townhouse. Walker was such a sweetheart for letting me stay here, and I know that Forrest wasn't keen on the idea initially. But as I watch him from behind a curtain as he walks up to the door, dressed in dark-blue denim, a black shirt, and a brown leather jacket, freshly showered, I'm hoping he'll let that little detail slide.

He knocks, and I take a deep breath before answering the door. "Hi," I say when our eyes meet.

But then his lower, taking in my entire body. His hand comes up to cover his mouth as he groans. "Fuck, Shauna."

"Is something wrong?"

I watch his pupils dilate, and his chocolate-brown eyes become darker as he assesses me from head to toe again. "I don't know if I'm going to be able to concentrate on playing with you wearing that."

Pleased with myself, I turn around so he can see my backside in this dress as I grab my purse from the entry table. And the growl I hear come from him lets me know that Evelyn's suggestion about forgetting subtlety was right on the money.

The rust-colored sweater dress clings to every curve of my body. The brown leggings she gave me today complement the color perfectly, and I paired the entire outfit with light-brown heeled boots. I wore my hair down in soft curls since I know that's how Forrest used to love it, and I put a few extra spritzes of perfume on for added effect.

I turn around, patting his chest playfully as I walk past him. "I'm sure you'll be fine." He shuts the door behind me, waits for me to lock it, then leads me out to his truck with his hand on the small of my back.

Touching me intimately already? That's a good sign of a date even though he's not calling it that.

When he opens my door and helps me inside, I glance over at him. "Thank you."

He grunts and then shuts the door before rounding the hood and hopping into the driver's seat. "Have you eaten?"

"I did. I wasn't sure if this little adventure included food, so I didn't want to be starving."

"Sorry. I guess I should have clarified."

Reaching over, I grab his hand and squeeze it. He lets me, which sends relief through my body. "It's okay."

When he looks over at me, he asks, "Well, do you still have room for dessert?"

"Always."

"Good. I'm craving something sweet, anyway."

Forrest exits the neighborhood and heads toward the highway. We sit in comfortable silence for a while before he finally speaks. "Did you get a lot done today? At the ranch, I mean?"

"I spent most of the day on the phone, but yes. Things are coming along. You?"

"Fridays are usually a pretty slow day. Mostly, it's just processing billing and tracking profit."

"Sounds fascinating," I tease.

"It's actually the part I hate the most. Sometimes I miss working with my hands."

"Well, that's what the music is for, right?"

He nods. "Yeah."

"Do you ever get nervous before you play?"

"Not usually. I am tonight, though."

"Why?"

"Because you'll be there."

My optimism begins to deplete. "You can take me back home if you want, Forrest. I don't have to go."

He shakes his head before turning into a shopping center, coasting along as he finds some place to park. "No, it's not that I don't want you there, Shauna," he says as he shifts the truck into park and then faces me head on. "It's that I do."

"And that makes you nervous?" I whisper.

"Being with you again feels just as nerve-wracking as it did when we were teenagers."

"You must have been good at hiding it back then because I never would have guessed that."

"I was better at hiding it then, but I think that's because the stakes were lower." He grabs my hand again, rubbing his thumb over the top of it. His touch sends electricity racing down my spine.

"There's no pressure, Forrest."

He nods, still staring down at my hand. "Friends, right?"

"Yup," I agree reluctantly.

"Well, friends can get ice cream together, correct?"

I look up at the shop in front of us, appreciating his suggestion. "Absolutely, as long as one friend doesn't give the other one shit about their flavor choice."

"No guarantees." He winks at me and then opens my

door, escorting me into the shop for us to each grab a treat for the drive.

After Forrest gets his scoop of chocolate in a cone and I have my scoop of rainbow sherbet—only ever in a cup, of course—we hop back in the truck and head for Perryton.

"What made you stop for ice cream?" I ask around a mouthful as we coast along the highway. Music is playing softly through the speakers, just loud enough to hear it but not so loud that we have to talk over it.

"You mentioned it last night when we were working." He shrugs before taking another bite. "It sounded good, and then I thought about how I couldn't remember the last time we got some together."

"It has been a long time. Probably before I moved to Vegas."

"I think so, too."

"Something in the Orange" by Zack Bryan begins to play as I place my empty cup in the small trash can Forrest keeps in the truck. And as the melody continues, I close my eyes and try like hell not to let my emotions get the best of me.

But Forrest catches the shift in my demeanor. "Are you okay?"

"Yeah, I'm good." I exhale, staring out the passenger window as my eyes fill with unshed tears.

Dammit. The last thing I wanted was to cry tonight. But this song, this artist . . . it gets to me every time.

"Are you sure?"

"My dad loved Zach Bryan," I manage to say, fighting the lump building in my throat. "He wasn't as big back then as he is now, but every time one of his songs comes on, this rush of emotions just hits me."

"I can change it if you want." Forrest reaches forward to skip the song, but I place my hand on his forearm, stopping him.

"No. It's okay. I like hearing him sing. It just takes me by surprise sometimes. I wasn't prepared for that to happen tonight."

Forrest settles back into his seat. And then he surprises the hell out of me when he says, "Tell me about him."

"Who?"

"Your dad."

My bottom lip begins to tremble, but I keep my composure. "Are you sure?"

"I wouldn't have asked if I didn't mean it, Shauna." He continues to stare out the windshield, but I can tell that he's waiting for me to speak, so I do.

Evelyn said I would know when the time was right to open up to him and discuss the past, and Forrest just gave me my chance.

"Well, he passed away about three years ago. His cancer came back several years after he went into remission, and he was just too weak to fight it a second time."

"I'm sorry."

"Me, too, but at least I got the time with him that I did." I look at Forrest dead on. "I don't regret that for a second."

He casts me a knowing glance. "You shouldn't."

I let out a sigh. "Meeting him was surreal, though. My mother kept very few pictures of him when I was growing up, you know? But when I met him face-to-face, I saw why he hid his diagnosis from us. He wasn't the same man . . . physically, anyway."

"Why did he hide it from you guys?" Forrest shakes his head. "I guess I never understood that part."

"He didn't want to be a burden to me and my mom. I was little, and he figured I was better off remembering him for the man he was then as opposed to the one he was destined to become. I made sure to tell him how I felt about that decision when the time was right."

Forrest grins. "Good for you. And what about your mom? What did she say when she went out there?"

Forrest and I broke up just before my mother flew out to Vegas and I told her everything about my father. I never got to tell him how it went because he was long gone by then and I couldn't handle our breakup *and* the shift in my family life at the same time.

It was all too much for a nineteen-year-old to take on, and I realize that now. But I don't think I would have made many of those decisions differently looking back— except maybe being truthful with Forrest from the start. However, I still wouldn't have left Vegas with him. The time I got with my dad was necessary and something I won't allow him to make me feel guilty for, no matter what.

"She was furious with me, so pissed that I lied and went behind her back. And when she spoke to my dad, she screamed. I think seeing him broke her heart all over again because he led her to believe he was unfaithful when he left. He thought it would make it easier. They spent a lot of time working through that dishonesty and becoming friends again before he passed."

"I'm glad."

"His Parkinson's progressed quickly, but it was the pancreatic cancer that ultimately took him from us." I sniffle but refuse to let tears fall, ruining my makeup.

Forrest reaches over, grabs my hand, and kisses the top of it. My heart leaps in my chest as if jumping on a trampoline, trying to launch itself toward him. "Thank you for telling me that. You have to know that your father is proud of you, right?"

"I hope so."

He glances over at me quickly. "What's not to be proud of, Shauna? You stuck to your guns, went against your mother and me because your gut told you to do so. You followed your intuition and healed wounds between your parents." He lets out a long sigh. "I get it now. Why you did what you did."

And that's what makes a tear fall. "Thank you," I whisper.

"You shouldn't be thanking me, Shauna. Fuck, I'm pissed at myself right now for holding a grudge against you for so fucking long for choosing your family over me," he admits. "But I think if the shoe was on the other foot, I'd have probably done the same. I know you think I don't appreciate my family, but if I had a limited amount of time with my dad, I'd spend it with him, too."

"It wasn't easy, Forrest. But I'm glad I did it."

As the song wraps up with the singer begging his love to turn their car around and come back to him, he kisses my hand again. "I'm glad you did, too."

CHAPTER ELEVEN

Forrest

"How's everybody doing here tonight?" Leland yells into the microphone as the walls of the bar rattle from the crowd's applause.

My gaze drifts over to Shauna for the thousandth time since I had to leave her to set up for our performance, mesmerized by how stunning she looks in that dress. But her smile is the real star of the show—bright, larger than life, and natural—everything about that woman that I missed.

"I sure hope we have some country fans in the audience," Leland continues as the crowd agrees. "Awesome.

So let's start with a little George Strait then, yeah?" The crowd goes wild as I begin to play the introduction to "Check Yes or No." Every other night, I use the music to block out my thoughts. But tonight, they're focused on one thing only: Shauna.

Like I told her in the car, I was nervous to have her here because I wasn't sure how I was going to respond. The skintight dress she's wearing obviously didn't help my dick from reacting, even though he always gets excited when she's near. But music helped me move on, move forward, all those years ago. Now the question is: Can I let it do the same for both of us this time?

I think that's why I wanted her here, to share a part of me with her that no one else knows about. It's what friends would do, but the more I spend time with her and talk to her, the more we address our past, the more I know deep down I could never just be friends with this girl.

The song ends, and we jump right into the next one, "It's a Great Day to Be Alive" by Travis Tritt.

Every now and then, I cast my eyes over to watch Shauna singing along to the songs we're playing and sipping on her whiskey and coke. Initially, she said she wasn't going to have a drink tonight, but I encouraged her to since I would be driving us home later. Part of me just wanted her to relax after that conversation we had in the truck earlier.

I knew we'd have to address it eventually, so when

that song came on, the one that reminded her of her dad, I couldn't miss the opportunity to bite the bullet and get it over with. Listening to her talk about how that whole thing went down with her parents made me realize how selfish I was being back then. Of course, if she had been honest with me from the get-go, it would have been easier to understand. But I also don't know that I would have at that age. The only thing that mattered to me at the time was her.

But there's one thing she said that stood out the most: that she didn't regret her choice because it gave her that time with her dad. And as I told her in the truck, I know I would have done the same thing if the situation were reversed.

Realizing that felt like a weight had been lifted from my shoulders, and now, as I watch her laughing with the couple she's sitting next to, winking at me when our eyes lock every so often, I know discussing that matter eased some tension between us.

"Thank y'all so much! We're gonna take a short break and then be back in just a few minutes with the second half of our set for you," Leland announces as we end our eighth song of the night. He walks offstage, and Max, our drummer, follows him before I can get my guitar strap off my neck.

"Hey," a familiar voice calls out to my left.

I turn around and find Tina, the woman from last time, batting her eyelashes up at me.

"Hey, Tina. How's it going?"

"Good. How about you, Forrest? Looking good up there." She eats me up hungrily with her eyes.

"Thanks." Setting my guitar behind me, I prepare to let Tina down easy, but when I turn back around, a man approaches Shauna at her table, stealing my attention. I'm pretty sure Tina is still talking, but I have no idea what she's saying. My eyes are locked on the guy leaning into Shauna across the table as they speak, her eyes casting down as she laughs at something he said, the way his hand reaches out to touch hers.

And that's when I just react.

"Excuse me," I say to Tina as I jump down off the stage right beside her, ignoring her question while I stalk over to Shauna's table. And when I arrive there just seconds later, I grip the guy by the back of the shirt and pull him up from his chair.

"What the—"

"Forrest!" Shauna gasps. "What are you doing?"

"The woman is taken," I declare as the man about to lose his limbs darts his eyes between me and Shauna.

"Funny. She didn't say anything about it," he challenges, which was a very stupid fucking move.

"Well, I'm saying it for her. Now, before you start something you can't finish, I suggest you walk away."

He looks over at Shauna once more, and thankfully, she speaks up. "He's right, Paul. I'm here with him."

He holds his hands up and shakes his head. "Not

worth it," he mumbles before walking off. A few patrons who were watching the whole thing unfold go back to their own conversations, but Shauna grips me by the bicep and pulls my attention toward her.

"What the hell was that, Forrest?"

I reach over and take a large drink from her freshly made whiskey and Coke. I definitely need a drink after that.

That sure was a caveman move from someone who says he just wants to be friends with this woman.

"He needed to know his place."

"I mean, we were just talking. It wasn't like I was going to go home with him. There was no reason for you to get all possessive like that."

I drop my head so our mouths are inches apart. "Isn't that what you wanted, though, Shauna? Isn't that why you're here . . . to get me back?"

Her eyes drop to my lips. "Well, yeah, but . . . I wasn't sure if you were still on the fence about that."

"I may still be figuring out how to move forward, but I'll be damned if I stand by and watch some man flirt with you while I do."

Our eyes meet, and she licks her lips. "I'm not interested in anyone but you." She reaches up and cups my face, dropping her eyes to my lips again. But before she can say anything else, I pull her up from her stool, grip her hand in mine, and drag her down the hall that leads to the rear exit. Once we're out the back door, I spin her around, press her up against the wall outside the bar and claim her like I've wanted to since that night we reconnected in Vegas.

Even my dreams don't hold up to the reality of kissing this woman again.

When our lips meet, I lose all control. I release all of my restraint with this kiss, fucking her mouth with my tongue, unleashing fifteen years of pent-up need. Shauna meets my every movement, clinging to my shoulders, digging her hands into my hair, moaning every few seconds. The sound travels straight down to my cock.

We make up for lost time—gripping, squeezing, clawing at each other like wild animals—before we finally come up for air.

Yeah, friends don't kiss like that.

"Fuck, Shauna," I mumble against her neck between kisses, pressing my hips into her stomach so she can feel what she's done to me, what she's always done to me.

"Stop talking, and just kiss me."

Our tongues meet once more, and I lean into her so hard I'm afraid her ass is going to make an imprint on the wall behind her. Luckily, Leland interrupts our moment before we can get too carried away.

"Oh, uh . . ." He clears his throat, alerting us to his presence. I pull away from Shauna to find my friend smirking at both of us. "It's time to go back on."

I wipe my bottom lip with my thumb but stay

standing in front of Shauna to spare Leland a front-row seat to my dick on full display. "I'll be right there."

He laughs and then says, "Take your time. I'll stall if I need to."

"Thanks."

When he walks back inside, Shauna stares up at me, her eyes wild and darker than the vibrant blue they normally are. "Forrest..."

"We can talk more later, okay?" I'm not sure what to say at this moment, anyway, because all of my blood has rushed down to my dick and my brain isn't functioning properly. But I gave in to our physical connection, and I don't know if that was the right thing to do just yet.

I know I want her. Hell, that's never changed. But rushing into the physical stuff isn't going to help us in the long run.

It sure as hell felt good, though.

She smiles, lets out a long sigh, and nods. "Okay."

After a few moments to let my dick calm down, I walk back inside the bar, still holding Shauna's hand. When I step onto the stage and find my stool again, I grab my guitar and stare over in Shauna's direction.

Her smile blinds me once more, and then we get back to the music. A few songs later, I grab Leland's attention from the front of the stage and whisper a song suggestion in his ear. He confirms with Max, and then I start to play the opening notes to "Something in the Orange."

Little did Shauna know that we've been working on

this one. But after the drive out here, I knew we had to play it for the first time tonight.

I look over at my girl, hands tucked under her chin, eyes filled with unshed tears, and hope radiating from her as we play the song.

I can barely take my eyes off her.

The entire bar grows quiet as Leland sings the words about two lovers, one asking for a second chance, and I don't think I've resonated with a song before as much as I do now.

Then it hits me.

Second chances rarely exist. But more importantly, sometimes we expect them to look like the first chance we took.

The thing is, they never do, and if we don't take advantage of the opportunity to change our circumstances the second time around, the regret only builds.

Shauna took a chance moving out to Vegas to meet her father, and she took another coming back here for me.

I took a chance when I faked my injury back in college and another when I tried to stop her wedding.

So if we're both here now, wanting the same thing, this is our chance to get something right together. The question is: Can we do that? Or are we doomed to repeat our mistakes?

"Goddammit, woman," I groan as Shauna grinds her pelvis over my cock once more. With the driver's seat leaning back as far as it can go, Shauna straddles me and gyrates her hips, making the decision not to rush things between us harder and harder to uphold.

The second I pulled into her driveway, she launched herself at me across the center console of my truck. Needless to say, I gave in to her rather quickly.

The last time we did something like this, we were teenagers, but I think that's what makes it even more thrilling.

"God, I missed this," she mumbles against my lips, scraping her fingernails up the back of my neck.

"Shauna, we need to stop."

She leans back and stares down at me, her hair and eyes wild. "Why?"

I pinch the bridge of my nose. "I can't believe I'm saying this because I'd love nothing more than to bury myself inside you, but we need to take things slow."

Her bottom lip juts out. "Well, that's no fun."

Laughing, I pull her face back down to mine and bite her bottom lip. "Shauna . . . I'm trying to be a gentleman here."

"That doesn't sound like the boy I used to know. He would have taken full advantage of what I'm offering," she teases.

"I'm not that boy anymore, Shauna. And the last thing I want to do is fuck this thing up between us again." She rocks her hips over my cock again, making me groan once more. "Fuck, babe. Please..."

Sighing, she stops moving and leans back. "Okay..."

"It's not that I don't want you, because believe me, I do. I just..."

She cups the side of my face. "I get it, Forrest. I may not like it, but you're probably right." She plants a soft kiss on my lips, and then I help her back over the center console as she untangles the hair I had my hands buried in moments ago. "I guess watching you play got me all riled up."

"Not a bad problem to have." I grip her chin and direct her attention back to me, resting my elbow on the center console. "Thank you for coming tonight."

"Thank you for inviting me," she whispers.

I plant one more soft kiss on her lips and then exit the truck, walking her up to her door.

"Will I see you Sunday at the ranch?"

"Yeah, I'll be there. In fact, your mother has a big idea for the festival she wants to talk to the whole family about."

"Joy."

"Oh, stop. Your mom loves that ranch and just wants to make this event as magical as possible."

"I know." I roll my eyes and then press her up against the door and slant my mouth over hers once more. Tasting her again is like fulfilling a craving I can't stop thinking about. Cupping the side of her face when we part, I murmur, "Guess I'll see you then."

"Goodnight, Forrest. Talk to you soon."

I watch her lock herself inside and then head back to my truck, thinking about how quickly things turned around for us this evening and wondering now how that's going to affect us moving forward.

CHAPTER TWELVE

Forrest

"What the hell did I just walk into?" Hands planted on my hips, I stare at my brothers who are both dressed as elves, bells on the tips of their shoes and all.

"Oh, don't worry. Mom has one for you, too," Wyatt says, shooting me an annoyed glare. Meanwhile, Walker is shaking his ass and listening to the music he's making as he moves around.

"The fuck I'm wearing that."

"Oh, but you will," my mother sing-songs as she walks over to me, holding up my very own elf outfit. And I hate that the first question that comes to mind is: How in the hell did she find one big enough to fit me?

"Mom, look . . . I love you and all, but—"

"Told you he wouldn't go for it," Shauna interjects, coming into the barn now with arms full of fabric.

"Hate to say it, but she's right, Mom."

My mother frowns. "Come on, Forrest. Your father is going to be Santa, I'm going to be Mrs. Claus, and we need elves. I didn't have three boys for nothing." She plants her hands on her hips. "Need I remind you what you and your brothers have done to my body?"

I rip the outfit from her hands and grumble to myself as I head toward the bathroom to change. I swear, my mother knows how to lay on guilt like smooth butter on a biscuit.

This is not the morning I envisioned when I was heading over to the ranch this Sunday. No. My ideas involved me and Shauna making up for lost time with our mouths in between working on the pieces for the festival.

Yet, sadly, I'm now involved in a Christmas-themed fashion show.

After I squeeze into the outfit, I force myself to look in the mirror before showing my family. "My God."

I look like a modern-day Peter Pan, but a giant one. This suit barely zipped up the back, and it looks like the seams are about to rip apart. One wrong move, and my dick is going to be greeting kids and their families, which isn't the type of Christmas magic I'm thinking they're looking for.

Shaking my head, I put on the hat and slowly walk out to where the rest of my family waits, careful not to move too fast so this thing doesn't self-destruct.

Kelsea folds in her lips as Evelyn covers her mouth with her hand, stifling her laugh. Just great. Even the girls are aware of what a spectacle I am.

Shauna spins around and sees me next, but her reaction isn't one of amusement. Nope. Her eyes drop right to my crotch, and then her lips curve into a pleased smile, the kind that could make my dick hard—which would make this situation even worse.

"Stop looking at me like that. This costume is barely holding itself together right now."

She eyes me up and down, walking around me, assessing me from all angles. "Damn. Who knew I had a thing for elves?"

"Ha ha. Very funny."

Giggling, she reaches up and adjusts my hat. "This look suits you, Forrest."

"You knew about this, didn't you? This was Mom's great idea, huh?"

She licks her lips and then says, "Maybe."

I pinch the bridge of my nose. "Fuck. All the women are out to get me now, I swear."

Momma comes back in, clapping her hands as Walker

and Wyatt follow closely behind. "Oh my gosh! You three are gonna look so perfect!"

"I think this classifies as child cruelty," I reply.

"Oh, it's not that bad," Shauna says. "And it's going to add to the ambiance. Everyone is going to love it, and seeing you three dressed like this might bring people in from town just so they can witness it for themselves."

"I feel like we should start our own leprechaun band," Wyatt mutters, pulling the fabric from his crotch. He must be feeling the same crowding that I am. "Too bad none of us play an instrument, though."

"Forrest does," Kelsea says, and then she covers her mouth, widening her eyes as her admission floats through the room.

I shift my gaze to her. "What did you just say?" I ask, my pulse rapidly firing. *How the hell did she know that?*

"You play an instrument?" Walker turns to me. "What the fuck? How come we didn't know that?"

Kelsea glances over at Shauna and mouths, "I'm sorry."

I glare at Shauna now as my heart races even faster. "You told her?" I let my guard down, let her in, and now it's about to blow up in my face.

"Told her what?" Wyatt prods. "What the hell is going on?"

"I mean, yeah . . . I told the girls that you were taking me out to see your band play, but . . ."

Anger courses through me as I feel everyone's eyes on me.

"You play in a band, Forrest?" my mother asks now, her voice soft but full of hurt. Silence fills the barn before she continues, her voice full of hurt. "Why wouldn't you tell us that?"

My heart hammers as I feel everyone's eyes on me. "Because I didn't want anyone to make a big deal out of it," I grate out. *Fuck. I don't need this right now.*

There's a reason I didn't tell my family—I wanted something in my life that was separate from them, something that was only for me. And after sharing that part of me with Shauna the other night, I thought she understood that. Turns out, she's intent on not only inserting herself back into my life but airing details of it to my family as well.

"How long?" my mother continues as everyone looks on.

"Since I moved back home," I answer her, wishing I could rewind time right now. "It's just the guitar. It's not a big deal."

"Holy shit," Wyatt mutters as he shares a look with Walker.

I glance back at Shauna now, who's chewing on her nail. "Forrest, I—" But before she can say anything else, her phone rings. She digs it out of her pocket and instantly grimaces. "It's my mom. I need to take this." She glances back at me, worry etched on her face before heading outside for privacy.

"Forrest, just so you know, Shauna only told us

because she was so excited that you wanted to take her out," Kelsea explains once Shauna is gone, slowly approaching me.

I don't say anything in return because I'm not sure what to say. Part of me feels betrayed, and then part of me knows that Shauna's intentions weren't malicious. I just hate all of this attention on me right now. I've avoided it for a reason.

"She asked us not to tell Wyatt and Walker, either," Evelyn adds. "And obviously we didn't, hence their reactions."

"You kept this from me?" Walker says to his wife. "What the hell?"

"Oh, stop. I don't have to tell you everything just because we're married."

"Uh, this isn't just anything, Evelyn. This is huge!"

"It's not that big of a deal!" I shout over their bickering.

"That's enough!" my mother yells over all of us. "Boys, go get changed. The outfits need some alterations, but we have time to get them done before the event." Then she turns to me, pulling me to the corner of the barn, a look on her face that tells me I've let her down.

I fucking hate that look.

"Forrest . . ." She shakes her head, disappointment in her eyes. "Why did you hide this?"

I stare off to the side, avoiding her gaze. But she grabs

my chin and forces me to look at her, even though I stand almost a foot taller than her. "It was private."

"Why?"

"Why does it matter?"

"Because you obviously found something you enjoyed after you and Shauna broke up and you lost football, and we could have been there to support you through that. We could have cheered you on and watched you find joy again," she replies as if the answer is so simple. "You've pushed us away for years because you thought it would be easier for you, but all it's done is hurt us."

Regret courses through me. "I just wanted to be alone."

"Well, that's never going to happen, Forrest, because as long as you're part of this family, you won't ever be alone, you hear me?" she says, releasing my chin finally but her eyes are still locked on me, piercing my resolve like daggers.

"Yes, Momma."

"And that woman out there is part of this family, too. All she wants is time with you. She didn't mean to spill your secret, so you'd better not hold it against her because it shouldn't have been a secret in the first place."

I clench my jaw, knowing my mother is right. After my and Shauna's night together, things finally seemed like they were getting back on track. But this little development reminds me that letting her in isn't going to be as easy as I wanted it to be.

I have a life here that I've created since we broke up,

but is it much of a life? Is my mother right? Did I shut my family out because I thought that being alone was better than letting people in again?

This entire spectacle just reminds me of what Shauna said to me in my office that day, too. Do I really take my family for granted? I never used to be that way...

But what happens when you let people in? You get hurt, that's what.

Exhibit A: the woman who helped me learn that lesson standing right outside this barn. She's the one who hurt me the most.

"Go get changed, and talk to Shauna," my mother says, pushing me toward the bathroom.

I take a few steps away and then turn to face my mother, who is still watching me. "I'm sorry, Momma."

"You'd better be, Forrest Eli. And wearing this elf costume will be the first step to proving just how much."

Letting my smile take over my lips, I head back to the bathroom to change and find my brothers there, waiting for me.

"You play the fucking guitar?" Walker asks again as if he can't comprehend the fact.

"Yeah," I mumble as I start to peel the spandex off my body.

"That's so fucking cool!"

"It's not a big deal," I say for the thousandth time.

"I wanna see you play," he continues. "When do you play next?"

I keep my eyes focused on the ground as a foreign feeling takes root in my chest. Is that nervousness? Anxiety? Does the idea of my brothers watching me play make me excited or want to hide some more?

"Next month. We just had a gig and only do one a month since we're all busy."

"Maybe your band can play at the brewery sometime," Wyatt suggests, pulling my eyes over to him.

My heart is hammering once more as I realize that my brothers aren't mad I kept this from them, not at all. It actually seems like they want to be a part of it, and I'm not sure what to think about that yet.

I slide my jeans up and fasten them before pulling on my t-shirt. "I'll talk to the guys, see if they'd be interested."

Wyatt nods. "Sounds good."

"And just for the record, you know you can share shit with us, right?" Walker adds.

"I know, I just—"

"—don't like talking about your feelings," Wyatt finishes for me. "We know."

"Look, I need to talk to Shauna." I shove the costume back in its bag. "Catch you guys later."

I don't wait for them to reply before walking out of the bathroom and heading outside. My brothers can wait to dissect this further, but my focus is on the woman who just blurted my secret to my entire family.

"Look, I can't get into this with you right now. I'll call you in a couple of days when we have more time to talk," I hear Shauna say as she stands off to the left of the barn. I don't say anything and just listen to her side of the call instead. Her frustrated sigh is so loud it carries over the wind. "Love you, too. Bye." When she spins around, she jumps at the sight of me. "Oh my God. Forrest . . ." She places a hand over the center of her chest.

"Everything okay with your mom?"

"Yeah, just being dramatic about some things." Shauna's brows draw together. "I'm sorry about Kelsea and Evelyn. I shouldn't have said anything to them, but . . ."

"My music was private."

"I know. I'm sorry."

Closing my eyes, I put my hand on top of hers. "You make me feel too fucking much sometimes, woman."

"Sucks to be you, then, because I'm not going anywhere."

"You say that now."

And I think that's the root of all this uneasiness for me—the notion that she'll leave again once she realizes she's made a mistake, that what I have to offer her won't be enough. I sure as hell wasn't thinking about that when I stormed her wedding that day or the other night at the bar when that guy was hitting on her. But now that she's here, now that I see what we *could* be mixing with what we *were*, I'm having a hard time merging the two visions together.

Suddenly, all my insecurities start rearing their ugly

heads. "This is what I have to offer you, you get that, right?"

Her head swivels back. "What do you mean?"

"Small-town life, me playing in a band for fun, running a construction company. I'm not Brock, Shauna. I'll never wear a suit and tie for work or try to give you a life in the big city. It's not who I am."

She takes a step closer to me, placing a hand on my chest. "I know it's not, but that's part of the reason I came back because I didn't want that life. Don't push me away, Forrest. Please. I don't think my heart can handle that."

"I'm not trying to." But I retreat from her and take a deep breath. "But I have work to do, all right?"

"Okay," she replies reluctantly.

Before I can walk away, this innate need to reconnect with her comes over me. I push her against the outside of the barn, bury my hands in her hair, and cover her mouth with my own.

I'm not sure if kissing her right now is going to make these insecurities go away, but it at least drowns them out for the moment. The feel of her lips on mine, the sounds she makes as I twist my tongue against hers, the heat of our bodies as they press together—it all makes my anxiety from earlier start to dissipate.

"So you're not mad at me?" she asks when we part, breathing heavily.

"No. I can't really be. I guess it was time that everyone found out, anyway."

She pushes my hair back from my face. "You don't have to hide who you are anymore, Forrest. I, for one, want to get to know the man standing in front of me, not the shell of one who has been walking around for years."

"That shell has been protecting me from a lot of shit, Shauna."

"I know, and I know I played a part in that. But I need you to let me in."

"I want to . . . I just . . ."

She brings my lips back to hers and kisses away my doubt. It doesn't make it go away completely, but at least I know that we're headed in the right direction, even if this journey feels rocky already.

~

"How was your weekend?" Jill asks as she walks into my office Monday morning, but she doesn't miss the smile that forms on my lips as I think back to pressing Shauna up against the outside of the bar and stealing the oxygen from her lungs or the hot and heavy make-out session we had in my truck before she finally went inside her place alone. And even though Sunday was a rollercoaster when my family found out about the band, at least Shauna and I left the ranch on good terms.

"Oh! That good, huh? Would this have anything to do with the Miss Shauna who appeared in the office last week?"

"Maybe."

"So she no longer sees me as a threat, huh?" I told Jill about Shauna's jealous moment, and we both shared a good laugh about it.

"I guess not."

"If she played for my team, I'd invite her to join Becca and me."

"There's a visual I didn't need. Thanks."

"No problem." Then she pins me with her stare. "Just don't ruin it, Mr. Grumpy."

"What makes you think I will?" I ask, slightly offended.

She arches a brow at me. "Do I need to spell it out for you?"

"Spell what out?" Javi asks as he enters my office as well.

"Forrest and Shauna spent some time together this weekend, and I just warned him not to ruin it," Jill repeats, bringing him up to speed.

"Oh, he will, but at least things are moving forward, yeah?" Javi asks.

"I really appreciate all the faith in me in this room. Makes me feel all warm and fuzzy inside."

"I didn't know you were capable of feeling those things," Jill fires back.

Javi just laughs.

"Is there something you two need, or did you come in here just to give me shit?"

"Give you shit," they say simultaneously.

"Well, I don't pay you for that service, so if you could kindly get back to work, I would appreciate it."

Jill comes over and ruffles my hair. "I offer that service for free, Forrest. You should know that by now."

Javi stays in my office after Jill walks out. "So things are going well, then?"

My lips curl up again. "They're going. We went out Friday night, and . . . we kissed," I admit.

"Did you use protection?" Javi teases.

"Fuck you."

Chuckling, he says, "All joking aside, I'm pumped for you, man. Did you work through your shit yet?"

"Part of it," I say, not wanting to go into total detail with him right now. I'm still struggling with all of the fucking feelings racing through me, but day by day, I'm getting used to the idea of this being my new normal . . . hopefully.

"That's good. So where do you go from here?"

Before I can answer him, my phone vibrates on my desk. It's only just after eight, and Shauna is calling me. I hope nothing happened.

"Hey, I need to take this."

"Yeah, no problem. We'll catch up later."

I watch him leave, shutting the door behind him, and then I swipe across the screen to answer the call. "Hello?"

"Hey." Just the sound of her voice makes my body relax. She doesn't sound stressed or in trouble.

"Is everything okay?"

"Yeah, why wouldn't it be?"

"I don't know. You're calling me early in the morning, and I wasn't sure if something had happened."

I hear her small giggle. "Everything is fine. I just . . . I just wanted to hear your voice before I headed to the ranch this morning."

Smiling, I spin my chair around so I can look out my office window. "Is that so? Getting a late start this morning?"

"Yeah. I had some emails to answer and a few phone calls to make. When I moved out here, I handed off my accounts to Erin, one of my colleagues at Ember & Stone. But there are still some events' details I'm helping her with, so we talk every Monday until she can take them over completely."

"I'm sure you don't have to do that."

"I do, though. I'm the one who chose to leave." *To come out here for me, that is.*

"So you wanted to hear my voice, huh?" I ask, directing the conversation back to why she called in the first place while internally appreciating that even though she left her other job, she still is trying to make things right.

"I did." She lets out a wistful sigh. "I keep thinking about Friday night."

I clench my jaw. "Me, too."

"Watching you play, the way your fingers moved over that guitar . . . kissing you again . . ."

My dick takes on a life of its own, pressing against my zipper almost instantaneously. "Fuck, Shauna. Why are you bringing this up?"

"It just made me realize how much I missed your hands, what they used to feel like on my body. Do you ever think about that?"

"All the fucking time, but..."

"How long are you going to make me wait until you touch me like that again, Forrest?"

"Shauna..." Closing my eyes, I rub my cock through my jeans and momentarily debate how long it would take me to drive from the office to her townhouse to tie her to the bed for making me hard at work.

"I'm on edge, Forrest. I have been for months."

"You're tempting me, Shauna."

"I'm just being honest."

I glance back at my closed office door, and then I walk over and flip the lock. "Are you wet right now?"

"Yes..."

"Fuck. Then this is what we're going to do. You're going to get yourself off on the other end of this line, and I'm going to listen."

"Are you going to join me?"

"Do you want me to?" I ask as I pop the button on my jeans before sitting back in my chair again.

"God, yes."

"Then take your pants off." I drag down the zipper of

my jeans, shimmy them and my briefs down my thighs, and grip my aching cock, giving it a good squeeze.

"I don't have any on. I haven't gotten dressed yet," she tells me, her voice low and seductive. She knew exactly what she wanted with this little phone call, and right now, I'm not even going to complain.

"Then lay down on the bed, put your fingers in your panties, and touch yourself, Shauna. And don't hold back. Let me know how wet you are, how good it feels."

She's silent for a minute and then a long breath fills the line. "I wish it were you, Forrest. I want your hands. I'm aching for you."

"It will be me soon, but this is what you get for right now," I grate out as my hand continues to move up and down my length, pinching the tip every time I hit the top. Just listening to her breathing has me ready to blow my load.

"I'm so wet."

"Is your pussy shaved? Soft and slippery?"

"Yes. I remember you didn't care either way, though."

"Still don't. I'd eat you out no matter what because I'm addicted to the taste of you."

"I want to taste you, Forrest. Suck your cock until you come down my throat."

"Jesus. You want that?" We never did that when we were younger, but hearing her say those words just reminds me that we still have so much more to explore with one another.

"So much."

"Circle your finger around that pretty little clit, Shauna. Soft circles . . ." I pick up the bottom of my shirt, holding it beneath my chin so I don't get cum on it in a minute.

"I loved it when you used to do that," she mewls. "I still think about you when I touch myself, Forrest. I never stopped."

"You've always been the woman in my fantasies."

"Oh God . . . I'm getting close," she moans as her breaths become harsher.

I pick up my speed, stroking my cock while trying to focus on not dropping the phone. Instead, I hold it between my shoulder and ear so I can use my other hand to pull on my balls, working myself over before I explode. "Fuck, I'm there, Shauna. Let me hear you, baby . . ."

"Oh God, Forrest! I'm coming . . ." She screams through her release, and I follow her over the edge, grunting and spilling cum all over my hand and stomach.

Our labored breaths fill the line, and then, finally, I hear her giggle through the phone.

"That just happened, didn't it?"

I take a tissue from the box on my desk and clean myself up as I reply, "It did."

"I still wish it was you touching me instead."

"Shauna . . ."

The truth is, I'm not sure how much longer I'm going to be able to hold out after that little experience. I could almost close my eyes and see her come even though I wasn't there, drawing on our time together before and all of the visions I have had of her since then. But now, I wonder how much sexier she looks, how much less inhibited we'd both be now that we're older, how much fun we could have rediscovering each other's bodies.

We have a lot of time to make up for.

So then why are you waiting, Forrest?

Because we still have shit to talk about.

"Okay, I'd better be going now, or I'm going to be late."

"Make sure you put some pants on, yeah?"

I can almost hear her eyes roll. "Yes, sir."

"Fuck, Shauna. Don't say shit like that."

"Oh, yeah? Does that little honorific do something for you, Forrest?" she teases me.

"It makes me want to spank you for taunting me, if that answers your question."

Chuckling, she says, "Noted. See you tomorrow night at the ranch?"

I'm going over earlier this week to work on the projects since this Thursday is Thanksgiving. "Yes. I'll be there."

"See you then."

When we end the call, I lean back in my chair and wonder what the fuck just happened, but it doesn't take long for me to realize that woman still has a hold over me—she always has. And she can make me do uncharacteristic things, just like she did back then.

CHAPTER THIRTEEN

Shauna

"These maps turned out just darling." Momma G holds up the Winter Wonderland maps I just got back from the printer. They show the entire ranch and where each activity, food vendor, and experience will be set up.

"Aren't they cute? I'm so glad you love them."

"They're perfect. We can hand them out at the entrance, that way everyone knows where they can go. The signs will help, too, of course." She looks back up at me. "Have you painted those yet?"

"That's on my list of things to do today, actually.

Forrest finished a few of them last night, but he wasn't able to complete them all." The three hot and heavy make-out sessions we had while we were alone together are probably the reason they aren't done. I guess I can take full responsibility for that, but after revealing his musical secret on Sunday, I was desperate to feel like I didn't ruin all of the progress we'd made. Luckily, he was on board with that idea, too, but he's still holding back from me, and I'm starting to question why.

"I see." Momma flashes me a knowing smile, but I turn my back to her. I'm not sure she wants to know everything that her son and I have been up to lately, especially the phone sex.

After last weekend, my body kicked into overdrive. The desperation I feel to be connected to him again physically took over, and then the phone sex on Monday happened. Part of me can't believe we did that, but the other part thinks it was a worthwhile way to keep moving forward since the man refuses to sleep with me just yet.

I know he thinks it will cloud our minds, redirect our focus from repairing our relationship to only focusing on sex. But at this point, I'm tempted to argue that it would help. I think it's healthy to want each other as much as we do. And I know he has aggression built up toward me—I just want him to take it out on my vagina already.

"Well, I'm sure he'll get everything done in time for the event. Thanksgiving is this week, though, so there won't be any working on Thursday. I know I'll have to remind Randy of that about a hundred times, but if he knows what's good for him, he'll listen." Momma G stands from the couch. "Would you like hot tea, Shauna? I think I might make a pot. It's getting chilly outside."

The wind has been whipping the trees outside the windows all morning. "Sure."

As Momma G walks into the kitchen, my phone rings. I pick it up from the coffee table to find my mother's picture on the screen. "Hi, Mom."

"Shauna . . . did you forget to call your mother this morning?"

Slapping my palm to my forehead, I groan. "I'm sorry. I did. I was in a rush to get to the office supply store this morning and completely spaced." I might have also been daydreaming about Forrest, my go-to distraction lately.

"Well, you definitely gave me a bit of a heart attack wondering where you were. I guess that small-town life is sucking you back in harder than I thought."

"I'm fine, Mom," I say, rolling my eyes. My mother was always one for the dramatics. "And you will be, too."

"I miss you, honey. How are things going out there?"

When I told my mom I was moving back to Newberry Springs, she had a lot to say about it. And after I ran out on my wedding to Brock, I told her what happened, how Forrest and I reconnected in Vegas and how he showed up the day of the wedding. She wasn't pleased and accused him of trying to infiltrate my life again. I told her that I was having doubts about marrying Brock even before we reconnected, which made her even more upset.

My mother and I haven't had the best relationship since I brought my father back into our lives. It took both of us a long time to come to grips with everything that happened. She managed to create a friendship with my father again before he passed, but she also became hyperfocused on my life, like she had to prove to me and her both that we made the right decision leaving Texas, which included leaving Forrest, too.

After Forrest and I broke up, it took me a long time to think about dating again. I was focused on my career, and then after my dad died, my mother finally encouraged me to take a chance on love. She didn't want me to end up alone like she was for the better part of my childhood. So when Brock came into the picture, she was ecstatic.

Part of me wonders if I stayed with him just to please her. And even after the wedding fiasco, one of the challenges in our relationship is that my mother still sees Brock on a regular basis since he works at the same firm as my stepfather. That's actually how we met.

However, she's the *only* one of us who's seen him since our wedding because he still refuses to talk to me.

"Things are going well. You should come out here for the event. It might help you get in the holiday spirit," I reply, focusing back on our conversation.

My mother scoffs. "Going back there doesn't interest me in the slightest, Shauna. You know that." I sigh. "But that's actually why I was calling you . . . to see if you'd be willing to come back here. Brock . . ."

"Brock, what?" My heart drops.

"He says he's ready to speak with you."

That rush of anxiety quickly morphs into irritation. "Well, how generous of him. It's funny, though, because I've been trying to speak with him since our wedding, and he couldn't be bothered to reply, even to let me know he wasn't ready to speak with me yet."

"Shauna, can you blame him? What happened was embarrassing for him and our family."

I amble down the hallway, further away from the kitchen for some privacy. "It would have been worse if I had gone through with it and changed my mind after. I'm sorry, but I know I did the right thing."

"That's still debatable, Shauna. But I also feel for Brock. He was your husband-to-be. Your stepfather and I formed a connection with him, too, and we will always consider him a part of this family. He's hurting, honey. But he approached Frank the other day and asked where you were. He went by your place to speak with you, but I guess you didn't tell him that you left."

"Was I supposed to? We aren't engaged anymore, and I was tired of waiting for him to communicate. And there was a timeline involved with me coming out here, anyway."

"I told him as much. But I think you owe it to him to come back here and put some things to rest."

I know my mother is right, which is why I tried to do that months ago, but I guess I can't blame Brock for pushing me away after what I did. The problem is, now I'm knee-deep in my life and obligations here. I can't just get up and leave because Brock is ready to talk to me.

"I don't know when I'll be able to get out there. I'm busy and have a lot going on, but let me look at my schedule and consult Momma G and see what I can do."

"You can't put this off forever, Shauna." My mother grows quiet and then asks, "Does that mean I won't be seeing you for the holidays this year, then?"

My eyes land on a family picture of the Gibsons hanging in the hallway I'm currently standing in. Randy and Elaine look proud as their boys surround them, their smiles covered in braces and hair perfectly combed. This picture is from when Forrest was in high school, but it seems like just yesterday.

Those five people staring back at me were just as much my family then as they are now, and it feels so surreal to be back here with them. And as much as I love my mother, my heart is telling me that this is where I'm supposed to be right now.

"Probably not. If I'm able to make it back to Vegas, it will likely be after Christmas. The Winter Wonderland event runs until Christmas Eve, and that is my priority right now."

"You could fly in that day..."

"I'm not making any promises, Mom," I say, hoping

that appeases her.

"Fine. Well, please keep the Brock thing in mind, at least. I think there's a lot you two need to talk about, and maybe talking to him will help you come to your senses."

"I've already done that, but thanks for the support."

"You know I only want what's best for you, Shauna."

The idea of reliving my thoughts and emotions leading up to the wedding makes my skin crawl, but I know it's necessary for me to move on completely.

I just hope Forrest understands that I have to do this when I tell him and that my mom respects my decision when I choose to fly back.

"I know." I see Momma G head back to the couch with two cups of tea through the end of the hallway. "Look, Mom. I've got to go."

"All right, sweetie. Thanks for letting me know you're alive."

"I'll call you this weekend, okay?"

"Sounds good. Love you."

"Love you, too." I end the call and then rejoin Momma G in the living room. "Sorry. That was my mom."

"No need to apologize," she says before blowing on her steaming mug of tea. "How is your mother? I haven't seen her in years."

"She's doing well, just making me feel guilty as always." I swear, it's one of her hidden talents, the ability to layer on guilt so easily I barely notice it's lurking under the surface until it just starts seeping out of my pores.

"How so?" Momma G takes a sip of her tea and then sets her cup on the coffee table in front of her.

I momentarily debate how truthful I should be with her, but she already knows how I arrived at the decision to come back to Texas, so it can't hurt to explain what's going on. "I might need to go back to Vegas for a few days, but I want to wait until after the event."

"Is everything okay?" Her brow furrows.

"Yes. It's just that my ex-fiancé wants to see me."

"Oh?"

Sighing, I plop back into the sofa. "The thing is, I never got a chance to speak with him after I called off the wedding. He refused to communicate with me at all, but now I guess he's ready."

"And do you not want to go?"

"It's not that," I say, looking her in the eyes. And because the woman has the intuition of a fortune teller, she sees my reservations almost instantly.

"You're worried about Forrest."

I nod. "Yeah."

"I see." She picks up her cup again, takes a sip, and places it back down. "Shauna, did I ever tell you that I was dating someone else when I met Randy?"

I sit up taller in my seat. "No . . ."

"Well, I was. His name was Evan, and we were together for over a year. It was a serious relationship, but Randy and I were just friends at the time, so his presence didn't create any doubts for me. Turns out, Randy overheard that Evan was preparing to propose to me, so he admitted his feelings to me before Evan could ask. I was so mad at Randy, but as soon as he told me how he felt, I couldn't deny that I felt something, too. It was always there, but I was too blind to see it."

"So what did you do?"

"Making that decision was one of the hardest things I've ever done in my life. I knew that if I married Evan, I would be happy, that he would give me a life that was comfortable and loving. But he wasn't Randy. And even though I was taking a huge risk to find out what was between Randy and me, I knew that I had to. So I broke Evan's heart."

"Why did you never tell me this?"

Momma G smiles at me. "It's not like you've been around, honey." She reaches out and grabs my hand, squeezing it. I can feel the sting of tears build, but I blink them away. "But when you came back and told me what happened, I knew I'd share this with you eventually."

"How did Evan take it?"

"He was crushed, furious . . . got a little nasty at first. We all lived in the same town, so it was impossible not to cross paths at one time or another. But I was honest with him, told him that even though I loved him, I wasn't the woman he was supposed to marry."

Her smile spreads wide. "But I never regretted it for a second. Look at the life I have because I took that leap of faith," she says, fanning her hand out. "But I think what made it easier to handle was that I was truthful with him, told him exactly how I felt, and that I loved Randy with a strength I didn't know was possible. I loved that boy even when I didn't realize what love was. Ultimately, Evan accepted it and even went on to get married and have a big family. But when Randy and I started building our life together, it left me with a sense of peace knowing I did the right thing."

I brush a tear away that fell down my cheek while she was talking. "I don't want Forrest to think that I still have feelings for Brock or that I'll change my mind after talking to him, Momma."

"It's hard to say what my son will do or think because I'm still trying to figure that out and he's thirty-four." We share a quick laugh. "But if he truly loves you and wants to move forward with you, he'll understand your need to do this." She squeezes my hand again. "You've got to do it, Shauna. Make a clean break, that way you can move on without an anchor of your past tying you down."

"Thank you." I swipe away another tear.

"Of course. Besides, I may be a little partial, wanting things to work out between you two. Put my son out of his misery, and give me one more daughter-in-law to pass my biscuit recipe down to."

Smiling now, I reach for my tea. "You know I always wanted it. I still do."

"I know. But we've got to make you a Gibson first."

CHAPTER FOURTEEN

Forrest

"Aw, come on!" Wyatt shouts at the television, clutching his beer between his hands as he sits on the couch beside me and Walker. "That was pass interference!"

"Totally," Walker agrees, draining the last of his beer before standing. "You two want another one?"

"Yeah," we both echo, our eyes still focused on the screen in front of us.

It's Thanksgiving, and in true Gibson fashion, the boys are in the living room, huddled around the television watching the football game while the girls hang out in the kitchen.

Turning around, I glance in that direction, and a wave of contentment comes over me. For years, it was just Kelsea and Momma in there, cooking and laughing beside each other. But now, Evelyn is a part of our family—and Shauna is here, too, right where she belongs.

It's only been three-and-a-half weeks, but when I think about how much my life has changed in that span of time, all I can do is shake my head to ward off the disbelief. Three weeks ago, I thought I'd be alone forever, resigned to the fact that the woman I've always loved got away, and I had no one to blame but myself.

Now, she's standing in the kitchen next to my mom and sisters-in-law, spending Thanksgiving with my family—just goes to show that life can change in an instant.

"I hope our refs for the championship game next week aren't as blind as these morons," Walker says as he comes back into the living room, handing out beers to me and my brother. My father has a glass of scotch in his hand—his drink of choice on special occasions such as this—as he rests in his recliner.

"We've been pretty lucky this year in that regard, so I think we'll be okay." Wyatt pops the cap off his beer and tosses it onto the coffee table.

My brothers and I play in a men's football league

between the neighboring towns of Newberry Springs every fall. It's a way for all of us men to relive our youth and have an excuse to act like boys again. At first, I wasn't sure if I should participate since my family always thought my reason for leaving college was due to an injury, but I've been able to pass off a decent recovery that allows me to play at about ninety-percent capacity.

Still, it bothers me to be lying about it to this day.

"Don't focus on the refs, and just play your game. You'll be fine," my dad interjects.

"You gonna be there, Dad?" Wyatt asks.

"I'd never miss getting to see my boys play," he says, lifting his glass to the smug smile on his lips. "But if you lose, I will disown all of you."

Walker barks out a laugh. "Same. We can't lose to Lexington. We never have. If we do now, they'll never let us live it down."

Lexington is the town east of Newberry Springs, and for the past five years, it's been us and them in the championship game. We've won every time. Losing to them now would be a huge upset.

"Then we'd better pick up some pointers this Sunday at the Bolts game," I say, popping the top on my new beer.

"Uh, about that," Wyatt says. "I can't go anymore."

My eyes snap over to him. "What? Why?"

"Kelsea's dad is coming home, and he's been gone for over a month. She wants us to have a late Thanksgiving with him." He shrugs. "Sorry, bro. Wife trumps football."

"Yeah, I can't go, either," Walker adds.

I stare up at him from the couch. "Let me guess . . . the wife?"

Walker doesn't even try to hide his smile. "Yeah. She, uh . . . convinced me last night to stay back so we could do a few projects around the house. She can be very persuasive when she wants to be," he continues, bouncing his eyebrows up and down. My father laughs from his recliner.

"Well, what the hell am I supposed to do now? Go by myself?"

"You ask Shauna to go with you," my father says like it's so obvious.

"Oh, shit. That's brilliant," Walker agrees. "You know that woman loves football. I'm sure you could use the time alone anyway, right?" He bounces his eyebrows again. "I'm sure she can be very persuasive, too."

"Watch what you say about Shauna," I grate out.

Chuckling, he adds, "Calm down. All I'm saying is here's the perfect opportunity to do something fun together. Don't overthink it, just do it."

"I hate to say this, but my annoying twin brother is right. You guys have barely spent any time together since she's been here, and I don't know what you're waiting for." Wyatt tips his beer bottle toward me.

"We've hung out," I argue but don't offer more details than that. I don't need them involved in the intimate details of my love life. And they sure as shit don't need to know about the other things we've been up to that have me jerking off every morning to thoughts of her. "She went and saw my band play, and I'm helping build shit for the Wonderland thing, remember?"

"Okay. And while you're doing that, are you talking?"

"No. I stay mute and make her try to figure out what I'm going to say." I flick my head back and forth between my younger brothers. "What is this? You two offering up relationship advice?"

"As crazy as it sounds, I think your brothers are right here, Forrest." My dad tucks the foot rest of his recliner away before moving to stand. "You'd be a fool not to use this opportunity. Just ask her." He pats my shoulder before making his way into the kitchen.

Walker leans down next to my head, resting his hand on my shoulder. "Did you hear that? Dad says we're right. God, that feels good."

I swat him away. "Get the fuck out of my face." Standing from the couch, I drain half my beer and then head toward the kitchen where the girls are all standing around the island giggling.

"What's so funny?" I ask as I reach for a deviled egg and pop it into my mouth.

"Oh, just sharing stories about you boys," Kelsea answers.

"I don't want to know, do I?"

Evelyn stifles her laughter behind her hand. "Probably not."

I turn to Shauna. "You busy?"

"She's not," my mother answers for her. "Go on, get out of here, you two. Go do something. We still have about thirty minutes before dinner is ready, and Kelsea and Evelyn can help me get the rest of the food ready."

"Are you sure, Momma?" Shauna asks.

My mother widens her eyes at us both and shoos us away. "Go."

I reach for Shauna's hand, weaving her fingers in mine before leading her out the back door onto the porch. As soon as we're out of sight, I press her up against the side of the house and plant my lips on hers.

She frames my face with her hands, pulling me closer to her as our tongues meet.

Fuck, it's getting harder to stay away from her when she's so responsive to my touch—her nipples pebbling under my thumb as I brush my hand over her breast, her leg wrapping around my hip, and the sounds she makes as we kiss make me rock-hard in seconds.

"Well, hello to you, too," she breathes out as we part.

"Fuck, I needed that."

"I'm available anytime."

I squeeze her hip. "Don't tempt me."

"I swear to God, Forrest. If your family wasn't here, I'd let you fuck me right here and now." She bites my bottom lip, making me groan.

"You can't say shit like that, Shauna, when my family is

probably watching us through the windows at this very moment."

Giggling, she replies, "Well, it's the truth."

"I wouldn't do that, though . . . fuck you up against the wall like this."

"Why not?" she asks breathlessly as she reaches between us and rubs her hand over my cock.

I pin her hand in place with my hips, pressing her against the wall even more. "Because when I get you naked again, you're going to be splayed out on my bed so I can retrace every inch of your body with my hands and tongue and remind us of what we've both been missing."

She closes her eyes, breathing even heavier now. "Forrest . . ."

"Speaking of which, I need to ask you something," I say, nibbling on her earlobe, still pressed against her body.

"Okay?"

"How would you feel about coming to Arlington with me on Sunday? I have tickets to the Bolts-Cowboys game, and I want to take you. We could get a hotel room, stay the night—"

"Yes," she cuts me off. "Oh my God, yes." She slants her mouth over mine again, showing me how much she wants this. And now that I think about it, it would be the perfect opportunity to be alone together without my meddling family in the way.

"We can be home early on Monday so you don't miss the entire day and can still get stuff done."

She shakes her head. "I don't care. First of all, you know I love football." I grin, remembering how passionate she can get about a game. "And secondly, you and me in a hotel room? Alone? I think I might combust just waiting for it."

"Fuck, Shauna." I kiss her again while thinking about everything I'm going to do to her once we're in that room—bending her over the bed, slamming into her from behind, eating her pussy until she's screaming my name so loudly that the entire hotel can hear her. I'm ready to claim her as mine again, and that night will be the perfect time to do so. Perhaps it will give us a chance to talk some more, too. "We're gonna have dinner with Maddox Taylor and his wife, too, while we're there," I say between kisses.

"Oh my God! Seriously? You still talk to him?" She stares up at me, eyes bugging out.

"Hell yeah. How do you think I got the tickets?"

"Okay, now I really can't wait. Maddox Taylor! The number one quarterback in the league? Who would have thought we'd know a future professional football player back in the day?"

I stare down at her, concerned about her level of excitement. "Should I be worried about how excited you are right now?"

She pushes against my chest, and I finally stand back, creating space between us while adjusting myself in my pants. "I don't know, Forrest. Maybe you should." She smirks at me.

I frame her face with both of my hands and lower my nose to hers. "Don't worry. I'll make sure you remember who you're there with that night. You can count on that."

"Can't wait."

When we part, I lead her back inside just as Momma is taking the turkey out of the oven. "Shauna? Do you mind making sure everything we need is on the table, honey?"

"Sure, Momma." Shauna lets go of my hand, gives me a knowing glance over her shoulder, and then saunters off as I watch her ass sway in the pair of leggings she chose to wear today. They're the same ones she had on the night at the bar but navy. At this rate, I'd buy her some in every color of the fucking rainbow just so I can see her ass displayed like that every day.

Once Momma and the girls bring all of the food to the table, everyone takes their seats.

My father raises his glass of scotch as he sits at the head of the table. "Before we dig into this lovely meal, I'd like to say a few words."

Everyone grabs their drinks, settling in as we wait for him to continue.

"Elaine and I talk a lot about how blessed we are, but as we grow older, we realize that it's not the physical things that make us feel blessed—it's the people surrounding us day in and day out. Now, obviously our sons don't have much choice in the matter," he says as my brothers and I grumble and the girls laugh. "But the women in their lives have enriched ours as well. Kelsea, you were already like a daughter to us, but you brought Evelyn and Kaydence into our world as well, and lord knows there probably wasn't another woman out there who could handle Walker."

Evelyn laughs. "Don't forget, he was the one who pursued me."

"Even so, you were meant to be a part of this family, dear. And we are so grateful to have you here with us this year on this holiday."

Walker leans over and kisses her head. "Couldn't have said it better myself, Dad."

Then my father turns to me, flicking his eyes back and forth between me and Shauna. "There is one addition to the table this year that warrants celebration as well. Shauna, you have always been a Gibson, sweetheart, since the moment Forrest brought you here to meet us all those years ago. And I think I speak for everyone when I say it feels right having you back here."

Shauna wipes away a tear. "Thank you for welcoming me back in."

"You're always welcome here, even if this bozo here ruins things again," my father jokes, tossing his thumb at me.

"Thanks for the faith, Dad," I mutter as everyone snickers.

"You two are meant to be, and I hope you can find

your way back to each other like you always should have been."

"To family and happily ever afters," my mother adds, raising her glass of wine.

I'm not going to lie, my dad's speech makes nerves build in my chest as I realize I'm not the only one who stands to be hurt if things don't work out this time with Shauna. And I know I shouldn't think about that, given how far we've come since she arrived and the steps we're taking to move forward, but I definitely feel some pressure as our family sits around the table together right now.

I shove down my reservations, and we all clink our drinks together and dig into the meal, handing out compliments to my mother with every bite of food. Momma is a genius in the kitchen, but I think this may be her best Thanksgiving yet.

I sure as hell know it's mine because Shauna is right beside me.

When everyone finishes eating, I help remove plates and dishes, bringing them into the kitchen. Every year, I'm the one who helps clean up since Walker usually has to leave for a shift and Wyatt spends time with Kelsea out on the property after we eat. They usually sneak off somewhere, and I don't bother asking what they're doing since I'm pretty sure I already know the answer to that question.

That leaves me alone with my mother in the kitchen,

which is usually time I cherish. But I can tell by the look on her face right now, I'm about to get an inquisition.

"The food was amazing, Mom," I start, hoping to butter her up so she'll take it easy on me.

But she sees what I'm up to and narrows her eyes at me. "I know."

Laughing, I begin scraping the green bean casserole into a dish to store in the fridge. "Glad to know that subtlety isn't your strongest quality."

"No need for it when you're my son and I'm tired of watching you make decisions out of fear."

"What do you mean?"

She places her hands on her hips and lowers her voice. "What do you mean, what do I mean? Shauna told me about Vegas, Forrest. How come you didn't?"

Shaking my head, I clench my teeth together. I should have known Shauna wouldn't keep something like that from my mom, but I still wish she would have had the decency to tell me that she told my mother everything. "Not exactly a moment I'm proud of, Mom."

She places her hand on my forearm, making me freeze. "Well, that's a damn shame because it sure as hell made me proud of you."

"What?"

"You took a huge risk going out there, Forrest. Probably the biggest one I've ever seen you take. You followed your heart, took your life into your own hands, and chased after the woman who has never left your soul. How could I not be proud of you for that?"

"But it didn't end well," I argue.

"Maybe not at first, but what about now? This is your chance, Forrest. It's always been her, and she's here."

"Yeah, because of your meddling," I fire back at her in a playful tone. I was pissed at my mother at first, but I can't deny that the past three weeks have been eye-opening, and part of me feels whole again just having Shauna here.

"Meddling is a mother's job, a delicate balance between meddling too much and not enough," she tosses back with a playful smirk before she turns serious again. "I don't regret bringing that woman back into our lives. But you're out of your mind if you waste this chance to get your happily ever after."

"I'm working on it," I mutter, focusing back on my task.

"Are you? Because it seems like you're still keeping her at arm's length."

"I'm taking her to the Bolts/Cowboys game this Sunday. Does that sound like keeping her at arm's length?" I shoot a glare over my shoulder.

"It's a start. You need to show that girl what she means to you, what she means to all of us."

"There's still a lot to work through, Momma."

"Then what are you waiting for? What's holding you back?"

"This job is temporary, right? Her reason for coming back here?" I drop my eyes to the counter in front of me. "So what if she decides to leave, Momma?"

She takes a step closer to me, looks up into my eyes, and says, "You've got to give her a reason to stay, then, Forrest. Because believe me—you'll regret it forever if you don't."

CHAPTER FIFTEEN

Shauna

"This place is amazing." I look around at the thousands of fans packed into the Cowboys' stadium for the game. We're wearing Bolts attire, of course, so we are definitely outnumbered. But I don't even care because Maddox got us seats just a few rows up from the field, right at the fifty-yard line. No one else around me exists right now, anyway, except for Forrest.

"You've never been here, huh?" Forrest asks me, clapping as the refs call holding on the Cowboys.

"Nope. I went to a few games out in Vegas once they built the new stadium, though. It sucks my father didn't live to see it. He wanted to go to a game with me before he passed."

Turns out my love of football was ingrained in me from birth since my father was a big fan as well. Being here makes me think of him, but it's more joyful memories than sadness.

Forrest leans over and kisses my temple. "I'm sorry."

"It's okay." Plastering a smile on my face because I refuse to allow today to be tainted by sad memories, I stare back out at the field. "Thank you again for bringing me."

"Well, Walker and Wyatt were supposed to come, but their wives convinced them otherwise."

I lean back, gasping dramatically. "So you're saying I was second choice?"

Forrest smirks. "Not intentionally. Besides . . ." He leans closer to me and lines his lips up to my ear. "You've always been first choice when it counts, Shauna. Especially for me."

I turn my head and line my lips up to his. "Good answer."

When our mouths meet, all it does is wake my body up and remind me of how badly I want this man. Brock and I weren't exactly very physical with one another, especially toward the end. So it's been a while for me, and no one ever knew my body as well as Forrest did, even though we were young the last time we were intimate. The difference was, he made me comfortable and was so eager to please me and figure out what I liked—*so fucking eager.*

I wonder what new tricks he's learned since then.

"What are you thinking about?" he asks, grinning as he stares down at me.

"Oh, nothing."

Pinching my ribs, he pulls me into his chest so my back is to his front, allowing us both to see the game again. "Liar."

I giggle. "I guess you'll just have to find out later."

"Don't worry. I plan on edging you until you tell me all of your deepest, darkest secrets."

Well, there *is* something I haven't discussed with him yet, but today is not the day for that. My mother and I spoke again yesterday, and she prodded me relentlessly about when I would be returning to Vegas. I still haven't given her an answer.

We focus back on the game, biting our nails as the score stays tied at three and three until the end of the fourth quarter, when Maddox throws a Hail Mary pass and Hayden Palomar sweeps it up in his arms right in the end zone, giving the Bolts the win.

"Hell yeah!" Forrest yells beside me. We scream and celebrate around a bunch of broken-hearted Cowboys fans and then make our way out of the stadium.

"Where are we meeting Maddox and Penelope?" I ask as Forrest leads me out to the car, our fingers intertwined.

"The Mercury Chophouse. Maddox already took care of the reservation and told us to go ahead. He and Penelope will be there within the hour."

We make our way to the restaurant and, once inside, are seated in a private room next to the kitchen, out of view of the other customers. I assume these are the types of perks you get being a professional athlete, and part of the experience makes me wonder if Forrest could have had this life, too, if he hadn't been injured.

Forrest asks me to choose a bottle of wine to drink while we wait, and once our glasses are poured, I turn to him. "This is nice. I don't think we've ever experienced a night quite like this one with such a fancy dinner."

"What about Vegas?"

"I don't count that. That was old friends catching up. But this . . . this is more, Forrest."

He leans forward, nuzzling my neck with his nose. His lips find my skin, lightly nibbling. "I don't know who I was kidding thinking I could just be your friend anyway, Shauna."

I lean back and look into his eyes. "Do you ever wonder where we'd be if things had gone differently?"

"All the time, but I'm really fucking tired of doing that." He takes a sip of his wine and stares down at the table.

"I was just thinking about how your life would have turned out if you hadn't gotten injured. Do you think you'd be living a life similar to Maddox?"

A pinch in his brow develops. "Maddox has told me over the years how hard it was to trust people the more popular he became, how hard it was to find a woman who genuinely wanted to be with him for who he was and not what he could buy them." He shakes his head. "I didn't want that. The only thing I wanted back then was you. Nothing else mattered."

I reach out and cup his face. "Well, I'm here now."

"Yeah, you are." He lifts my hand and kisses the back of it. "And later, you're going to be flat on your back and reminded of how I felt when you left."

Heat flashes all over my body. "I'm so ready."

"I hope we're not interrupting anything," Maddox announces from above us, pulling our attention to where he's standing next to the table with his wife, Penelope, right by his side.

"Oh, it's obvious we were, Maddox. By the way Forrest was just looking at her, I'd say he was about to eat her for dinner right here on this table."

I nearly choke on my saliva as Maddox shakes his head at his wife and Forrest laughs. He stands and then greets them both. "Good to see you, man." He and Maddox shake hands, and then he hugs Penelope. "Pen, always a pleasure."

"I know." She smirks. "And who do we have here, Forrest? I do believe this is the first time you've brought a woman to dinner with us?"

Forrest grabs my hand, helping me stand from my chair. "This is Shauna."

Penelope's eyes widen. "*The* Shauna?"

I glance back at Forrest. "I take it you've spoken about me before?"

"Oh, honey. I can get anything out of anyone when I want to," Penelope interjects. "All I had to do was get this grumpy one drunk at dinner one night, and then I couldn't get him to stop talking about the one who got away." She winks at him. "Seems you've found her again."

"Something like that."

We all settle into our seats, reading the menus now since Forrest and I didn't bother before. Once we've ordered, Maddox and Forrest start talking football, leaving Penelope and me the chance to get to know each other.

"So, what do you do, Shauna?" Pen asks, taking a sip of her wine.

"Well, I was in event planning for almost twelve years, primarily weddings. But right now, I'm helping out on the Gibson Ranch."

Her eyes light up. "I keep telling Maddox I want to visit there the next time we're in Texas, but our schedule is always so busy. I head up the PR for the Bolts now, so time is limited during the season."

"I know." Bashfully, I admit, "I follow you two on social media. I love your interactions, and most importantly, I love watching you keep Maddox in line. Back in high school, he always was a little mischievous."

"Oh, believe me. He still is." She smiles, hinting at her thoughts, and glances over at her husband. "But he is the best man I've ever known. The camp he puts on for the kids in Newberry Springs is one of his favorite ways to give back to where he came from. He speaks so highly of that little town and what those people did for him, shaping him into the man he is today."

"I can imagine."

Penelope's eyes light up again. "Oh my God, why didn't I think of this a few seconds ago?" She takes one more drink of her wine and places the glass on the table. "Maddox's cousin, Leslie, heads up the camp and foundation right now, but she's looking for help. Is that something you might be interested in, given your experience?"

A rush of anxiety runs through me. "I—I don't know. I'm kind of here temporarily right now," I say, glancing over at Forrest who's oblivious to my and Penelope's conversation at the moment. But the idea of working for a nonprofit, giving my time to people who don't have money to throw around, has a need building inside of me that tells me this might be what I've been searching for.

"Oh. I thought . . ." Penelope's eyes shift over to Forrest for a second.

"It's complicated. We're kind of working through a few things at the moment, so I'm not in the position to give a yes or no answer. But I'm very interested," I tack on, managing to find a smile again. "Can we exchange numbers so I can let you know?"

"Of course. Sorry for assuming..."

"Oh, it's not your fault. It's just that history doesn't always stay in the past, you know?"

Penelope tilts her head at me and sighs. "I know that better than you might think."

Dinner comes out just as we wrap up our conversation, and then the four of us are back to engaging as a group.

"She got you back on a horse?" Maddox asks Forrest around a mouthful of food.

"Yeah, and believe me, my ass was sore for days."

"Oh, kinky," Penelope snickers, making me laugh.

"When's the last time you rode a horse, Maddox?" I ask him before taking another bite of my steak with garlic butter, which melts in my mouth as I try not to moan out loud.

"The last time I was home, actually, so this past summer. And I remember that soreness. I do some pretty physically demanding things, but I forgot how much my body is affected by that."

"Well, Shauna hopped right back on as if no time had passed at all," Forrest explains.

"I told you, I was volunteering at the horse rescue out in Vegas, so I was still riding on and off over the years. And I'm glad, because I really missed it. There's nothing like riding on the ranch, though."

Forrest reaches for my hand under the table and squeezes it. I look over at him, and he's smiling, something he's been doing much more of lately.

"Horse rescue, huh?" Maddox asks, breaking through our moment. "You know, I have a contact for one out in Perryton. I can give you the information if that's something you'd be interested in doing again."

All of the opportunities presented to me tonight are beginning to overwhelm me, but in the best way. Without showing too much excitement, I simply reply, "That would be amazing. Thanks."

"No trouble at all. I'm sure you have other things to keep you here in Texas, but if you ever need anything or want me to put in a good word for you, just let me know." Maddox nods across the table at me.

"I appreciate that."

"Of course. It's not every day I can help out a friend of mine, let alone the girl he faked an injury for."

I freeze, wondering if I heard him correctly. Leaning forward in my seat, I say, "I'm sorry . . . what did you just say?"

"Shit," Forrest mutters under his breath beside me.

Maddox laughs. "What?" But then he reads my expression, and his face falls. "Fuck. I thought—"

"You thought I knew, right?" I laugh through the words, trying to find humor in this development but failing. "Because that would be the logical assumption . . . that Forrest would have told me by now that he also had some secrets in our past." I turn to him, but Forrest's eyes remain on the table in front of him. "Is it true?"

He twists to look at me, his face hard and his eyes narrowed. "Yeah."

I can't believe this.

"Just lovely." I remove my napkin from my lap, tossing it onto my plate, no longer hungry. "I'm sorry, but I need to go." Standing from the table, I look at Penelope. "It was so nice to meet you. Thank you for being so welcoming."

"It was great to meet you, too." She flashes me a sympathetic smile.

"Shauna . . ." Forrest speaks, but I ignore him as I spin on my heels and head for the front of the restaurant.

I'm not sure where I'm going to go. Forrest drove us here and we haven't even checked into the hotel yet. But I push open the door to the restaurant, and as the frigid air outside hits me, I take a deep breath to help calm the fury running through my veins.

Forrest lied to me. All those years ago, he withheld the truth, too, and yet he had the nerve to be pissed and blame the end of our relationship on me. If I had known what he'd done—hell, I'm not even sure if it would have changed things for him. It certainly wouldn't have for me. There was no way in hell I was leaving Vegas at that time. But he made such a big deal about me keeping things from him, when in reality, he's been doing the same.

"Shauna," he calls out as he pushes through the door. I don't turn toward his voice, but I can feel him walk up to me without looking. "Shauna, please . . . can we just talk about this?"

"I don't want to talk to you right now," I say as tears fill my eyes.

"So what are we going to do? Just not talk for the rest of the night?"

"I—I don't know. I'm just . . ."

He reaches for my hand, and I let him take mine in his, but I still don't meet his eyes. "I know what Maddox said caught you off guard, but—"

"But what? What on earth can you say to me right now that negates the fact that you lied, too, Forrest? You lied and jeopardized your entire future for me." Shaking my head, I yank my hand from his grasp and head toward the truck.

Forrest doesn't reply, but I hear him follow me, hot on my heels. When he unlocks the truck, he still opens my door for me and makes sure I'm buckled up before heading to the hotel.

The drive is filled with silence, neither of us even looking at each other, but the tension is so thick I could cut it with a knife. Ironically enough, a song by Zach Bryan comes on, which has me fighting back even more tears, the kind that want to spill from anger rather than hurt.

I stand behind him in the lobby as we check in since the room is in his name, and I'm sure the woman behind the counter wonders if I'm here against my will from the look on my face. Forrest grabs the keys to the room and then leads me to the elevator, where we once again remain silent until he unlocks the door to our room and holds it open for me to walk inside.

I set my suitcase in the corner and then stand there, not sure what else to do. I have so many emotions flowing through me that I'm having a hard time pinpointing which one needs to take precedence.

"Shauna," Forrest pleads again, his voice cracking. I close my eyes, not wanting to cry any more over us. I'm so tired of never feeling like I'm on solid ground with this man. Being with him is like being on a rollercoaster full of bumps, twists, and turns, and my stomach and heart can't take much more.

"Shauna, please let me explain."

I twist to face him, meeting his eyes for the first time since before Maddox let his secret slip.

"I don't even know what to think right now, Forrest." Shaking my head, I let a tear slip down my cheek. "All this time . . . all this time, I've relived that night in my apartment over and over again, feeling so much guilt for not telling you about my dad, for pushing you away. And then tonight, I find out that you lied to me, too. Why would you do that, Forrest? Why on earth would you fake an injury and lose your scholarship? Do you realize how different your life could have been if it weren't for me?"

Guilt.

That's the emotion that stands out above the rest right now.

Guilt over how my choices have dictated this man's life.

His face hardens right before my eyes, and then he closes the distance between us, anger rolling off of him in waves. "I don't understand how you can't see the reason I did it. Nothing else mattered without you, Shauna. I had everything *but* you. That's why. I would gladly give up everything else in my life over and over again if it meant that I had you. That's all I wanted, all I needed, but you still pushed me away."

God, how did we get here? How have we spent so much time lying to ourselves about what we felt and what we wanted?

"You were so angry with me, made me feel like the worst person in the world for what I didn't tell you . . . but what about what you didn't tell me?"

His next sentence nearly stops my heart. "Well, now I'm telling you that I'm about to fuck you into next week and make you mine again. How do you feel about that?"

I suck in a breath. "Forrest—"

He slams his mouth over mine before I can reply and pins me against the wall, diving his tongue deep, showing me with his touch how possessive he is of me, how all the time we've been apart never changed how we feel about one another.

There have been mistakes, countless lies and choices we made thinking it was best for the other person, but none of them changed us—the fact that we belonged to one another, heart and soul—and that's what ultimately matters.

"God, woman. You're so fucking stubborn."

"No, I think you're the stubborn one," I mumble against his lips. "You jeopardized your life, your education, your passion."

"I'd do it all over again. Now shut up and let me fuck you. I need to fuck you, Shauna."

I drag his bottom lip between my teeth. "Then fuck me, Forrest."

Forrest lifts the bottom of my jersey and tank top, pulling them over my head before tossing them to the side. He reaches behind me, pinches the clasp on my bra, and yanks that from my body as well, staring down at my breasts like a lion that's been starved.

"Jesus, you're fucking perfect. Still so fucking perfect," he says before bending his knees and drawing one of my breasts into his mouth. His tongue circles my nipple as he pinches the other one, making them harden even more than they already were as I bury my hands in his thick hair, pulling on the strands while he nibbles and sucks, heating my body up.

"Oh God."

"Not God, baby. Me."

I pull his head up and plant my lips on his once more,

framing his face in my hands. "This is really happening, isn't it?"

"Hell yes. God, the amount of times I've dreamed of being with you again should be illegal."

I reach for the bottom of his shirt, lifting it up until Forrest grabs the neck from behind, tearing the entire thing from his body in one smooth movement.

And mother of God.

His body—muscles full of sinew, veins popping through his tanned skin, pecs hard and full, biceps bulging as he stands there, letting me soak up every inch of him with my eyes—the boy I knew before is all man now.

And he's mine tonight—*hopefully forever.*

I lean forward and press my lips to his chest, kissing his taut skin before dragging my tongue over his nipple, remembering how much he loved when I played with them before.

"Fuck, Shauna." He pulls me back to him, encasing me in his arms as we fall to the bed, devouring each other's mouths once more.

When he pushes himself up on his elbows, hovering over me, his eyes trail all over my body. "I need you naked. Now."

He stands from the bed, popping the button on his jeans as I do the same, shimmying out of mine and tossing them to the floor. When he pushes his briefs down and his cock juts out, I suck in a breath. "God, yes. That's what I want."

He strokes his length and smirks down at me. "He's all yours, baby."

But then my eyes land on the tattoo on his thigh. "Forrest? Is that . . ."

He stops moving his hand, taking a few steps closer so I can get a good look. I trace the image on his skin—a woman riding on a horse, her hair whipping behind her. She looks free, happy, and in control.

She looks like me.

"I got it two weeks before we broke up," he says, staring down at the ink and then glancing up at me, garnering my reaction.

"Is that . . ."

"You?" He nods. "Yeah, baby. It is."

I stare up at him in awe while my heart threatens to break my rib cage.

I've been inked on his skin this whole time, and I didn't know it. But I think the true reality is that we've both been inked on each other's hearts since long before this moment.

"Come here." I curl a finger at him, prompting him to pick up where we left off because the war of emotions and lust rushing through me is too much to process all at once.

I'm choosing to let lust take over at this moment. We can deal with the emotions later.

He leans over me again and our mouths meet once more as he reaches between us, stroking me through my soaked thong. "Fuck, you're drenched."

"I want you. I'm so ready." Even more so now that I know how long this man has kept me in his heart.

He steps back and hooks his thumbs in the strings at my hips, peeling the fabric down my legs so slowly I think I might die. But then he drops to his knees, pushes my thighs open, and licks my pussy from bottom to top without any hesitation. My eyes roll back in my head from the sensation. "Fuck, I missed this pussy. *My* fucking pussy."

"She missed you, too," I say, glancing down to watch him eat me. Our eyes meet, and it's one of the most erotic moments of my life.

"Fuck, you taste like heaven. Sweet, sweet heaven, Shauna."

"Forrest . . ." I let out an embarrassing moan when his tongue finds my clit and circles my bundle of nerves perfectly. "Don't stop."

He keeps his eyes locked on me, sucking on my clit while slowly inserting a finger into my core. Time feels like it stands still as I watch him lick me, with precision and intention I can feel in his touch and see in his gaze. The feeling of his fingers and tongue makes my climax build in record time, embarrassingly so, but I'm so ready to hurl myself over that cliff.

"Come on my face, Shauna. Show me who this pussy belongs to."

My hips start moving of their own volition as I rub myself up and down Forrest's mouth. His fingers keep sliding in and out of me as he flicks my clit with his tongue, and a few seconds later, I see fucking stars.

I scream through my release, shouting his name as I fall over the edge. And when I'm just about to fall back completely, Forrest catches me.

He drags a hand across his face, wiping most of my arousal from his face and scruff, and then hovers over me, kissing my cheeks, jaw, and neck. "Jesus, Shauna."

"Fill me, Forrest. Fill me up with your cock, please," I beg, not wanting any more time to recover. All I care about in this moment is reconnecting with this man completely.

Forrest lines his cock up to my entrance and pushes inside, sliding in with little effort since I'm still dripping and more than ready for him.

We groan in unison once he reaches my end, resting his forehead on mine before he retracts his hips and thrusts in again, setting a pace we both agree to.

"Fuck. *Fuck.*" His hips keep meeting mine, his thrusts powerful, our bodies slick with sweat.

"God, I missed this. I missed us."

"This is heaven—being buried inside of you again—which means I've been living in hell for the past fifteen years, Shauna," he grates out, slamming his hips against me, working my body over like he never forgot how.

My body prepares for another orgasm as the tip of his cock rubs against my G-spot again and again.

"I can feel you getting close. Are you going to come all over my cock?" he asks, murmuring the words in my ear.

"Yes . . . God, yes . . ." And within seconds, I'm exploding again, clutching his arms as I ride out my high.

It's even better between us now, and it was more than fucking magical back then.

"Jesus, your pussy is squeezing me so tight, Shauna," he says before kissing me deeply, flipping us over so I'm on top now. When we part, he stares up at me, brushing my hair from my face as our ragged breaths fill the room. "I wanna see you ride me."

"Then don't stop looking up."

He chuckles and then points to the full-length mirror in the corner. "I wanna watch us. You up for that?"

A shiver runs down my spine at the notion, but I nod, because ultimately, I'd do anything for this man.

Forrest helps me up and then sits on the edge of the bed, pushing his knees out wide. He guides me by the hand and helps me straddle him so we're facing one another. Rubbing his cock through my pussy, he coats himself in my arousal and then slips back inside, holding me to his chest as he faces the mirror while my back is to it.

"Goddamn," he groans as I start to lift up and down his

length, feeling him deeper the harder I fall on his lap with each thrust. "Your pussy is sucking me in, Shauna. Like a fucking glove."

"I wanna see," I say, glancing over my shoulder in the mirror, watching my body move. It's so erotic, watching us together, seeing how intimate we're being, sharing our bodies with one another.

It's one of the most erotic moments of my life, but then Forrest takes it to another level.

"Here." He lifts me off him, spins me around so I'm facing the mirror now, and slides me back down on him so we both get a front-row seat. "There. That's my pussy. There she is," he grates out in my ear, holding me by the hips to help guide me up and down.

"Oh God. Your cock, Forrest . . . God, I've missed you." Twisting to face him, I look him in the eye and then press my lips to his, speeding up my movements.

"You're mine, Shauna. You always have been."

"I am yours, Forrest," I whisper against his lips as he reaches a hand around my waist and finds my clit, circling the nub softly.

"I wanna watch you come on my cock again, baby."

"Me, too."

Our eyes shift back to the mirror, locking on one another's gaze in the reflection, and then my body takes over, chasing my release while staring at the man in the mirror who possesses me, heart and soul.

It doesn't take long before that orgasm works its way

through my body, and then I detonate, clenching Forrest's thighs as I fight to stay upright.

"Jesus, fuck." He keeps his eyes on me while he lets go, spilling his cum inside me. We didn't use a condom, but I don't even care at this point. I didn't want anything between us, anyway.

"Shauna . . ." he whispers in my ear as he pulls us back onto the bed. After a little rearranging of our bodies, I lie on my side, my head resting on his chest.

"Forrest . . . I'm so sorry," I croak out as all of the emotion from this evening catches up to me.

His lifts my chin so our eyes meet. "No, I'm sorry. I'm sorry for lying to you, for placing all of the blame on you, for holding a grudge for so long."

"I just want to move forward, Forrest."

"Me, too, baby." He presses his lips to my forehead as I feel my body relax. "Me, too."

And even though tonight didn't go exactly as planned, I still ended up in this man's arms, lying in bed next to him, and that's exactly where I want to be.

CHAPTER SIXTEEN

Forrest

"God, this ass." I feel like a fucking animal as I smack Shauna's cheeks again. My hips continue slamming into her from behind as she clutches the sheets in front of her, letting her body relish in the pain and pleasure I'm giving her.

"Spank me again." She looks over her shoulder, watching me fight for control as my hand comes down on her ass once more. "Harder."

"Mine," I grate out as my hand connects with her ass again. "This ass is mine, Shauna."

She leans down on her forearms, changing the angle I'm reaching inside her. "Oh, fuck. Keep going."

"Soak my cock, Shauna. Give me all of it." I refuse to let up, hitting her deeper and deeper with each thrust, and then she's screaming as her orgasm rolls through her body. A minute later, I join her, emptying myself inside her before collapsing on the bed.

Lying there, our breaths shallow, Shauna starts to giggle. "Good morning."

"That's the best fucking way to wake up, baby." I look over at her while still lying on my back. Then I yank her to me by the hips and kiss her hard. "Are you sore?"

"A little, but I don't care." She smiles up at me.

Shauna and I had sex four times last night, and before I opened my eyes this morning, she woke me up with her mouth wrapped around my cock. It was one of my many fantasies come true. And even as we lie here, I think about all the times I wished for this moment, having her back in my arms and in my bed.

"We should get going." I brush her hair from her face.

"Yeah, but I don't want to." She pouts, so I lean in to kiss it away.

"Me, neither, but I have to go into the office for a little bit today so I don't fall too far behind, and I know you have work to do, too."

"When will I see you next?"

"Probably at the ranch this week when I come over to work on the pieces for the event."

Her excitement fades further. "Oh."

"Look, last night was amazing, and I don't regret it for a second, Shauna. Everything is out in the open now, but I have this huge project that I need to focus on for a couple of days."

It's not that I don't want to spend more time with her, buried inside of her, but last night was a lot. My chest is tight as I fight with what my heart wants versus what I think I should do.

As we lay down to go to sleep last night, I wanted so badly to feel at peace. Shauna knew the truth about my injury now, I knew the truth about her dad, and she was finally back in my arms.

But then I remembered—there is still uncertainty to face. And the last thing I want to do is be blindsided again by our reality.

She pushes herself out of my arms and stands from the bed. "No, I understand. I have a lot to get done."

I reach out and grab her hand before she gets too far away. "You okay?"

"Yeah, I guess I just thought . . ." She shakes her head. "Never mind."

I want to ask her to finish that thought, I do. But my phone rings, pulling me back to reality, reminding me that even though Shauna and I are working through our past, the present is still here, needing to be dealt with, too.

Freshly showered from the gym, I step into the Gibson Brewery, scouring the room in search of my brother. Wyatt wanted to talk to me about the championship game this Saturday, but our schedules weren't lining up. So I offered to come by on Tuesday after my workout, knowing I could take care of one of my obligations while getting a decent dinner as well.

"Hey, Forrest," Kelsea greets me from behind the long, wooden bar that lines the back wall. All of the beer taps are behind her, the windows on the walls giving customers a view of the holding tanks beyond that.

"Hey. Where's your husband?"

"Oh, he's around here somewhere." She looks around the room, clearly not locating him, either. "Can I pour you a beer while you wait?"

I take a seat in one of the empty stools. "Sure. I'll take the stout, please. Thanks."

"No problem." Kelsea pours my beer with very little foam, like the expert she is, and then slides the glass over to me. "So how was the football game?"

I smirk at her over the rim of my glass. "Good."

"That's all I get?"

"Consider it payback for telling everyone about my band." I place my glass back on the bar.

"Oh, come on. That wasn't my fault, it was Shauna's."

"Funny how during that conversation, you said I shouldn't blame her for sharing my business with you girls."

She sighs and then leans over the counter. "I know, I just want to know how things are going with you two, is all."

"Things are going, Kelsea. It's hard, though..."

"How so? You wanted her back, right? And here she is. What's holding you back?"

"I just get the feeling that her past isn't still in the past. And her mom..."

"What about her mom?"

Groaning, I down another large gulp of my beer. "Forget it."

Kelsea slaps her palm on top of my hand. "No. You can't do that anymore, Forrest. I'm gonna tell Momma that you're holding shit in again."

I narrow my eyes at her. "You think that scares me?"

"It should."

Sighing, I admit, "Her mom wasn't always my biggest fan. I know that if we're going to be together, I'm going to have to confront her, and given that I crashed her daughter's wedding and told her to walk out on it, I'm guessing she's not my biggest fan right now, either, even less so than before."

"I see. So now that you finally have her back in your life, you're going to let her mother stand in your way?"

Irritation builds in my chest. "It's not that simple, Kelsea. Shauna's mom is all she has left. Her dad was gone for most of her life, and then when she finally got him back, he was sick. He died three years ago. The entire reason she went to Vegas was to have a relationship with him."

"Yeah, I know. She told Evelyn and me."

"So I can't ask her to choose between me and her mom, Kelsea." And I think that's why I needed space from her after this weekend. The glaring obstacles still ahead of us became apparent as soon as the sun rose yesterday morning.

"Well, I hope you two figure it out."

I drain the last of my beer just as Wyatt comes out from the back of the brewery. "Yeah, me too."

"Hey," Wyatt says as he comes over to where I'm sitting. "Sorry to keep you waiting. I was on the phone with one of our suppliers. They fucked up my order."

"No problem. Kelsea was just prying information from me like the wizard she is."

Kelsea smiles. "It's a gift, what can I say?"

Wyatt kisses her temple and then holds up our playbook in his hand. "You ready?"

"Yeah."

He leads us over to a high-top table in the corner, and we spend the next thirty minutes going over our game plan for this Saturday.

"I like it. I don't think Lexington will know what hit them."

"It requires you to do some running, though. You up for that?" Wyatt asks out of concern for my knee—the one that was never really messed up to begin with.

Fuck. I think back to Shauna's reaction the other night, and the last thing I want is for that secret to slip out, too. So without any preparation, I tell Wyatt the truth.

"My knee is fine, man."

"I know. You always say that . . ."

"No, I mean there was never anything wrong with my knee, Wyatt."

He stares at me, confusion etched into the lines on his face. "I—I don't understand."

"I was never injured. I faked it, told you guys that was the reason I came home from college, but it was a lie. I dropped out to be with Shauna because I missed her too damn much, but when I went to Vegas to repair things, we broke up instead."

He shakes his head. "Jesus."

"I know. I'm sorry I lied, but I was desperate back then. All I wanted was her and me back together in Texas."

"Wow. Well, I can't say that I'm too surprised because you always made decisions with her in mind."

I huff out a laugh. "Yeah."

"But I appreciate you telling me. Does Shauna know?"

"She found out this weekend. Maddox let it slip when we were at dinner."

"Shit. How'd she take it?"

"Not well—blamed herself when she has no reason to."

"Well, I can see how she might think that way. Your entire life changed trajectory because of that decision."

"I know, but I didn't care at the time."

"I get it. I'd choose Kelsea over many things in life."

"Took you long enough to realize it, though," I tease him.

"Yeah, but at least I figured it out eventually. My question to you is: Have you figured out what you want with Shauna yet? Have you shown her the house?"

I clench my jaw and drop my head. "No." It's one thing I don't think I'm ready to share with her just yet, not until I know we're both on the same page.

"Why the fuck not?"

"Because I don't want her to choose me because of our past, Wyatt," I blurt out, surprising myself. "I mean, obviously we have that history, but we can't change any of that, and it honestly shouldn't affect our future. She's only here temporarily, anyway."

"That's not what Mom said."

My curiosity piques. "What?"

"She told Kelsea that she offered Shauna the event coordinator position full-time."

"Did she accept it?"

"Not yet."

"Why not?"

He gives me a deadpan glare. "Why the fuck do you think?" I stare at him, still not grasping what he's laying down. "You, you idiot!"

"Me?"

"Yeah. Why would she take that job if she didn't know

you two were back together? Would you want to work for your ex's family when you still have feelings for that person? I sure as fuck wouldn't." He shudders.

"Jesus. Shit keeps piling up."

"Only if you let it. Fucking talk to her, see what she's thinking, and then make some fucking decisions, for the love of God."

I shove him in his chair. "I know you're married and think you can dish out relationship advice, but sometimes shit isn't simple."

He nods. "You're right. Sometimes it's not. But here's what I know." He leans closer to me. "If she's the woman you want, then walking through all that shit and coming out the other side of it together is all fucking worth it, Forrest. Trust me. That I *do* know."

CHAPTER SEVENTEEN

Shauna

"How's it going over there?" I glance over at Forrest as he lines up two more pieces of wood, getting ready to hammer them together.

"It's going."

"Oh. Okay."

That's it.

That's the most I've been able to get from him since he arrived tonight. It's Thursday, so we're stuck in this barn together, working on the pieces for the Winter Wonderland event, and I feel like something happened in the past three days that I'm not privy to.

Sadly, the only way I can figure out how to fix it is if Forrest starts talking, but that's like counting your chickens before they hatch.

"Can you hand me that box of nails over there?" he asks, breaking me out of my mental spiral.

"Uh, sure." I grab the box and walk it over to him, but he doesn't even meet my eyes when he takes it from me. And that's when I snap. "Okay, what the hell is going on?"

He continues to avoid my eyes. "What do you mean?"

I smack the box of nails out of his hand, and that has him standing to full height now, peering down at me.

"I mean you're being standoffish and won't even freaking look at me, Forrest. Three days ago, you were buried inside me, telling me I'm yours, and now, you're avoiding me! What the hell happened?"

He shoves his hand through his hair. "Fuck, Shauna." Tossing his hammer on the table beside him, he looks at me with a vulnerability in his eyes that I haven't seen in years.

"Talk to me. Tell me what the hell is going through your head."

He straightens his spine and locks his eyes on mine. "Why didn't you tell me that my mom offered you a permanent job here and not just a temporary one for this event?"

My head rears back. "Excuse me?"

"You heard me."

"Are you honestly mad at me about that right now?"

"Yeah, because I thought we didn't have any more secrets between us. I thought we were past that."

I narrow my eyes at him. "How dare you! How dare you try to make me out to be the bad guy when you're the one that has done nothing but push me away!" I shake my head and plant my hands on my hips. "Fine. You want to know why? Because I wasn't about to take a full-time job here if you weren't going to let me back in. There! Does that make you happy?"

"No," he simply states.

"Then what will? Because all I know is that we spent an amazing weekend together, said a lot of things, and then you ran. What changed?"

"I just don't understand how this is gonna work!" he shouts, burying his hand in his hair.

His admission nearly knocks the breath out of me. "What? Why?"

"Where do we go from here, Shauna? We slept together. It was fucking incredible, but now we have to make these decisions, figure out the future, and I don't know where your fucking head is at."

I take a step toward him and then lower my voice. "Then *ask* me, Forrest, you big doofus." I shove his chest, and he catches me off guard when he wraps his hand around my wrist, holding me in place.

The pinch in his brow almost unnerves me, but the tone of his voice is what really has me holding my breath. "What do you want, Shauna? Do you want to do this job permanently? Or are you going to find something else to take you away from me again?"

Everything becomes clear in an instant. "Your indecision is because you're worried I'll leave you?"

"Wouldn't be the first time, baby."

Sighing, I step into him as he releases my hand. I lift my fingers to brush the hair from his face, sprinkled with sawdust and paint, feeling his shoulders start to loosen. "Forrest, I'm *not* going anywhere. I came back for *you*, and I've never lied to you about that."

He closes his eyes and inhales deeply. "Okay."

"But . . . Just so everything is out on the table . . ."

His eyes pop back open. "What?"

"I do have to go back to Vegas after the event."

"Why?"

I take a deep breath and then put everything out in the open. "I have to talk to Brock."

"The fuck?" He takes a step back from me, his shoulders tense before he pinches the bridge of his nose and turns his back to me. "God, I feel like I'm nineteen all over again."

"Look, it's not what you think, but I've hurt people, Forrest. I've made decisions in my relationships that make me question whether I'm a good person. Do you see how hard that is? And then I came here, asking for your forgiveness when I'm not sure that I deserve it. I haven't spoken to Brock since the wedding, Forrest. He didn't want to talk to me, wouldn't reply to my calls or emails, and then when I got the job offer to come out here, I knew I wasn't going to wait around for him to be ready. Having your mother post that job opening was a sign, and I had to listen to it, but I have to be able to put my past to rest so I can focus on our future."

"So he doesn't know about me?"

"Not entirely, although I'm not sure what my mother has told him."

"Does your mom know what I did?"

"Yes, she does."

"Fucking great." He pinches the bridge of his nose again. "She must really hate me now."

"She doesn't *hate* you . . ." Hate is a strong word, but my mother certainly has her opinions about the boy from the small town who stole my heart all those years ago—the boy she thought I had left behind for good.

Forrest snorts. "Sure. And now I find out she still talks to your ex?"

"Brock works with my stepfather, Frank. That's how I met him, and yes, my parents still speak with him."

"But he wouldn't talk to you himself . . ."

"I wounded his pride. Can you blame him?"

"Yes," he replies instantly before inhaling deeply, letting it out in one large breath. "So where does this leave us? Because if memory serves me correctly, your mother didn't like me back then, and I'm pretty sure she's not a fan of mine now. And you haven't even made a decision about whether you're staying here or not."

"First of all, let me handle my mother. And second, I haven't brought our future up with you because I've been trying to respect your pace in all of this. We can talk about that now if you want, but honestly, I'm just glad that you finally said more than two words to me."

He sighs loudly. "Fuck, Shauna. I'm sorry. I'm a fucking mess. Having you here is everything I wanted, but now I'm not sure I was aware of all of the shit we'd have to work through. It's killing me thinking that this could all vanish again, that I could go back to being the shell of a man I've been walking around as for years."

"Then don't. Don't be that man again, but shutting me out isn't going to help you and neither is shutting out your family." An idea dawns on me. "Maybe you should invite them to your gig this Friday night?"

Forrest's band is playing again this weekend, earlier in the month than normal because of the holidays.

"What's that going to do?"

"Do you not remember how hurt they were when they found out?"

"They wouldn't have if it weren't for you." I twist his nipple, making him shriek. "Hey!"

"Yes, they would have. Because even if you never told them, they would have found out eventually. You've spent so much time hiding in your life, and I refuse to let you do that anymore if I'm going to be a part of it. So yes, they found out, but this is your chance to share it with them."

"Are you going to be there, too, then?" he asks, his

voice lowering as if he's afraid of my answer. I have every reason to keep this argument going, but the man standing in front of me is shedding his armor, and I'd be a fool to make him put it up once more.

"Of course, babe. I wouldn't miss seeing you play guitar again," I say, dragging my hands through his hair, leaning into his chest. "I want to be there for you, Forrest. Plus, you know what seeing you play does to me . . ."

"Fuck, Shauna." He leans down and gives me his mouth, kissing away the uncertainty from before.

Yes, we have more things to figure out, but none of that can happen if he keeps pushing me away. And even though his stubbornness makes me want to scream, I'd gladly have the same fight with him over and over if it means having him back in my life.

CHAPTER EIGHTEEN

Forrest

"Jesus, there's a lot of people out there tonight."

Leland glances over at me from behind the stage. "No more than usual. What's gotten into you?"

"My fucking family is here, man."

"Oh, shit. They've never seen you play, huh?"

"Nope."

He pats me on the shoulder. "Don't be nervous, brother. You're fucking awesome. They're going to see that, too."

"Yeah, I guess."

If I thought I was nervous when Shauna saw me play last, nothing beats the way I feel tonight having my parents and brothers in the crowd.

I'm a thirty-four-year-old man still afraid of disappointing my parents. How fucked up is that?

I guess it's not entirely far-fetched, since I've made choices in my life they didn't necessarily understand, but something about sharing this with them has me bracing for criticism.

I stare out over the crowd again, landing on my family and Shauna, who's busy talking to Kelsea and Evelyn. And just the smile on her face helps ease my anxiety.

Our talk the other night helped ease it, too, but I'm not going to lie—knowing she has to go back to Vegas to confront her ex makes me want to pound the guy into a pulp.

I get being angry, having your pride hurt—because this woman has done that to me, too. But now? Now, I get that the decisions she made back then weren't about me. They were about her.

And that's exactly who she chose when she walked out on their wedding.

Sure, I probably gave her a nudge by showing up. But she already knew that he wasn't the man she was supposed to be with.

Does it suck for him? Hell yeah. But is it better she

figured that out before they tied the knot so they both have the chance to be with the people they're meant for? Absolutely.

I didn't get a chance to talk to her more about it the other night, but tonight, I'm going to let her know that if she's going back to Vegas, I'm going with her.

"You ready?" Leland asks me as Max glances up as well.

I nod, steadying my heart rate. "Yup. Let's do this."

Leland slaps me on the back as I follow him and Max out onto the stage. The crowd goes wild with their cheers and applause, and my eyes land on the people in my corner.

It hits me then—I've never had people I care about watching me before. And fuck, it feels kinda nice.

"How's everybody doing tonight?" Leland asks the crowd as whistles ring out.

"Awesome! I just wanted to let you guys know that we have some special guests in the crowd tonight," he says. "Our guitarist here, Forrest . . . well, his family came all the way from Newberry Springs to see him play. Why don't we give them a round of applause, yeah?"

The crowd goes nuts as my mother practically bounces in her chair, waving her hands. "That's my boy!" she shouts, making the rest of my family laugh.

And fuck. I laugh, too.

Shauna mouths at me, "See? They love you."

And that's when I know that I love them—*and her*—too.

"Well, now I feel like Wyatt and I have to learn to play something so we can start our leprechaun band," Walker says as I stand next to my brothers at the bar.

"They're fucking elf costumes, Walker," Wyatt mutters, closing his eyes. "And I'm not learning to play an instrument. I have enough going on, thank you very much."

"Party pooper," Walker declares as I laugh at these two. "But seriously, that was fucking awesome, Forrest."

"Thanks."

"You guys don't want to try to make it big?"

"Oh, hell no," I reply, taking a sip of my water. I didn't drink tonight since I still have to drive Shauna and myself home. "We knew going into this it was just going to be about fun."

Wyatt shakes his head. "I still can't believe you've kept this from us all this time."

"I know," my mother interjects, pushing her way between me and Wyatt to frame my face in her hands. "My son is so freaking talented!"

"Thanks, Momma."

She wraps her arms around me, so I do the same to her. "I'm so proud of you. You were amazing. God, I didn't think I would still feel this way watching my kids do something they love for the first time, but it seems there's no limit to the age at which that happens."

"What do you mean?" Walker asks.

"Well, when you were younger, it was watching you play football, learning to ride a bike . . . you know, things like that. Now, as you've gotten older, I get to watch you be husbands and fathers, which is a totally different type of feeling. But watching you play tonight . . ." She stares up at me. "It gave me the same feeling I used to get when you were little. And I guess it just reminded me that you're all growing up too fast." She starts crying.

I hold her closer to me. "I'm glad you're here," I whisper in her ear.

"Me, too."

"Elaine, honey. It's time to go." My father comes up to us now, reaching out to shake my hand. "Proud of you, son. Hell of a set. Who knew you had the musical talent in the family?"

"One of us had to," I reply, letting my hold on Momma go. "You gonna be okay?" I ask her.

"I'm fine. Just had a moment, you know."

"We know," my brothers and I echo.

"Come on, honey. You can cry about how big our boys are on the way home," my dad says to my mom, leading her away.

"Yeah, I hate to say it, but I think Kelsea and I are gonna take off, too. We have the game tomorrow, and I want to rest before then." Wyatt stretches his arms above his head.

"Yeah, same, especially since I have to go back to work the day after," Walker adds.

"Shauna and I are gonna head out of here in a minute, too. I'm taking her home with me tonight."

Wyatt's eyebrows pop up. "Oh, shit. Really?"

"Yeah. We talked through some shit the other night about the job and her mom. I know we're not fully on the same page yet, but it's time."

"She's gonna flip," Walker says, patting me on the back.

Nerves race through me, wondering what her reaction might be. I can't see her not liking it because the vision came from her mind, but I still have reservations about what she might think. I mean, I fucking built the house we talked about when we were in high school, years after we weren't together anymore. Does that speak of romance or desperation?

I guess I'm about to find out.

"There you are," Kelsea says, spinning into Wyatt's arms. "You ready to go home?"

"Yeah, seems we're all leaving soon."

"Perfect. Evelyn and Shauna are still in the bathroom, but they'll be here in a minute." Kelsea turns to me. "I loved watching you play, Forrest."

"Thanks, Kels."

"I know Shauna did, too." She bounces her eyebrows. "The girl was squirming in her seat the whole time."

"He's taking her to his house tonight," Wyatt says, making Kelsea gasp.

"Finally!" She turns to Wyatt and says, "You know, watching them tiptoe around each other and refuse to admit their feelings is how people must have felt about us, babe."

"It is," Walker declares, smirking. "But you two got there, and so will Shauna and Forrest."

"Shauna and Forrest what?" the woman in question asks as she approaches the group.

"Nothing. My brothers and Kelsea were just about to start minding their own business," I say instead of letting anyone else speak.

Evelyn snorts. "Yeah, like that will ever happen."

The six of us say our goodbyes, and then I lead Shauna out to my truck. Once we settle inside, I turn the ignition before turning to face Shauna over the center console. "I have something I want to show you."

"Okay..."

"Feel like coming home with me?"

She instantly smiles. "I didn't bring any pajamas with me."

I reach over and pluck her bottom lip with my thumb. "Something tells me you aren't going to need them."

"You sound pretty sure about that," she teases. And then she leans forward, cupping my jaw. "I'm proud of you, Forrest."

"For?"

"For letting everyone in tonight."

I swallow down the lump in my throat. "Thank you for pushing me to do that."

"You're welcome. But I think you would have gotten there by yourself."

I shake my head. "No way. That was all because of you. Everything you said to me since you've been here has helped me see how closed off I've been. But I'm kind of tired of that, babe."

"So what do you propose you do?"

"I think it's time to show you just how long my heart has been yours."

∼

When we pull into my driveway, I wipe my sweaty palms on my jeans and then turn to take in Shauna's reaction.

Her mouth is agape and her eyes are laser focused on the house in front of her. "Forrest . . . is that . . ."

"Come on." I hop down from my side of the truck, racing over to her door to help her from her seat. When her feet hit the dirt, I grab her hand and pull her toward the front porch steps.

"It's beautiful," she whispers as our footsteps echo off the wood. "It's white . . . with blue shutters."

"It is. I built it five years ago."

Her head whips back to me. "You did?"

"Well, High Performance Construction did. I put in

some labor myself, but after I took ownership of the company, I knew I wanted to build a home that had everything I wanted. I lived in a townhouse beforehand, one very similar to Walker's, but this property was too good of a deal to pass up. And I had a vision in mind of what I wanted my house to look like..."

What I wanted *our* house to look like.

I unlock the front door and lead her inside, shutting it behind us before flipping on the lights.

Shauna spins around, taking in the open floor plan—the living room with high-vaulted ceilings to her left, the kitchen just behind it featuring a massive center island with dark marble countertops and cherry-stained cabinets, and the formal dining area in the far left corner. To our right is the hallway that leads to the four bedrooms and den that I've turned into a bit of a man cave. I have a pool table, a pinball machine, and a poker table in there. They don't get used nearly as often as I'd like, but I haven't exactly wanted to be social over the past few years.

I think it's safe to say that my mind has changed about a lot of things recently, though.

"This has to be a dream, right?"

"There's something else I want to show you." I lead her to the back door that opens out to the wraparound porch and turn her to the right where a wooden bench swing hangs, facing the back of my property.

"Is that..."

"It was one of the first things I put out here." I watch her walk over to the swing, her fingers dancing along the wood as she stands next to it.

"I can't believe you did this," she whispers, finally looking over at me.

I see in her tear-filled eyes that I had nothing to worry about bringing her here. If anything, having her here helps bring everything into perspective.

So I let her know that.

"How could I not, Shauna? Even when we weren't together, you were a part of everything I've done, every choice I've ever made." My admission rests between us, but it's the fucking truth.

Shaking her head, she walks back over to me and rises on her toes, planting her lips on mine. "It's perfect."

"I'm glad you think so. I was afraid you wouldn't approve."

"How so?"

"Well, it's been years since we spoke, but I still built this fucking house for us. That vision never left my mind."

"It never left mine, either."

"So you could have appreciated that or thought I was a hopeless schmuck who never gave up hope when he should have."

She runs her hand through my hair as I pull her into my chest. "I'm glad you never gave up hope, Forrest, because one of us had to keep it. If you hadn't shown up in Vegas, I probably would have gone through with the wedding." Her confession makes my heart race. "But seeing you only once told me everything I needed to know. It's always been you."

I stare down into her blue eyes dancing in the overhead light. Not ready for the night to end, I say, "Would you like to have a drink out here with me, then?"

Her smile nearly blinds me. "I'd love that."

Once we're inside, I fill two wine glasses and then steer her back out to the swing where we settle in to enjoy the chilly night.

"I have a question for you."

Shauna has her legs tucked up under her as she leans into my chest, my arm around her shoulders. "Okay . . ."

"Why weddings?"

She looks to the side so our eyes meet. "Why did I plan them?"

"Yeah. I almost asked you that night in Vegas, but I don't think I was thinking straight." She chuckles. "But for the girl who never wanted the big ordeal, I find it odd that you made a career planning those big parties for other people."

She contemplates her reply for a minute and then takes a drink before answering me. "The romance, I guess. You know I loved romantic movies, and I guess I wanted to believe that those type of love stories were possible. But I quickly realized that real-life love is not like it is in the movies."

I snort. "I could have told you that."

She elbows me in the ribs. "Anyway, I would work with these women who paid thousands of dollars on a party to impress other people, on details of their wedding that honestly very few people care about. When in reality, I think most of them were oblivious to the fact that the most important detail was the man at the end of the aisle they're walking down." She clears her throat. "You know that movie *The Wedding Planner* with Jennifer Lopez?"

"How could I forget? You made me watch it about a dozen times."

She elbows me again. "Well, that's what my life was like. My colleagues and I would actually take bets like that, too, about how long a marriage would last. I almost always won."

I huff out a laugh. "How did you figure it out?"

She stares up at me, her blue eyes twinkling in the overhead light, and says, "I used to see if the groom looked at the bride how you used to look at me."

My heart starts thrashing. I tuck her wavy hair behind her ear, drawing my fingertip down her cheek. "Am I looking at you that way right now?"

"Yeah, you are. But you're also looking at me like you're about to fuck me again."

"Seems like you can still read my mind, then."

I take our wine glasses and set them on the small table next to the swing before grabbing Shauna by the waist and helping her straddle my lap. She's wearing a dress with leggings so it's easy for her to spread her legs, and I dive my hand under her dress to rub her pussy through the fabric.

"Forrest..."

"I wanna fuck you out here, Shauna... on this swing. You up for that?"

"It's a little cold," she says as a shiver runs through her body.

"Don't worry, baby. I'll warm you up really quick."

Our mouths meet, and then no more words are spoken. Shauna buries her hands in my hair as our tongues twist and tangle. Every moan she lets out goes straight to my dick and, as if she's reading my thoughts again, she breaks our kiss and stands from the swing, taking off her boots and peeling her leggings down her legs.

Once her bottom half is nearly bare, she straddles me again, reaching between us to pop the button on my pants. I help her push my jeans and briefs down, freeing my cock. She doesn't waste any more time before pulling her thong to the side, lining me up to her entrance, and sliding all the way down my cock.

"Holy fuck," I groan, tossing my head back as Shauna moves her hips up and down, rubbing her wetness all over me.

"God, you feel so good," she mewls, giving me her lips again as I hold her to my chest. "I don't think I'll ever get enough of this," she murmurs against my lips.

"Me, either, Shauna. Fuck, woman. Ride me . . . ride me hard."

Crickets chirp in the air around us, and a light wind whips across the porch, but I keep Shauna in my arms and help her chase her release as she continues to move over me.

She pushes against my chest and then leans back, resting her hands on my thighs, staring at me with a twinkle in her eye. I look down, lift the bottom of her dress, and watch my cock slide in and out of her pussy, glistening with her arousal.

"Fuck, that's hot." She's stretched around me, pulling me in with each thrust. "I love watching you take me, Shauna . . . watching that pussy suck me in, squeeze me tight." I close my eyes as that familiar tingle travels down my spine, resting in my balls.

"I'm close, Forrest. Touch me, please."

I slide my fingers through her folds, locating her clit and gently rubbing circles around the nub. I can feel her tighten, her breathing get more shallow, and then she throws her head back and curses as her orgasm rips through her body.

I thrust up under her and find my own release just seconds after she detonates, and then she falls forward against my chest.

"So good," she mumbles into my shoulder.

"Agreed. God, woman. How have I gone this long without you?"

"I don't know because I feel the same way."

I bury my nose in her hair, breathing her in.

I'm so in love with her, even after all these years, but this time feels distinctive. We're different people, more aware of who we are and what we want, more open and honest. I sure as fuck am.

So I decide right then and there to stop second-guessing this.

"I'm all in, Shauna," I whisper in her ear. "I'm so fucking in." She lifts her head off my shoulder and searches my eyes. But I cut her off before she can reply. "This time is different. There are no more secrets. We know what we both want, and I want you, baby. I want you to stay. Stay here with me."

"Are you sure?"

"Yes. And I know you have to go back to Vegas, but I'm going with you," I tell her, deciding there's no reason to beat around the bush.

"You don't have to, Forrest."

"I know, but I want to. I need to talk to your mom. I can't avoid her forever, and I want to be there for you with Brock. And if need be, I can punch him in the face, too. I know it would make me feel better since the man touched what's mine."

Shauna chuckles. "You know, the caveman thing shouldn't be hot, but it kind of is."

I smack her ass, making her shriek. "Don't worry. There's plenty more where that came from."

Her smile falls. "You're sure that you want this? There's no going back, Forrest. It's now or never. I can't handle losing you again."

"I'm sure, Shauna. I've had everything I could want in my life. Everything . . . but you. And now that I have you again, I'm never letting you go."

CHAPTER NINETEEN

Shauna

"Come on, boys!" Kelsea shouts beside me as she, Evelyn, and I stand side by side in the stands at Newberry Springs High School. The score is tied seven to seven, and it's nearly halftime during the men's league championship game.

Evelyn pulls her coat tighter around her body. "I'm so glad I didn't bring Kaydence out in this weather. I'd hate for her to get sick before her party next weekend."

"I agree. Besides, you know Momma G would much rather watch her than be out in this cold, anyway." Kelsea nudges her from the side, making her bump into me as well.

A ref blows the whistle on the field, signaling the end of the first half.

"Should we try to get some food at the snack bar, or will the lines be out of control?" I ask them, not sure if it's worth the wait.

Evelyn leans down and digs through her bag. "I have snacks if you're hungry. Granted, it's Goldfish crackers, but I have a one-year-old, so . . ." She shrugs as she stands again, handing me a pack of crackers.

"That'll work. I don't want to ruin my appetite, anyway, since Forrest and I are having dinner after this." I take the bag from her, tear it open, and shove a handful of crackers into my mouth.

Kelsea smirks over at me. "And how are things going with you two?"

I didn't share any relationship details with them at the bar last night since Forrest's parents and brothers were there. And I've been so busy since Thanksgiving—getting things ready for the Winter Wonderland event—that we haven't had any girl time, so I haven't had the chance to bring them up to speed on what's happened between us. But here we are, finally alone, so I'm eager to get their opinion on things.

"Things are"—I fight the smile on my lips—"good," I say, bouncing my eyebrows. "Really good."

Evelyn squeals. "Yes! So does that mean you're staying? For good?"

"I think so."

Kelsea squeals. "Oh my God, I'm so happy."

"Me, too." I sigh wistfully. "Forrest showed me his house last night, you guys, and well..."

Kelsea interjects. "It's beautiful, huh?"

"Stunning."

"Wyatt was one of the only people who knew that it was modeled after what you two talked about when you were younger."

Evelyn spins to face me. "He built you a house? Like, your dream house?"

I shrug my shoulders, still smiling. "Pretty much."

"Ugh. It gives me *The Notebook* vibes." She sighs dramatically.

"Totally," Kelsea agrees.

"Well, it was extremely romantic, and I think we're finally on the same page. Except..."

"What do you mean 'except'?" Evelyn admonishes.

As soon as the smile drops from my face, the girls' lips turn down as well. "There's one more obstacle."

"What's wrong?"

Sighing, I turn to face them head on. "I have to go back to Vegas in a few weeks. My ex wants to talk to me."

Kelsea's eyebrows pop up. "Why?"

"We haven't exactly talked since the wedding," I say, shoving more Goldfish in my mouth.

"And let me guess . . . Forrest isn't happy about it?" Evelyn asks.

"Not exactly, but he's going with me."

"That's good, though, right?" Evelyn asks. "At least he's trying to be supportive . . ."

"I know, and I love him for it. But we also have to deal with my mom."

Evelyn curses under her breath. "Fucking moms . . ."

"I love my mother, I do. I'm so grateful for everything she's done for me and supported me through. Lord knows I haven't been the perfect daughter, either. But she is not very supportive of Forrest and me."

"Why not?" Evelyn prods.

"Well, remember how I told you my dad left when I was young?" They nod. "My parents were high school sweethearts, met in a small town in Alabama. And when he left, she always told me to avoid young love because she believed it would only end in heartbreak."

"I mean, I see her perspective, but that's not fair to Forrest," Kelsea says.

"I agree. But then we broke up at nineteen. And when I started dating Brock, she thought I would be creating a life like the one she always wanted. Little did we both know that Forrest would come back into the picture and wreck all of that."

"So she resents him because he expressed his feelings and made you admit yours?"

"Kind of?" I groan and dump the rest of the Goldfish

crackers in my mouth. "I don't know. I just know that it's not going to be pretty."

"Well, Kelsea and I aren't exactly the people I would recommend to give you advice on dealing with mothers, but if Forrest is who you want, then you have to stand up for him. Your mother needs to stop projecting her life onto you."

"Yeah, I know. And I know Forrest is anxious about it, too, but we haven't had a chance to make a plan yet. We have time, but I just hope he doesn't shut down on me again."

"Make him talk to you when you're ready. Strip in front of him naked and tell him he's not allowed to touch you until he talks," Evelyn suggests. "He'll buckle so fast, and then you're both winning."

Kelsea snorts beside me. "Normally, I wouldn't condone my best friend's sex-based advice, but she just might be onto something here."

Laughing, I look back out at the field just as the men are returning to start the second half. "I'll think about it, but right now, I'm just trying to focus on today, too, you know? Like this." I wave my hands around. "It's been fifteen years since I've been in this stadium, staring down at this field. I spent two years of my life here, cheering on Forrest down on the track and staring up into the crowds with the lights gleaming down on us." My eyes find him on the field, standing there with his hands on his hips, hyper focused as the team prepares for kickoff. "It feels so right being back here."

Evelyn wraps her arm around me from the side. "Then enjoy, Shauna. And just keep the faith that everything will work itself out."

Kelsea stares at her best friend, mildly confused. "Before you fell in love with Walker, I would have never heard something like that come out of your mouth."

Evelyn smiles back at her. "Well, love can change a person, right?"

No truer words have ever been spoken.

"You did so good," I mumble against Forrest's lips after the girls and I stormed the field, celebrating yet another championship win for the team. The end score was fourteen to seven, and the last touchdown was made in the last five minutes of the game. It was a nail-biter, for sure.

Mr. Gibson came down to congratulate his boys and then left to head back to the ranch and beat the traffic.

Forrest chuckles. "Thanks, babe."

"And it was so hot watching you play again." I drag a hand down his sweaty chest. "Brought me back to high school, you know?"

He reaches up and adjusts my beanie to cover my ears. "Do we need to relive what we used to do after those games, too?" He waggles his eyebrows.

"Yes, please. As long as your old man knees can take it."

He pinches my waist. "These knees are just fine, remember?"

"Have you ever thought about telling your brothers your injury was fake?"

He lifts his head and looks over mine at Walker, Wyatt, Evelyn, and Kelsea also celebrating the win. "I did. I told Wyatt last week and Walker shortly after."

"I'm proud of you for doing that," I say, cupping his jaw. "Then what about your parents?"

He furrows his brow at me. "I will when the time is right."

"And I'll be there if you need support, okay?"

He dips his mouth to mine. "I appreciate that."

Before he gets a chance to say anything else, the twins and the girls come over to us.

"Great game, bro," Wyatt says, reaching out to shake Forrest's hand.

"Likewise, boys. Couldn't have won without you."

Forrest plays quarterback, Walker is a running back, and Wyatt plays wide receiver. As much as they fight and bicker outside of football, when they play together, they look like a well-oiled machine. Anyone can see their bond —on and off the field.

"What are you guys up to for the rest of the night?" Forrest asks his brothers.

They both blink at his question.

"Well, we were going to pick up Kaydence and head home," Walker replies.

"Kelsea and I were gonna celebrate at home as well," Wyatt says.

"Well, how about you guys come over to my place and celebrate with me and Shauna? I'm sure Mom would hold on to Kaydence for a few more hours. We can order some pizza and pick up some beer," he offers.

Wyatt and Walker share a look and then glance at their wives for their approval.

"Let's do it," Kelsea says with a grin. "We can pick up some beer from the brewery and then head over after Wyatt showers."

"Yeah, let me clean up, too, and then Evelyn and I will be there within the hour," Walker adds.

Forrest nods. "All right. See you then."

We all disperse to our cars. Forrest and I walk hand in hand to the parking lot after he grabs his bag from the locker room.

"Why did Walker and Wyatt act surprised that you invited them over?" I ask once we settle into his truck.

Forrest exits the parking lot and then says, "Probably because I haven't done that before."

"Ever?" I practically shriek.

He shrugs and continues to drive. "Not in a really long time, at least. I've been a bit of a recluse over the years, remember?" Reaching over the center console, he grabs my hand and kisses the back of it.

"So what changed your mind?"

"You," he answers simply. "You've changed everything, Shauna."

And I don't even reply because hearing those words tells me that everything is going to be okay.

~

"Happy birthday, dear Kaydence! Happy birthday to you!" Everyone cheers and claps as Evelyn and Walker tell Kaydence to blow out her candles. The sweet little girl tries to grab the flames instead, making everyone gasp until Evelyn yanks the cake away from her and blows out the candles herself.

I've never been to a one-year-old's birthday party before, but seeing the joy on everyone's faces is making me feel a tad emotional. Surviving the first year of parenthood has to be a momentous task, and watching Walker and his family only makes me yearn for that feeling one day as well.

Maybe I'm closer to getting there than I think.

"Yay!" I stand there clapping, admiring the three of them smiling and laughing just as I feel two strong arms wrap around my waist.

"Hey, you." Forrest presses a kiss to my temple and then rests his chin on the top of my head.

"Hey there, yourself. Where have you been?"

"Talking to my dad. Running through a few things for

this week, making sure we have a plan in place. How are you feeling about it?"

"Nervous but excited. Ready to see it all come together but also kind of ready for it to be done so I can think straight for a while."

"It's gonna be great. Everyone knows how hard you've been working, Shauna."

"I hope it turns out to be everything your mother imagined."

It's the Saturday before the Winter Wonderland event starts this coming Monday, and nerves and stress are high amongst Mr. and Mrs. Gibson and me. This week has been chaotic and filled with a bunch of long nights, but it's also been full of laughs and moments with the Gibsons that remind me this place is home.

Forrest stares across the room at Momma G as she slices Kaydence's cake, clearly happier than a pig in mud. "You know, I don't think Momma will even care if things go awry."

"Why is that?"

He nods in that direction again. "Because this is what she ultimately wants—her family together. And that family includes you."

I close my eyes and lean back into his chest. "I feel that way, too."

Forrest has taken on a big responsibility this week as well by helping me make sure things are running smoothly. And honestly, it just makes me fall in love with him even more. We haven't exchanged those words again yet, but I feel them—in every touch, in the way his eyes hold mine, in every breath and moment I spend with him and his family—and I can't wait to just move past my obligations this month and focus on what comes next for us.

We're so close I can almost taste it, but we've also been ignoring the obstacles waiting for us in Vegas soon. Our tickets are booked for right after Christmas; that way, we can be back before January first to start the new year with our past completely behind us.

"That little girl is pretty freaking cute, I must admit," Forrest speaks softly behind me, pulling me out of my thoughts.

Twisting in his arms, I glance up at him. "Yeah, she is."

"I used to think I wouldn't have kids after we broke up. But now, watching my brother be a dad and having you back . . . it makes me want those things again with you, Shauna."

I spin to face him completely, weaving my hands around his neck. "Really?"

"Hell, yeah." The smile he flashes me melts my heart. "Little girls with your stark blue eyes and dark hair who will be just as wild and driven as you. Little boys I can teach to fish, build things with their hands, and love this ranch like we do." He looks up, assessing everyone in the room, and then grabs me by the hand. "Come here."

Forrest leads me to the back door. "Where are we going?"

"Just follow me."

I pull my coat tighter around my waist as Forrest leads me out past the barn where the Winter Wonderland event will be taking place. We already have a few things set up, but we can't do much more until the morning of.

As we trek through the wind, I really hope the weather decides to cooperate.

Forrest opens the door to the warehouse we've been building and painting in, pulling me inside, out of the cold.

"Why'd you bring me out here?"

"So I could give you this," he says before slamming his lips to mine. He spins me around and pushes me up against the wall just inside the door, pinning my hands above my head.

Every pass of his tongue over mine heats my body up so fast I almost forget we were just out in the cold.

"Got anything else in there?" I tease him when we part.

He takes one of my hands and brings it to his denim-covered erection. "No, but I've got something in here if you're interested."

"I'm always interested."

Forrest finds my mouth again and then reaches for the button on my jeans. He pops it open swiftly, releases my other hand, then bends down and helps me take off my boots and pants, slowly sliding my thong down as well. The chill in the space hits my skin, making it pebble, but then Forrest starts kissing his way up my calf, past my knee, and to the juncture of my thighs, swiping his tongue through my slit.

"We're supposed to be at a one-year-old's birthday party eating cake," I moan out as Forrest starts sucking my clit between his lips.

"Who needs cake when I have the sweetest dessert in my mouth right now?"

I tangle my fingers in his thick hair, pulling him into me, grinding my pussy on his lips as I realize I'd much rather be here, anyway. "God, don't stop."

And he doesn't. He doesn't let up until I'm seeing stars and fighting for breath. Before I know what's happening, he lifts me up by my waist, wraps my legs around his hips, and lines himself up to my core, thrusting inside in one smooth movement. He must have undone his pants while I was delirious from that orgasm.

"You're fucking me against a wall," I murmur in his ear. "I thought you weren't going to do that?"

"I meant I wouldn't do that the first time. Now, as far as I'm concerned, we have a lot of places and positions to catch up on."

His crown hits that perfect spot deep inside me, making me moan. "I'm so on board with that plan."

Forrest sets a relentless pace, holding me in his arms,

kissing me between thrusts, telling me how perfect and beautiful I am as we race toward the finish line together.

I feel guilty about missing Kaydence's party for only a second, because my orgasm starts to blossom again, and all of that guilt flies right out the window as my entire body tenses.

"Fuck, I'm close, baby."

"Then come inside me, Forrest. Fill me up . . . please."

"Shit," he grates out, and after he pumps a few more times, he stills, emptying his release inside of me as my own pleasure ripples through my limbs.

Once his breath is more steady, he sets me down, kisses me passionately again, and then helps me get dressed.

"Well, that was unexpected. Everything okay?" I ask once we are both fully clothed.

Forrest frames my face with his hands. "Yeah, I just needed a moment alone with you. This past week has been crazy, and the next one is about to be even crazier."

"I know, and then once the event is over, we have Vegas."

He nods, but his brow tells me he's still deep in thought. "Fuck. I just can't wait for this to all be over so we can move on."

"And what are we moving on toward?"

He plants his lips on mine in a soft, reverent kiss. "Our future, babe. No more going back, Shauna. I want a life with you—holidays with my family, having you in the audience when I play music, horse rides on the ranch. Like I said, we have a lot of time to make up for."

"I know what you're saying, but I wouldn't trade that time apart if it meant getting to where we are now, Forrest."

"How come?"

"Because I think when you lose love and then find it again, it makes you appreciate it even more the second time around."

The corner of his mouth tips up. "That's one way to look at it."

"That's how *I* want to look at it. And in a few weeks, we can sit down and figure out all of the particulars, but I'm with you—we just need to get through this week."

"I'm proud of you, baby," he tells me, pulling me into his chest again. "This event is going to be the talk of the town."

"I hope so. It's been a lot of work, but it's probably the most fulfilling thing I've done in a long time." I stare up into his eyes. "I was missing this, Forrest."

"What exactly?"

"Purpose," I say.

"Yeah, I was missing mine, too."

"Did you find it?"

"Yeah. It's standing right here in my arms."

CHAPTER TWENTY

Forrest

"Make sure that gate is locked. If I have to chase reindeer around the ranch one more time, I'm going to lose my shit." I watch Gary secure the latch on the reindeer pen and then double-check it myself.

"All good, boss."

"Thank you. Now go refill the gas tanks in the tractors for the hay rides, please."

I watch Gary saunter off and then readjust my beanie on my head. It's day four of the Winter Wonderland event, and part of me is glad that it's almost over.

The other part of me, though, is not looking forward to the trip that's following it, but at least we have two days of rest and festivities with the family before then.

However, we still have three more days of these shenanigans to go, and my elf costume might not be in it for the long haul.

Pity.

Every day this week, from four to nine at night, families have ventured in from all over town to partake in the experience Shauna and my mother have created. My dad has been thoroughly enjoying his role as Santa for pictures with the kids, the reindeer petting zoo has been a hit, and the hay rides to check out the light displays have been keeping us busy all night. Vendors are happy to be making some money right before the holidays, and the ambiance on the ranch is nothing like I've ever seen before—lights, fake snow, twelve-foot Christmas trees, and fake poinsettia plants everywhere.

It's truly magical, and Shauna made it happen.

I walk over to the main gate to check that the new maps made it over there. I had to run to the printer this morning to get more because we ran out yesterday. I don't even think my mom and Shauna were prepared for that. But it's a little less than an hour before we open again, so I want to make sure we're ready. I anticipate the crowd will be biggest these next three days leading up to Christmas as well. Kids are out of school and people are taking time off work. It's the perfect excuse to come get in the holiday spirit.

I meet up with Barrett, one of the high school kids who's been working the gates for us, to ensure that he secures the maps so they won't blow away, and then I head back up to the main house, desperate to refill my mug with hot coffee again. The chill in the air is unmatched, and the extra caffeine is necessary to get through the evening.

Between work and helping out at the event, Shauna and I have barely seen each other. She's come home with me every night, but by the time her head hits the pillow, she's out. I think all of the anticipation and planning is catching up to her, so I know she'll need lots of rest when this is over. And as soon as it is, I'm moving her in with me permanently.

That house has always been ours, but it's time to make it official.

"More coffee?" my father asks as I meet him in the kitchen. I walk over to the coffeepot and pop the lid off my thermos.

"Yup. Say, did Mom know that this week would make us all pray to slip into a coma when it was over?"

My father chuckles. "Forrest, even if she did, that woman is all about making others happy. Have you seen her out there this week? She's emulating Mrs. Claus so well, you'd think she was competing for an Oscar."

I huff out a laugh. "Yeah, you're right."

"How's Shauna doing?"

"She's tired but really happy with the way everything turned out."

"As she should be." He turns to face me now as I secure the lid on my thermos. "And how are the two of you?"

I can't hide my smile. "Good, Dad. Really fucking good."

"So she's staying?"

"Yeah, I think so."

He nods in approval. "Does that mean you might still want to take over the ranch someday? I know that's what you two talked about back then."

A twinge of fear slashes across my chest, but I squash it before it grows. "I honestly don't know. I haven't had a chance to talk to her about it. We're kind of waiting until the festival is over to make decisions about what comes next for us. And we have to go back to Vegas next week to deal with a bit of unfinished business she has there, but then I don't want to waste any more time. I want to ask her to marry me, and I know we can sort out that topic then."

"As you should." He pushes up the sleeve of his flannel and flashes me his watch. "Then you can get one of these as well."

"What?" I take a closer look at the watch I've seen my father wear virtually every day of his life.

"Got it from my father on my wedding day, and I gave one to each of your brothers on theirs. Granted, Walker and Evelyn got married without anyone knowing, so it was a bit later, I guess."

Huh. I never knew that.

"I'm not a big watch wearer, Dad," I say wearily, not wanting to hurt his feelings in the event it sits in a box for the majority of my life.

"Yeah, I know, but it's tradition. And you've waited a long time for this. I mean, when you got injured, we thought you'd never crawl out of that dark hole you buried yourself in."

I rub the back of my neck.

He brought up my injury. My *fake* injury.

Well, it's now or never, right?

"Uh, about that..."

"What is it, son?"

"I—I never really got injured playing football, Dad."

His lips spread into a smirk so slowly, I'm afraid he fell asleep with his eyes closed. But then he says, "Took you long enough to admit it."

My mouth drops open. "You mean..."

"Forrest? Do you think your mother and I are idiots, son?"

"No..." I drag out.

"Then the next time you try to fake an injury, put in a little more effort, would you? For crying out loud, you didn't even have a bandage on your knee when you walked in the door. The only thing hurt was your damn heart, but you couldn't admit it, so you said it was your knee and, well? We just played along because, ultimately, we were happy to have you home." He shakes his head, laughing.

My shoulders slump. "Well, shit. I'm sorry, Dad."

"I'm not. You did what you had to do to give yourself permission to go after your girl, but your pride was bruised when it didn't work out the way you wanted it to."

That's a pretty accurate summary. "How did you know?"

"Shauna called us a few weeks later to check up on you. She told us not to tell you, so we didn't. But we kind of put two and two together."

I push my beanie off my head and drag my hand through my hair. "I'll be damned."

"That woman has always loved you, Forrest, but the time wasn't right back then. It is right now, though."

"I know. I'm not letting her go again, Dad."

My father smiles proudly. "Good." He picks up his coat off the back of the chair and slides his arms inside. "Now, it's time to get into character again," he declares, placing his red Santa hat on his head as well.

"You look good, Dad."

"I know. And even though this is all fake, the love is real, Forrest. Never forget that."

"Stop playing with your balls, Forrest." Shauna peers around me as I adjust myself in this damn elf costume for the thousandth time.

I tell you what, ditching this fucking getup will be the highlight of the event being over, *not* the amount of sleep I'm going to get afterward.

"You wanted this."

"I believe that attire was all your mother's doing."

"I know you were in on it."

She folds her lips in. "Okay, maybe a little."

I pull her into my chest. "You're lucky you're working right now, otherwise I'd take you into the barn and show you what I'm hiding in here."

"That sounds so amazing, but I might fall asleep in the middle of it."

"You sure you're all right? You've been run down all week."

"I know, but I think it's just stress and being more active than usual, you know?"

"You can go home, babe. We can handle things around here if you want?"

She shakes her head. "Absolutely not. I'm having the best time watching everyone's reactions. This is what I've been working toward, Forrest, and I'm not missing a moment."

"All right." I kiss her lips chastely. "Just make sure to eat something and maybe grab some coffee."

"I haven't eaten since lunch, so I think that's a good idea."

I watch Shauna walk off and then turn my head toward the main gate just as the clock strikes four. The gates open, and hundreds of townsfolk come wandering in. Each side of the street is lined with vendors, activities for the kids, Christmas trees decorated in different themes, and giant candy canes, with the end of the road leading to photos with Santa. Guests can spend hours decorating ornaments to hang on their trees, signing the wooden sign that my mother wanted to have as a keepsake for the event's first year, and purchasing cookies from the truck stationed off to the side, pumping the smell of sugar and cinnamon into the air.

"Holy shit. I heard the rumors, but I had to see it for myself." I spin around to find Javi, his wife, Sydney, and their two kids standing there. Javi grabs his phone from his pocket and snaps a picture of me, beaming. "Now I have blackmail if needed."

"Watch it."

Sydney steps forward to give me a hug. "Good to see you in the holiday spirit, Forrest. I take it you got conned into wearing that getup?"

"Yeah, by my mother and Shauna." I look over to find my girl talking to patrons and steering them into the line for pictures with Santa, where my parents are in full character, listening to kids and their Christmas wish lists.

"Is she staying for good?" Javi asks, looking in the same direction I am.

"Yeah, she is." *Fuck, I can't wait to make that woman mine permanently.*

"Happy for you, brother." He reaches out to shake my hand.

"Thanks. And thanks for being there for me when I was struggling to pull my head out of my ass."

Sydney chuckles beside him. "All of you men are the same, I guess."

"So I've heard." I turn back to face Javi again. "Hey, by the way, thanks for holding down the fort at work this week so I could be here as needed."

"No problem, man. That's what friends are for."

"Well, I actually have a business proposition for you," I say, piquing his interest.

"Okay . . ."

Resting my hand on his shoulder, I tell him, "But we can talk after the holidays about it."

I had an idea about how I want to handle my company moving forward, but it honestly depends on the conversation Shauna and I have later about our future plans. "For now, just enjoy the festival, guys." I bend down to speak to Javi and Sydney's daughter and son. "The hot cocoa is delicious. You should ask your mommy and daddy for some."

Ivy looks up at her father. "Can we get hot cocoa, please?"

"Thanks, man," he mutters to me out of the side of his mouth. "I'll make sure to bring her back to you when she doesn't go to sleep later." Then he looks at his daughter and says, "Sure, Princess. Let's go."

"Oh, Forrest." I spin around to find Jill nearly in tears standing next to her wife, Becca.

"Watch what you say, Jill."

"Or what?" She laughs out loud now. "You'll fire me? Yeah, I've heard that before."

Becca's eyes dip down to my crotch. "Damn. It's too bad I don't play for your team, Forrest, because with that bat, I feel like you could score a home run every time."

Shauna comes up beside me, sliding her hand around my waist. "Oh, don't worry. He does."

Becca nods in approval, and Jill finally gets her laughter under control.

"Shauna, you've met Jill. This is her wife, Becca," I say as Shauna reaches out to shake Becca's hand.

"Nice to meet you."

"Don't worry, Shauna. I have no desire to mount your elf man," Becca teases.

"I'm aware. And hell, I appreciate what this little outfit does for his body, too." She waggles her eyebrows.

Jill smirks at the two of us. "Glad to see you happy, boss."

I press a kiss to Shauna's head. "Thanks, Jill."

Becca grabs Jill's hand, dragging her away. "Come on,

baby. I want some peppermint cotton candy so we can eat it off each other later."

Jill licks her lips, her reply fading as they walk away. "Sounds like the perfect dessert to me."

Shauna presses up on her toes to kiss me. "Just wanted to say hello."

"You mean mark your territory in front of Jill, who's not even a threat?"

She shrugs. "You can never be too careful." Walking backward, she winks at me and then turns around and heads back in the direction she came from as my brothers come up to me from behind. The ringing is what gives them away.

Stupid bells on these stupid curly-toed slippers.

"These damn shoes. I can't wait to burn them," Wyatt mutters, adjusting his outfit. I swear, we spend more time doing that—making sure our junk isn't on display—than actually standing still.

"No, don't do that," Walker interjects. "Have Kelsea wear them while you're having sex. It's like making naughty music."

Wyatt and I both shoot our brother a deadpan glare. "You're disgusting." I take a step away from him, but Walker just shakes his head with a smile on his face.

"Don't knock it 'til you try it."

"How's Shauna doing?" Wyatt asks, changing the subject—*thank God*—and shifting his gaze to my girl.

"She's on cloud nine."

"As she should be. Everything turned out incredibly. I've had people in the brewery talking about it all week."

"I'll be sure to pass along the message."

"Are you ready for Vegas?"

"As ready as I'm going to be." Both of my brothers know about my reservations with Shauna's mom now, and it's felt really fucking good being able to confide in them.

"Just don't let the woman make you feel like you don't deserve her," Walker adds. "I'm telling you . . . when I told off Evelyn's parents for the way they treated her, I've never felt that protective over someone in my life. And that's how I knew I *did* fucking deserve her."

"I hope it doesn't come to that, but I have no problem being transparent with Dixie if she forces me to."

"And what about the ex?" Walker asks.

"Him I'm not worried about. He's long gone from our world, as far as I can see. But I hope he doesn't get nasty with Shauna, or I might have to give him a piece of my mind, too." I grind my teeth together, wishing the idea of her seeing him didn't make me so tense. But I can't help it. That man used to have the woman who has always been mine. I know she ultimately still is, but I don't want her to question that from something he may or may not say to her when they talk.

Which reminds me . . .

I turn to my brothers and look one and then the other dead in the eye. "You guys busy tomorrow?"

"Besides this, no," Wyatt answers. "I have Ben, my assistant manager, covering the brewery this week."

"I still have three days off. I've got to work on Christmas, but I don't have to report until the evening. Why—what's up?" Walker asks.

I take a deep breath and then say, "I want to go ring shopping, and I was wondering if you'd like to join me?"

Walker looks like he's about to cry. "Fuck, Forrest. Really?"

I shove him away. "Don't make it fucking weird, Walker."

Wyatt laughs and then nods at me. "'Bout damn time. I'll be there."

"Me, too, big brother," Walker adds. "When are you gonna ask her?"

"I think when we get back from Vegas. I don't want to start the new year without knowing she's going to be my wife. And I hate fucking waiting, but once she settles things out there, I know we'll be okay."

Wyatt pats me on the shoulder. "That's awesome, Forrest. I'm happy for you. You're finally getting what you want."

"Yeah. I think I fucking am."

∾

"Merry Christmas, baby." I turn over in bed, pulling Shauna into my chest as she pushes her ass into my erection.

"Merry Christmas, Forrest."

"I can't believe I'm waking up here with you in my arms. I guess Santa *was* listening this year."

Shauna giggles. "That was cheesy. You've got old man jokes."

"Don't start with that old man shit, Shauna, or I'll fuck you into next week and remind you of how young I still am."

She lets out a yawn. "How about the end of next week, that way all the traveling is done? I swear, I just woke up, and I'm ready to go back to sleep."

"I know, baby. But we made it. The Winter Wonderland event is over, and we just have seeing your mom and Brock to go."

"Ugh. Why did I agree to this again?"

I spin her around so she's facing me now. "Because you're someone who cares about other people."

"I'm not sure about that . . ."

"Well, I am. In fact, how come you haven't told me that you called my parents to check on me after we broke up?"

Her eyes widen. "They told you that?"

"My dad did the other night after I told him that I faked my knee injury. Apparently, I wasn't very convincing, because he and my mother already knew."

She slaps a palm to her head. "Jesus, Forrest. If you're gonna lie, at least do it right."

"You're one to talk," I say, tickling her ribs, making her squeal. "Now, answer my question."

Her eyes bounce back and forth between mine. "I was worried about you. Watching you walk away from me absolutely devastated me and made my chest ache for months. But I had to make sure that you were okay, that I hadn't broken you completely."

"The only thing you broke was my heart, babe. The rest I was able to put back together."

"I'm glad, but I've always felt guilty about that."

"That's why I know you care about others on an entirely different level. You may have made choices that hurt me and Brock, but you also righted them and always had our best interests at heart."

It's taken me a long time to get to this point, but it became clear to me after speaking with my dad: Shauna didn't set out to hurt me intentionally. She made a choice that she felt was best for her at the time. But then, she still held remorse for catching me in the crossfire. And she's doing the same thing for her ex.

Although, since I'm the man she chose, it's easier for me to see things this way.

"Brock deserves honesty from you, and I deserve the chance to show your mother that I'm not just the small-town boy who doesn't have anything to offer you."

"She doesn't think that . . ." I shoot her a deadpan glare. "I'm serious, Forrest."

"Come on, Shauna. Your mother didn't want me to suck you into this life because that's what happened to her."

"I know, but the problem is that she keeps holding that against me, like I'm doomed to the same outcome."

"I'm aware. So hopefully once she sees us together, she'll understand that this is what we want—and this time, it's forever."

"I hope so, too."

I smack her ass, making her shriek. "Now, we can either fuck in the bed or fuck in the shower. Either way, you're getting fucked."

"How about bed and also shower?"

I tilt my head back and groan. "Fuck, I love the way you think."

And then I show her just how much I love her with my body, holding on to the words for another day and time—a time I have planned out perfectly with the ring I bought two days ago.

∼

We arrive at my parents' house an hour later, the smell of freshly baked cinnamon rolls wafting out of the house the second we open the door.

"They're here!" Kelsea announces as Shauna and I

enter the living room. "Sorry to sound so enthusiastic, but Momma said we couldn't eat until you guys got here, and everyone is starving," she whispers as we walk past.

"Are we late?" Shauna asks, peering up at me. "You said nine."

"We might be a little late."

She pokes my ribs. "What the hell, Forrest?"

Kelsea rolls her eyes. "I'm sure he found plenty of ways to distract you, didn't he?"

Shauna's cheeks blush, which I find really fucking cute at this moment. "He did."

"Come on, everyone! Breakfast is ready!" Momma announces as our family gathers around the table for another home-cooked meal.

I notice Shauna push food around her plate after everyone is served. "Hey, you okay?"

"Yeah, I'm just not hungry. My stomach is feeling weird. I think I drank too much coffee the past few days, and the acidity is catching up to me."

"Maybe." I pass her a biscuit. "At least eat this, then. It will help soak it all up."

She takes a bite from the biscuit and moans, the sound traveling straight to my dick. I already had this woman twice this morning, but one sound later, and I'm wanting her again. "Oh, yeah. God, those are good."

I rub her leg under the table, and then, once everyone is done eating, we gather in the living room to exchange gifts.

The star of the show is Kaydence, of course, tearing wrapping paper off boxes once Walker and Evelyn show her how. My parents eat up every moment, taking pictures of each of my brothers and me with our girls, keeping the fire going with fresh logs, feeding us a charcuterie board that could satisfy twenty people, and spoiling us with hotel vouchers for couples' trips sometime next year.

Shauna falls asleep on me later while I'm watching the football game on the couch, and holding her to me brings a wave of peace over my very existence.

This is happiness—family, memories, time well spent.

And I'm really fucking happy.

For the first time in years, I have everything I've ever wanted.

Until one instant changes everything I thought I knew.

CHAPTER TWENTY-ONE

Shauna

"You sure you're okay?" Forrest asks as we buckle our seatbelts and the captain of the plane announces that his crew should prepare for takeoff.

"I'm fine. I think I'm just dehydrated." I twist the cap off my water and down almost half of it. "There. See?"

"You almost passed out this morning, baby. Maybe you need some juice to get your blood sugar up." He motions for the flight attendant to come over. When he secures an orange juice for me, he shoves it in front of my face. "Drink this."

"I'm fine."

"Just do it for me, please, Shauna."

The sound of desperation in his voice makes me comply without much of a fight. But honestly, I don't have the energy to fight him, anyway.

I down the juice and wipe my mouth with the back of my hand. "There."

"Thank you. Now, what do you think is going on?"

I cover up my mouth as I yawn again. "I don't know, Forrest. I think I'm still trying to recover from last week. I'm okay," I smile up at him, hoping to ease his concern. "But I'm tired. I just want to get some sleep on the flight, all right?"

His brows continue to pull together. "Okay."

Happy that he's dropping it for the moment, I grab my travel pillow, fluff it up, and then stick it between me and the window, ready to catch up on some sleep.

We have a three-hour flight to Las Vegas, and if I'm able to sleep the entire way, I should feel well-rested and ready to take on my mother. The thing is, Forrest is right. Something is going on with me. The bout of light-headedness I had this morning made me realize that after this visit, I definitely need to take some time to recuperate.

I've worked myself to the bone before, though, and I came out the other side just fine. Maybe the harsh winter weather we've been having in Texas exacerbated it. And perhaps all of the sex didn't help, either.

Knowing there's nothing I can do at the moment, I

close my eyes and let my exhaustion overtake me, eager to get some rest on this flight.

Right now, sleep is my best friend.

CHAPTER TWENTY-TWO

Forrest

"Shauna . . ." I gently stir her from her sleep, trying not to startle her. "Babe . . ."

"Huh?" She slowly opens her eyes and looks around the plane. "We're here?"

"Yeah, babe. We're here. You slept through the landing. I didn't know that was possible."

She wipes the drool from her mouth and sits up tall in her chair, slowly looking around the plane. Most of the people have left already, but I wanted to let her sleep as long as possible before I had to wake her.

Fuck, she looks pale.

"Shauna . . . you don't look good, honey."

"I'm fine," she grates out, grabbing her travel pillow and stuffing it into her bag.

"No, you're not. You're tired all the time, pale, and having bouts of dizziness." I stand from my chair, moving to the aisle so she can get out of her seat.

"I'm just worn down, Forrest. This has happened to me before." She slowly pushes herself up and slides across the row of seats to stand in front of me.

"It has?"

"I mean, yeah. Maybe not this bad, but sometimes I forget to take care of myself when I'm focused on an event."

"You can't do that, Shauna."

Her smirk eases some of my anxiety. "You don't need to tell me what to do, Forrest."

"Uh, yes, I do, if you're going to work yourself this hard and not listen to your body."

I hand her the bag she used as a carry-on, and then she starts heading toward the front of the plane. "You're going to try to boss me around for the rest of our lives, aren't you?"

Walking behind her as we hit the jetway, I reply, "Hell yes I am, woman."

"Eh. I guess there are worse problems to have," she says and then drops to the floor right in front of me.

What the fuck?

"Shauna!" I fall to my knees to catch her so she doesn't

hit her head, cradling her body in my arms as I give her shoulders a light shake, trying to get her to come to. "Shauna, baby." I tap her cheek with my hand, but she's out cold.

An airport security officer rushes over. "Is everything okay?"

"I don't know. She just passed out. She's been dizzy all morning and really fucking tired lately." I stare back down at her, making sure she's breathing by placing a finger under her nose. It's faint, but her breath is there.

"I'll call for medical assistance," the officer says as my heart tries to escape from my chest.

"Shauna." My eyes start to sting. "Baby, you gotta wake up. Fuck, you can't do this to me. We just found our way back to each other."

"Sir, let us take a look at her." Two paramedics approach me, arms full of equipment and a gurney behind them.

"She has to be okay," I tell them.

"We're going to check her out," they say as I hand her off and they get to work checking her vitals. I just sit there on my knees, oblivious to the world around me that's continuing to move.

Because my world just stopped spinning, and I'm afraid it might never start again.

∼

The beeping from the hospital machines keeps me on edge as I wait for Shauna to wake up. Turns out, her blood pressure was dangerously low and she was dehydrated, so they've hooked her up to an IV and have been letting her sleep while she's being monitored.

I don't think I've ever been so terrified in my life.

She collapsed right in front of me.

The woman who has made my life complete again has been sick for over a week, and all I feel is guilt. I should have taken her in sooner. I should have made her rest when I first saw the signs. I should have . . .

"Forrest?"

My head snaps to the bed where Shauna is lying, her eyes barely open as they peer down at me.

"Hey, baby."

Her head wobbles around. "What happened?"

"You collapsed. Fainted in the airport."

She groans and closes her eyes. "Oh my God, how embarrassing."

"More like fucking terrifying," I correct her. "Your blood pressure was dangerously low, baby."

"Shit."

"Yeah."

"Did you call my mom?" she asks. "She's going to be worried if we don't let her know we landed."

"I did. She's on her way here with Frank."

Shauna slaps a hand to her forehead. "Just great. Now, I can get a lecture from her for yet another thing."

I stroke her hand with my own, letting the adrenaline in my body start to burn off. "You fucking scared me, Shauna."

"I'm sorry, Forrest. I didn't do it on purpose."

"I know, but—" A knock on the door interrupts us.

"You're awake?" The doctor who has been monitoring Shauna since she was admitted comes walking through the door.

"She just woke up a minute ago," I explain.

"Good." She turns to the woman I love. "It's nice to meet you, Shauna. I'm Dr. Martin, one of the attendings on shift in the ER when you came in, and I wanted to talk to you about what happened."

Shauna struggles to sit up higher in the bed, so I stand from my seat and help her. "Okay," she says once she's comfortable, her hand still in mine.

The doctor's eyes slide over to me. "Are you comfortable with him being in the room for this conversation?"

Shauna turns her head to me as she squeezes my hand. "Yes."

Dr. Martin nods. "Okay. Well, your blood pressure was dangerously low, which is why you were feeling dizzy and eventually passed out."

"I told her that, Doc," I say.

Dr. Martin gives a quick nod. "Great. Well, I think we figured out why."

"Okay . . ." Shauna replies, and I can feel her bracing for bad news from here. Hell, we both are.

But the doctor smiles. "Congratulations. You're pregnant."

Shauna's mouth drops open. My heart nearly stops beating.

She's *pregnant*?

Shauna huffs out a laugh. "I'm sorry. Did you just say I'm pregnant?"

Dr. Martin smiles wider. "I did. Low blood pressure is often a symptom in early pregnancy since the blood flow is being rerouted to the fetus. By our calculations, based on the HCG levels in your blood, I'd guess you're about six weeks along."

Shauna sighs and closes her eyes. "I didn't even realize that I missed my period. I've been so busy."

Dr. Martin nods. "It happens more often than you think."

I look down at the love of my life lying in this hospital bed, letting the news finally hit me.

Shauna is pregnant.

She's carrying my child.

I'm going to be a father.

"I love you," I tell her right in front of the doctor, tears burning the backs of my eyes.

Shauna turns her attention to me, her eyes glistening as well. "Forrest..."

Dr. Martin clears her throat. "I'll give you two some privacy, but I'll be back to go over some next steps with you."

"Thank you," Shauna tells her before focusing back on me. I barely hear the doctor walk out. "Forrest, I—"

"I fucking love you, Shauna," I cut her off, holding her face in my hand, pressing my finger to her lips. "I love you so goddamn much, and we're going to have a baby."

She starts laughing and crying at the same time. "Oh my God. We are!"

"When my mother told me to give you a reason to stay, I don't think this is what she had in mind. But now, you're crazy if you think I'm going to let you get away again."

She shakes her head. "I don't want to get away. I want to stay in Newberry Springs forever—with you."

Leaning my forehead against hers, I take a deep breath, trying to get my pulse to slow down. All of the adrenaline from today is coursing through me again, and I'm afraid it might make me pass out, too.

"I love you, too, you know," Shauna whispers as we sit there, breathing the same air.

"I kind of figured."

She shoves me playfully, but I don't budge. "I didn't plan this, Forrest."

"I didn't say you did."

"I know. I just don't want you to think—"

I press my finger to her lips once more. "Don't even fucking finish that thought. What have we been fighting for over the past fifteen years, Shauna? Us, that's what. I don't care how this happened or why, but it would have eventually happened because you and I were meant to find our way back to each other. We are meant to be a family. It's going to happen a lot sooner than we planned, but I'm so fucking ready."

She takes a deep breath and blows it out. "I can't believe I'm pregnant."

"I mean, we *have* been having a lot of sex."

She chuckles. "Yeah, but if I'm six weeks along, then it probably happened the weekend of the football game."

"Again, lots of sex that night, baby."

She tilts her chin toward mine, and I bring my mouth to hers, kissing her softly, showing her that our love is worth every twist and turn. "I love you," she tells me again.

"I love you more."

A throat clearing breaks through our moment, directing our attention to the door where Shauna's mother, Dixie, and her husband, Frank, are standing.

"Sorry to interrupt," Frank says before Dixie rushes across the room to the bed.

"Oh, baby." Dixie lunges forward to hug her daughter as I step out of the way. I move to the other side of the bed so there's not much space between me and Shauna. The woman is carrying my baby now, so she'd better get used to me being overbearing.

And for some reason, I feel like I have to protect Shauna from her mother right now.

"I'm fine, Mom."

"You collapsed in an airport," Dixie argues.

"I caught her so she didn't hit her head," I chime in as Dixie's eyes lock on mine.

"Well, thank you. But I think it's safe to say that my daughter is working herself too hard."

"Mom..."

"Shauna." Her mother smooths Shauna's hair away from her face again. "I'm just happy that you're here. That you're home."

"Vegas isn't my home anymore, Mom." Shauna looks over at me. "Newberry Springs is."

"Shauna..." Dixie starts, but I decide now is as good a time as any to assert my position.

"Dixie, with all due respect, I hope you can accept the fact that Shauna and I are back together," I start as the woman standing on the opposite side of the bed glares at me.

"Yes, thanks to your meddling."

Me? A meddler?

Momma would be proud.

"I'm not going to apologize for that if that's what you're looking for because Shauna and I both knew that she wasn't happy with Brock. It took seeing each other again to make us both realize that our hearts belonged to one another and always have."

"My daughter deserves better than that small town, Forrest."

"That's a shame, because that small town is where

your daughter is happiest."

"Uh, hello? I'm right here," Shauna chimes in, glancing between us both. "And you know what, Mom? Just because you weren't happy there doesn't mean I won't be."

Dixie turns to her daughter. "But look at what happened when you left, honey. You went to school, made a career for yourself, found a man to take care of you . . ."

"That's what *you* wanted for me. The thing you're failing to realize is that all of those things came at a cost—losing Forrest." Shauna starts to cry. "I don't regret going after Dad, but part of my heart never left Newberry Springs. Because Forrest is there. And your grandchild will be, too."

Dixie gasps. "Are you . . ."

"I'm pregnant, Mom," Shauna says. "That's why I passed out. It's early, but my blood pressure was really low."

"Oh my God . . ." Dixie covers her mouth with her hand.

Shauna reaches for her mother's other hand, squeezing it. "I love you, but it's time for you to let me live my own life. I know what I want, and Forrest and Newberry Springs are it."

"I'm going to be a grandma?"

"You are," I interject as Dixie's eyes find their way back to me. "And I'm going to take care of your daughter and our child. I love her, Dixie. Shauna will be my wife and I, for one, don't want to fight you on that for the rest of our lives. So if you could learn to accept it and try to be a part of our family instead, I think that would make us all happy." I'm trying really hard not to clench my teeth as I stand my ground, and honestly, I'm surprised at how well I'm keeping my composure.

There are a million other things I could say, details I could use to help convince this woman that I deserve her daughter. But ultimately, I don't need to prove that to her because Shauna knows those things. That's all that matters.

"Honey . . ." Frank comes up behind Dixie, resting his hand on her shoulder. "Shauna has to live her own life."

Dixie brushes away her tears and then stares down at her daughter. "I've always just wanted the best for you, Shauna."

"I know, Mom. This *is* what's best for me." She reaches over and grabs my hand. "For the first time in fifteen years, I feel like I have everything I've ever wanted."

Dixie sighs but finally nods. "Then I will try to accept that."

Shauna smiles triumphantly. "That's all I ask."

"You can visit as much as you want," I interject. "We have plenty of room at the house."

Shauna looks at me as if I've grown two heads, but I think us living together is a forgone conclusion by now.

"I've always wanted to visit Texas," Frank says, and just like that, one less hurdle stands in our way.

CHAPTER TWENTY-THREE

Shauna

"I'll be right over there." Forrest points to a seat in the corner of the coffee shop where Brock and I agreed to meet.

"You don't have to be here. In fact, I think Brock seeing you might make things worse."

"I don't care. I want to be near in case he starts acting like a dick."

I'm not going to lie, having Forrest here has actually quelled my anxiety about this meeting, but I also don't want to rub the man I left Brock for in his face.

"Plus, you're carrying my baby, and wherever the baby

goes, I go." He points his thumb at his chest, acting like the Neanderthal he is.

God, I think I love it way too much.

I was released from the hospital two days ago, and we've been spending time with my mom and Frank since. Mom has warmed up to Forrest, and I can't deny that it's provided me with some much-needed relief. I spent the past two days resting and drinking lots of fluids, and for the first time in two weeks, I feel halfway normal today—which means I'm eager to get this conversation out of the way so Forrest and I can go back to Texas and start our lives together.

Oh, and tell his family there will be a new little Gibson joining us next summer.

"Easy there, Tarzan. The baby is fine. Nothing is going to happen to me just sitting in this coffee shop."

He cups the sides of my face. "You fucking collapsed right in front of me, Shauna, which scarred me for life. Do you honestly think I don't have a right to be overprotective of you?"

"I guess. But you can't be with me every second of every day, Forrest. What about when we go back to work?"

"I might just have to figure out a way to clone myself."

A throat clearing beside us breaks us from our conversation. Forrest keeps his hands on my face, but we both turn to find Brock standing there, eyeing us as if assessing the situation.

"Sorry to interrupt," Brock says, irritation in his tone. "I didn't realize you and I would have company, Shauna."

Forrest straightens his spine, appearing to be more intimidating than I know he really is. But I also know that this can't be comfortable for either of them.

"Look, I'm here to support her, okay? I'm gonna sit in the back and catch up on work, but if you try to get nasty with her, don't think I won't lay you out in this coffee shop."

"No need to threaten me. You've already won the girl. I'd say the fight is over." Brock shoves his hands in his pockets.

"If you don't realize she's worth fighting for over and over again until the end of time, then you didn't deserve her, anyway," Forrest says before planting a kiss on my lips and walking back to his seat.

"Shall we?" Brock gestures to the table.

"Sure. Sorry about that," I say as we both take our seats.

"I guess it's safe to say that you've moved on?"

"Yes. And look, Brock. I want you to know that I didn't run right into Forrest's arms, but seeing him again before our wedding was a huge wake-up call for me. It let me know I wasn't being true to my feelings."

Brock stares at the table in front of him. "I loved you, Shauna. I would have given you anything you wanted."

"I know, but the thing I wanted was something you *couldn't* give me. The truth is, I gave my heart away a long time ago, and ultimately, marrying you would have been wrong."

"I'm sorry I didn't reply to you right away, but I was so angry, so embarrassed, that I . . ." He shakes his head. "I couldn't bear the thought of looking at you and wondering where the hell we went wrong. Turns out, I guess I just wasn't him."

I nod. "That's the thing. You *didn't* do anything wrong, but I would have done us both a disservice if I'd married you while still loving someone else. I'm not the woman who is destined to make you happy, but I hope that you find her someday."

"Me, too." He juts his chin over to where Forrest is sitting in the corner. "Are you happy?"

I place my hand over my stomach, where my baby is currently growing—a child who is both part of me and part of Forrest. "I am."

"Then I'm happy for you." He flashes me a small smile, but I'll take it and the relief it offers, the weight it carries off my chest as it fades away.

"Thank you. And again, I'm so sorry for hurting you, Brock."

"Well, luckily a broken heart is a good way to figure out what you want out of life. I'm trying to work on that right now."

"Good for you. I hope you find what you're looking for."

Brock stands from the table and lets out a heavy sigh. "Good luck, Shauna."

"You, too, Brock."

I watch him exit the coffee shop and notice the door shutting behind him, closing that chapter on my life.

And then tears start to fill my eyes.

"You okay?" Forrest asks as he comes up behind me, placing his hand on my shoulder.

I sniffle, trying to keep my emotions in check. "Yeah. I'm okay."

"What's wrong? Was he an ass to you?" he asks when he hears my voice trembling.

I shake my head. "No, quite the opposite. Seems we both finally understand that we weren't meant to be."

Forrest comes around the table and sits in the seat that Brock just vacated. "Well, duh. You're meant to be mine, Shauna."

I lean forward and press my lips to his. "I know, and I'm so ready for all that entails."

CHAPTER TWENTY-FOUR

Shauna

"Are you sure about this?" I ask Forrest as I place the baby biscuit in the center of the oven. I made a batch of them myself at our house today and brought a few over here just in case I needed extras.

"I'm telling you, Momma is gonna lose it."

"I hate making your mom cry," I tell Forrest as I walk away from the oven so I don't look suspicious.

"It honestly doesn't take much, babe. But telling her she's going to be a grandma again? Tears are guaranteed."

We got home from Vegas last night, so Momma G insisted that we all come over for breakfast this morning since the family hasn't been together since Christmas. Forrest insisted we tell his family about the baby. At first, I kind of wanted to wait until I was further along just to make sure everything is okay. But he doesn't want to keep our child a secret."

Our baby is a miracle, a product of our love, and he wants to share the good news with everyone.

How could I deny him that?

"There you two are!" Momma G exclaims as she comes down the hallway toward the kitchen. "How was the trip?"

"It was interesting," I tell her before intercepting her hug.

"Interesting? Did something bad happen?"

"No, just jam-packed with a rollercoaster of emotions."

"Well, that's to be expected. Did everything go all right with Brock?" Momma asks, still holding my hand.

"It did, and I feel so much better now."

She squeezes my hand and gives me that motherly grin of pride. "Good. Time to move on now, right?"

"Absolutely," Forrest says, sliding up to me and kissing my temple as his mother moves deeper into the kitchen.

Walker, Wyatt, and Mr. Gibson come inside the house from the back door, followed closely by Kelsea, Evelyn, and Kaydence, sitting happily on her mother's hip.

Oh, God. That's going to be me in less than eight months.

"You're back!" Kelsea exclaims, walking over to pull me in for a hug.

"Yeah, we got in last night."

"How was it?"

"A lot warmer than it is here right now," Forrest says, making everyone laugh.

"Yeah, we went outside to let Kaydence see the horses, but it's just a little too cold," Evelyn says.

"Then let's warm everyone up with some breakfast. I'm gonna pop the bacon in the oven and fry up some eggs." Momma moves toward the oven as Forrest tenses up beside me.

Or maybe I'm the one tensing up.

Momma starts the oven to preheat, and recognition dawns on me and Forrest at the same time.

"Uh, aren't you going to check the oven before you turn it on?" Forrest asks his mom.

She twists around to face us, looking at him like he's lost his damn mind. "Why on earth would I check inside the oven before I turn it on, Forrest? Do you know how long I've been cooking in this kitchen? I never leave anything in there."

"I thought that was just safety protocol," I interject, which means the look of confusion on Momma's face is now directed at me.

"Did you two lose your marbles out in Vegas?" Momma shakes her head and then heads over to the sink, still ignoring the oven as it begins to heat up.

"I *really* think you should check inside, Momma." Forrest squeezes my waist.

Momma dries her hands on a towel and then throws it down on the counter in frustration. "I swear, you kids get older and think you can just tell me what to do . . ." She pulls on the handle of the oven and freezes when she sees what's inside. Grabbing an oven mitt from the drawer, she reaches in and grabs the mini biscuit that was sitting on a plate inside, removing the whole thing. "What the heck is this?" she asks as everyone stands around, watching.

Forrest's chest is bouncing with silent laughter, and then I hear Walker from the other side of the island.

"Oh, shit." He turns to us and asks, "Really?"

Forrest and I nod.

"Really, what?" Momma exclaims, placing the plate on the counter and picking up the biscuit. "All right. Which one of you girls tried to make my biscuits and failed, huh? This is a little embarrassing, ladies. You all know that size matters. I mean, come on."

Walker loses it. "Oh, Jesus, Mom. It's supposed to be that small. It's a *baby* biscuit."

Kelsea gasps. "And it was in the oven!"

Evelyn shrieks. "Oh my God!"

"What?" Momma shouts and then looks back over at me and Forrest. And I see the moment it finally clicks. "Oh my word . . ." Her bottom lip begins to tremble as tears fill her eyes, and all that does is spark my own. "Is this a baby biscuit in my oven?"

"Well, technically, it's in Shauna's oven, but yes, Momma," Forrest clarifies. "It is."

"I'll be damned," Mr. Gibson mutters.

"I'm gonna be a grandma again?" Momma G sobs.

"You are," I say, rushing over to her as she races to me as well, clutching her tightly to my chest.

"Holy shit. Congratulations, big brother!" Walker rushes over to Forrest, pulling him in for a hug as the entire family celebrates another Gibson coming into the world.

"That was not funny," Momma G chastises as she wipes the tears from under her eyes when we part.

"It was Forrest's idea," I say.

"I thought it was brilliant." He shrugs.

"It was," Wyatt agrees.

We spend the next thirty or so minutes answering everyone's questions about how we found out, how far along I am, and what comes next.

Later, after we've eaten, Forrest pulls me outside and guides me to the stables where Farbi and Karma are already saddled up. "Hop on."

"You wanna take a ride *now*?" I gesture back up to the house where the rest of the family is hanging out. "But I don't think I'm allowed to ride."

"The doctor said it's fine in the first trimester as long as you go slow." He winks and then pulls Farbi toward me. "So no racing today. But I wanna show you something, and horseback is the quickest way to get there."

"Okay..." I narrow my eyes at him, wondering what he has up his sleeve. As I settle into the saddle, he hops on his horse as well. "I can't believe I have to go slow."

"I think a slower pace is underrated sometimes."

And as I stare out across the land and absorb every detail of the ranch as we head toward the shack on the north side, I say, "Yeah, I think you're right."

The small building comes into view after a while, standing like a box that holds memories locked tightly inside. And it does, just like everything else this ranch holds for me.

"What are we doing out here?" I ask Forrest as our horses trot beside each other and we approach the hitching post.

"Just let me surprise you, will you?"

Rolling my eyes at him, he helps me down from Farbi, and then we secure the horses to the hitching post before he takes the key to the lock out of his pocket.

"It's got to be freezing in there, Forrest," I say as I stand behind him, waiting for him to unlock the door.

He jimmies the lock and then opens the wooden doors that creak as he pulls them apart. "I think we'll be okay."

I walk inside, and my mouth drops open. Gasping, I spin around, taking in all of the changes and renovations made to this little structure, and it instantly brings tears to my eyes. I don't even recognize the place.

"When the hell did you find time to do this?"

"I might have commissioned a few of my employees to do the major work, like installing the insulation, cabinets, and flooring. But the furniture and appliances I moved in earlier this week."

"Was I sleeping while this was happening?"

He closes the distance between us, wrapping his arms around my waist, and chuckles. "Yeah. But do you like it?"

"I love it." I move around the space, taking in every detail as he keeps talking.

"Remember how we talked about keeping this place for us to escape to? Well, now it's functional enough to do that, and in about eight months, we're going to need a little getaway at times."

In the corner to the left of the door, Forrest has created a small kitchen area with custom gray cabinets and a stove, fridge, and microwave. The far left corner contains a small bathroom with beautiful custom tile work in the shower and a sink and toilet. In the far right corner, where the air mattress used to sit, is a California king bed with teal bedding, gray accent pillows, and a gray padded headboard. And there's a small seating area to the right of the door complete with two teal cushioned chairs and a coffee table just big enough for two people to eat at comfortably. But the walls are white, which brighten up the space and make it appear so much bigger than it really is.

It reminds me of a studio apartment—an immaculately designed one.

"I can't believe you did this."

"I knew it was important, and I wanted you to see this before I talked to you tonight." The tone of his voice has me spinning back toward him, studying his face for any hint of what he has on his mind.

"Okay..."

He takes my hand, leads me over to the seating area, and we both sit in our respective chairs.

"Shauna," he breathes out, staring down at the table before leaning back in his chair. "I love you," he finally says as my eyes begin to sting. "I've always loved you, and having you back in my life has only solidified that for me."

All the oxygen leaves my lungs. God, it feels good to hear those words from him again, and I don't think I'll ever get sick of hearing them.

"I love you, too, Forrest," I say, my throat clogged with emotion. "So much."

He lets out the breath he was holding, and then he scoots his chair closer to me. "The past couple of months have been a tornado of emotions, but I need you to know where my mind is before the new year." I nod, still listening. "I want this life with you—all of your mornings and nights, all of the good and the bad in between . . ." He places his hand over my stomach. "All of the babies you'll allow me to give you. But I want you to be my wife more than anything."

He drops to his knees in front of me, and a fresh wave of tears develops.

He pulls a ring from the pocket of his jeans and holds it out to me, the princess-cut diamond sparkling in the overhead lights. "Will you marry me, Shauna? Will you build a life with me, love me even when I'm being stubborn, and prove to me that second chances do exist?"

I push from my chair and fall to my knees in front of him, wrapping my arms around his neck. "Forrest . . . I'm so ready to be your wife."

He lets out the breath he was holding. "God, I'm so ready, too."

He slides the ring on my finger and then slants his lips over mine, sealing our love with a kiss that has me melting into a puddle on the floor. If Forrest weren't holding me up in his arms, I'd probably collapse again—but this time from happiness.

"I love you, Forrest."

"Glad to hear it. But in case you needed any more convincing, I wanted to do this for us." He gestures to the space around us as he takes his seat again, pulling me onto his lap. "I wanted you to see our future, to remember that I listened to you all those years ago, to remind you that I will do everything in my power to make you happy."

Leaning my forehead on his, I whisper, "I could never forget that. You and this town have haunted my dreams for years. This is where I'm meant to be."

"Okay," he whispers back, and then we both lean away so we can find each other's gaze again. "So this brings me to my next question."

"Uh-huh..."

"I talked to my dad about the ranch, about taking over one day like I planned to all those years ago. But if you don't want that, I won't do it. I only want something we agree on, Shauna. I don't want you to feel like I'm making decisions for you."

The ranch. I can't believe I didn't think of that, the other part of our future I thought I wanted.

Do I still want that, or is there more for me out there? What about the horse rescue Maddox mentioned? What about working for his nonprofit?

I came out here looking for purpose in love and life. Is running this ranch what I really want?

I cup the side of his face and decide to see where he's at. "Is that what you still want? What about your company?"

"I can bring in a partner. Javi said he would buy in for part ownership in a heartbeat. I could work there part-time and manage things part-time here, especially since Dad won't be retiring for a few more years. We could also bring in a partner here, but my father would ultimately like the ranch to stay in the family, at least in part, if possible. But if we don't agree, then selling is still an option. I told him I wouldn't take on the responsibility unless I had your full support and agreement."

"I think the ranch staying in the family is important. And I mean, I can still plan events here, but I also want the opportunity to work in other areas. Maddox and Penelope brought up some career options for me that night, Forrest. I'm not sure I'm sold on any one decision at the moment."

"All right. That's okay. We can figure out everything later."

"Are you sure?"

He looks up at me from our seat. "Yes, Shauna. I told you, I want us to plan what comes next together, and now we have a baby coming that we need to think about, too."

"I know. Life is about to get crazy."

"But at least we have the shack to escape to now, right?"

I look around the room again, still in awe. "This is amazing. Could you imagine if we could have had this back in high school?"

"We never would have left here, Shauna." Forrest growls and then plants his lips on mine, kissing me deeply as he pulls me tighter to his chest. "Fuck, I love you."

"I love you, too."

He stands, still holding me in his arms, and then leads me over to the bed, tossing me onto it, making me squeal as I land. "Get naked."

Both of us start stripping, throwing clothes all over the floor before I toss the pillows aside as well, pull back the blankets, and watch Forrest crawl over me, his cock bobbing between his legs, hard and ready.

But he stops with his face between my thighs, kissing the inside of my legs teasingly as I grow more impatient for him. I need him desperately after days of feeling under the weather.

"Forrest, please."

"What, Shauna? What do you need?" He slides one finger up and down my slit, barely brushing my clit with each pass, teasing me even more.

"You."

"You need to be more specific, baby. Remember, communication is key."

Glaring at him, I stare down at his face between my legs and say, "Put your mouth on my pussy, Forrest. Now."

Smirking, he says, "Now, *that* I understood." He dives in, covering me with his mouth and sucking my clit between his lips with such enthusiasm, my eyes roll back in my head.

"Keep watching me, Shauna," he mumbles against me, sliding a finger into my core.

I open my eyes and keep them locked on him—the dark-brown irises that look almost black right now, the stubble on his face burning the sensitive flesh of my inner thighs, his hair standing on end as I pull on it, yanking him closer to me.

When he begins curling his fingers inside of me, my

orgasm builds so quickly that I can barely prepare for it. And then I'm coming, tossing my head back, chanting his name, and riding his face shamelessly.

When I come down from my high, I slump back into the pillows. "God, that was amazing."

"We're not done yet," he declares as he climbs over me, hooks my knees over his shoulders, and pushes inside me with one smooth thrust.

"Ah!" I shout, feeling him so deeply from this angle as his hips push my knees back to meet my ears.

"Fuck, baby. Take all of me . . . suck me in, baby."

"You're so deep, Forrest," I manage to squeak out between thrusts as Forrest sets a relentless pace, hitting me so far inside that it borders on pain.

"Good . . . because you're buried so deeply in me that I'll never survive without you, Shauna." He pushes my legs off his shoulders and falls on top of me so our chests are touching now. The pressure from before has waned, but something just as deep has replaced it—overwhelming love.

"Forrest." I grab his face with both hands and guide his mouth to mine, kissing him feverishly, tasting him as we chase our release.

I feel myself grow wetter, tighter, and the pressure builds in my core. Forrest knows I'm close, too, because he reaches between us to circle my clit, pinching and rubbing it, helping me reach the edge. And then, as his thrusts pick up pace, I know he's going to meet me there.

"Fuck, Shauna..."

"I'm coming," I announce, clenching around him and screaming through my release, digging my nails into his shoulders. I'm gasping for air as the waves keep going and going, and I feel like they're never going to end.

When Forrest finally stills, our bodies both unclench at the same time. He pulls out before collapsing onto the bed beside me.

"God, woman." He wraps his arm around my waist, pulling me into him so my back is to his front.

"I need a nap after that," I mumble, making him laugh.

"Sleep all you want, baby. I'm taking full advantage of having you all to myself right now."

"I guess I shouldn't complain about that, then," I say, rolling over as Forrest climbs back over me.

"The only thing you'll be complaining about by the time I'm done with you is that your clit is so fucking sensitive," he says, dipping his head between my legs, licking me again, over and over.

Smiling up at the ceiling, I say, "Eh. There are worse problems to have."

EPILOGUE

Forrest

"Damn, we clean up good!" Walker declares, adjusting his tie in the mirror beside me.

"The only reason I'm wearing a suit is because Shauna asked me to. Otherwise, you know we'd all be in jeans and boots," I reply, looking at myself in the mirror beside him.

It's our wedding day, and even though we're getting married at the ranch with just our close friends and family, Shauna begged me to wear a suit and tie. The last time she saw me in one was for our senior prom, and my goal in life is to make that woman happy, so if she wants me in a suit, I'm wearing a fucking suit.

Also, I'm hoping she tears this thing off me with her teeth later, which will definitely make wearing this for hours worth it.

At least it's more comfortable than that damn elf costume.

It's only been two months since I proposed, but neither of us wanted to wait that long to be married. Plus, Shauna was eager to walk down the aisle before she started showing too much because the dress she wanted to wear was very formfitting.

I can tell that her body has already started to change, and I fucking love it. But again, I wanted her to have the wedding she always dreamed of.

My dream wedding? That was always the one that had her walking toward me.

Nothing else mattered.

She moved in with me right after we got back from Vegas, and once I put the ring on her finger, she went into wedding planning mode.

Penelope reached out about Maddox's nonprofit again, and I could tell by the look on her face that her heart was dedicated to it before she even said yes. She's been working remotely so far and will continue to do so after the baby is born. But she's also planning weddings here on the ranch for the time being, especially since she wants the practice for when we take over.

My parents said they want five more years to run things, and then we'll draw up papers to transfer ownership of the business. The land will still be theirs, but my brothers and I decided to run things together. And Javi is going to become my new business partner early next year.

Life is crazy and wild, a stark contrast to how it was before. But I'll gladly take the changes and challenges if it means I have Shauna by my side.

"Where's Dad?" Wyatt asks as he glances toward the door. We're in one of the rooms in the main house, waiting until it's time to head for the barn. It's February, so the weather is still a little unpredictable, but luckily, we managed to have very little wind today—it's just cold. The barn is heated, though, so our guests will be nice and comfortable.

Perhaps Dad is checking on things to make sure they're in order.

"He said he'd be right here when I saw him a few minutes ago," Walker answers.

"I'm here," he announces as he steps into the room, his gray hair slicked back, his suit draped over the body that still commands a presence when he enters a room.

"Wyatt, Walker . . . do you mind if I have a moment alone with Forrest?"

My twin brothers share a look and then head for the door. "No problem, Dad. Go easy on the pre-wedding speech, will ya?" Walker says.

"Not like you got one," Dad fires back, making all three of us laugh. Once the two of them are gone, he walks over to where I'm standing near the window, peering out to look at the clouds. "How are you feeling?"

"I'm so fucking ready, Dad." Turning to him again, I look him dead in the eye. "I've been waiting a long time for this."

"I know you have, and I've been waiting for this day, too." He takes a box out from his jacket, and that's when it hits me.

The watch.

"I know that you knew this was coming, but there's a story behind it that you need to hear first."

I offer him a small smile. "All right."

"The day I married your mother, I was a nervous wreck."

"Really?"

"Yeah," he laughs. "But it wasn't because of doubt. It was fear—fear that we wouldn't last, fear that I couldn't give her everything she wanted."

I chuckle. "I understand that."

"Any good man, a man who loves his woman dearly, does. And my parents were always so happy, so in love. So I asked my dad what the secret was."

"And what did he say?"

"Thirty seconds."

"What?" I ask, my brows furrowing.

"Kiss her for no less than thirty seconds every day,

Forrest. That's how you make it last." He opens the box, extracts the watch, and flips it over to reveal the engraving on the back.

No less than thirty seconds.

"Doesn't seem long enough," I counter jokingly.

My father smiles. "I know, but trust me, once that baby comes and life starts to get in the way of the time you used to have together, you'll realize that thirty seconds is a lot. The thing is, though, it's also such a small thing you can do to keep that love between you alive. At the end of the day, you at least owe her that—thirty seconds of touch, of time, of love."

Swallowing the lump in my throat, I nod. "I hear you, Dad."

He places the watch on my wrist and secures it. "I'm proud of you, son. You deserve this day just as much as she does."

I pull my father into my arms, slapping his back as I choke back tears. "Thanks, Dad. I love you."

"I love you, too."

Thirty minutes later, my brothers, my father, and I head toward the barn that has been decorated in soft pink, dark green, and white. The room has touches of Shauna all over it, but the only thing that's missing is her.

When "Marry Me" by Train comes on, I take my spot up at the front after walking my mother down the aisle and eagerly await the arrival of my bride.

Evelyn and Walker come down first, staring at each

other as if they're the only two people in the room. Wyatt and Kelsea follow, grinning from ear to ear when they see me, and Willow, Shauna's best friend from college, glides down the aisle by herself, winking at me from across the aisle when she stands on the opposite side.

Javi's son comes down next, holding the ring pillow, and his daughter and Kaydence toddle down the aisle after that, tossing pink rose petals on the white runner.

And then I see her—my angel, my best friend, the mother of my child—*my everything.*

Shauna has either arm latched onto her mom and Frank as she makes her way down the aisle toward me. And when I see her dress, I nearly drool.

White silk drapes over her every curve, highlighting her hips and breasts. The top has a lace detail and thin straps, hinting at just a bit of cleavage. And her hair is down in loose curls with one side pulled away from her face with a diamond clip.

This is the way she should look as a bride, not like she did in the costume she was wearing last time.

When she arrives right in front of me, her mom and Frank give her away.

Things with Shauna's mom have been better since we said our piece in Vegas. She still has her feelings about small-town life, but she's grown more accepting that this is where Shauna and I will be. She and Frank have already talked about purchasing a home out here so they have somewhere to stay when they come to visit, and her mother won't stop buying things for the baby even though we don't know the sex yet.

"You look beautiful, baby," I tell her as she stands before me.

"That suit makes you look like James Bond, Forrest." She licks her lips. "I can't wait to tear it off you later."

After we exchange vows, I kiss my wife in front of all the people who matter to me, and then our reception gets underway.

We serve a meal of pasta, salad, and breadsticks. We laugh and cry during the speeches. And then it's time for dessert. And guess what we're having?

Cake with a side of chocolate ice cream.

Yes, you read that right. My wife's been craving chocolate ice cream, not rainbow sherbet. Seems like my baby has impeccable taste already.

Once we cut the cake and all of the dances are complete, I prepare for one last surprise of the evening.

"Excuse me. Can I get everyone's attention, please?" I announce into the microphone as I adjust my guitar strap on my shoulder. "I have a gift for my wife, but I need her to come sit up on stage with me to receive it."

Shauna shakes her head as she steps onto the platform, taking a seat in the chair next to me. "What are you up to?"

"Oh, just a little reminder for you that without you, life has no meaning."

I start strumming the opening notes to "Never Leave"

by Bailey Zimmerman, and then I do something none of my family, including Shauna, has seen me do before—*I sing.*

Shauna's eyes well with tears as I sing to her about the terrifying part of loving someone—putting trust in someone not to hurt you, not giving up on one another no matter what, and promising never to leave, even when things get hard.

I sing to her as if it's the first and last time I'll ever do it—publicly, at least.

And I sing to her knowing that without her encouragement and love, I never would have found the strength to finally be who I truly am.

By the time I'm done, there's not a dry eye in the place.

Shauna launches herself at me from her chair, planting her mouth on mine, and everything feels right in the world.

God, I love this woman.

I'd give up everything to have this moment with her over and over again.

Because without her, I have nothing.

Just like in that Zach Bryan song, looks like we finally turned those headlights back around.

THE END

Thank you SO much for reading Forrest and Shauna's story! If you enjoyed their story, PLEASE consider leaving a review on Amazon and/or Goodreads. It truly means SO much!

If you would like a glimpse into their future, download their Extended Epilogue here.

BUT WAIT!

Do you remember Willow? Shauna's best friend from college? The self-made millionaire who lives in Washington D.C.?

WELL, she's getting a book, which just so happens to be the start of my NEW SERIES coming next year!

Somewhere You Belong, the first book in my Carrington Cove series, is already available for pre-order HERE!

AND, you can keep reading for an exclusive sneak peek at her book!

I'll meet you in Carrington Cove 😉

Sneak Peek of Somewhere You Belong (subject to change before publication)

"I'm sorry. You're headed where?" Shauna, my best friend, asks for clarification as I continue to cruise down the highway, well more than halfway into my drive.

"North Carolina."

"And you said it's for an inheritance?"

"That's what the letter said. I don't even know who this man is, Shauna, but he said he knew my parents. Am

I crazy for even driving down there? What if it's a scam?"

Given that my company is a household name now, I've grown far more weary of people wanting to get close to me for the wrong reasons. And a long lost friend of my parents sounds like the perfect con to back me up into a corner, especially since my parents died when I was two and I haven't heard anyone mention them in a very long time.

I have no other family except for Mandy and Jason, my parents' friends that took custody of me per their will. My grandparents on both sides have passed since then, and I wasn't particularly close with them anyway.

But Mandy never mentioned the man who wrote me the letter—and since her and Jason divorced when I was five and she virtually raised me on my own—I figured I would wait until I know more to get her two cents. No sense in bringing up the past if this just ends up being a wild goose chase. Besides, Shauna is the first sounding board I turn to when I need to vent, and I know she'll tell me what I need to hear.

We met at UNLV and bonded quickly over our love of sarcasm and lack of interest in men. I was there to get my degree so I could start my business as soon as possible, and she had a high school boyfriend our freshman year that she ended up breaking up with when we were sophomores. From then on, it was us against the world—well, until she ended her engagement last fall to a man and went back to her hometown of Newberry Springs, Texas to reconcile with her high school sweetheart, Forrest. Let's just say, all went well and she's due to deliver their son any week now.

"If the letter came from a legal office, it's most likely legit, Willow."

See? That right there. There's the logical perspective that I needed.

"That's true."

"And it could be something small, but if it's a connection to your parents, you owe yourself to find out."

Shauna is the only person I've ever been honest with about how losing my parents has affected me. I might have lost them when I wasn't old enough to remember who they are, but that loss has haunted me and left a giant hole in my chest I've never quite filled. Add on a lack of a stable family and less than stellar luck in dating throughout my life, and it just became easier to shut off my feelings than try to deal with them.

But right now, it feels like someone is making the hole wider, digging roughly into the hard surface I've built to cover it as the anticipation of what awaits me grows the longer that I'm in this car.

"I know. I just…I don't have time for this. You won't believe what happened with my company the other day. And business is so crazy. There are so many accounts we have pitches and campaigns to get ready for."

"Well, you have time and so do I waiting for this kid to come out, so spill all of the details."

I spend the next several minutes recounting the morning wakeup call of a dick on screen three days ago.

"Do you think he was jacking off during the meeting then?" she asks through her laugh.

"I mean, that's what it looked like. You could see the mess that he made and it looked fresh. Perhaps the dogfood campaign they were working on really got him fired up and horny?" Shauna cackles as I switch lanes. "But if stuff like that is happening, that just goes to show that the last thing I should be doing right now is following a wild goose chase."

"First of all, you can't control if and when a man chooses to whip out his dick, Willow. That's beyond the scope of running a company, and I think any other CEO would agree."

The corner of my mouth lifts. "Fair point."

"And secondly, you and I both know that you're a work-a-holic, and you do much more than you really need to in the scope of your company."

"That's a matter of opinion."

"It's the truth." Shauna lets out a big sigh. "Look, I know you have all sorts of questions right now, but you won't have any answers until you meet with the attorney tomorrow. So, figure out the details and make decisions then. But please, Willow, at least enjoy the change of scenery. When's the last time you took a day off?"

I start thinking back, searching desperately for a date to tell her.

"Your lack of a response is your answer. It's been too freaking long."

Sighing, I flip my blinker on and move into the lane on my right. "Fine. You're right. I just hate not knowing what's going on."

"Oh, I'm aware. You're the biggest control freak I know. But believe me, sometimes life can throw you a curve ball right at the perfect time, and not all curve balls are bad. Look at me and Forrest."

"I'm pretty sure you ran into Forrest again two weeks before you were about to marry another man, and then you ended up leaving that man at the altar. How is that not disastrous?"

She laughs, but replies, "You're right. It was disastrous at first. But then it led me back to the man I never stopped loving and in a few weeks, we're going to be parents. I'd say that's pretty serendipitous, don't you?"

I hum in agreement, knowing that I've never seen or heard my best friend be so happy. "Yeah, I guess."

"Always the optimist." She pauses and then says, "Just breathe, Willow."

I let out the breath I was holding. "How did you know?"

"Because that's what you do when you're stressed. I'm sorry I can't be there with you, but it's going to be okay."

"And what if it's not?"

"Then you tackle whatever comes your way because you're Willow Fucking Marshall and that's what you do. You're a survivor."

"Thank you," I mutter as I feel the sting of tears. But I fight them down and focus on the road.

Shauna lets out a yawn. "I'm always here. However, I am exhausted so I'm going to let you go so I can take a nap."

"Fine. I guess you can go and continue growing my nephew."

"Thanks for your permission. Text me when you get there safely."

"I will. I still have a while to go though."

"Enjoy the ride, Willow. I have a feeling you're in for one hell of one."

How come at this moment, I get that feeling in my gut too?

Somewhere You Belong, the first book in my Carrington Cove series, is already available for pre-order HERE! Don't miss out on this new series 😉

MORE BOOKS BY HARLOW JAMES

The Ladies Who Brunch (rom-coms with a ton of spice)
Never Say Never (Charlotte and Damien)
No One Else (Amelia and Ethan)
Now's The Time (Penelope and Maddox)
Not As Planned (Noelle and Grant)
Nice Guys Still Finish (Jeffrey and Ariel)

The California Billionaires Series (rom coms with heart and heat)
My Unexpected Serenity (Wes and Shayla)
My Unexpected Vow (Hayes and Waverly)
My Unexpected Family (Silas and Chloe)

Newberry Springs Series (smalltown, brothers)
Everything to Lose (Wyatt and Kelsea)
Everything He Couldn't (Walker and Evelyn)
Everything But You (Forrest and Shauna)

The Emerson Falls Series (smalltown romance with a found family friend group)

Tangled (Kane & Olivia)
Enticed (Cooper & Clara)
Captivated (Cash and Piper)
Revived (Luke and Rachel)
Devoted (Brooks and Jess)

<u>Lost and Found in Copper Ridge</u>
A holiday romance in which two people book a stay in a cabin for the same amount of time thanks to a serendipitous $5 bill.
<u>Guilty as Charged (Javier and Sydney)</u>
An intense opposites attract standalone that will melt your kindle. He's an ex-con construction worker. She's a lawyer looking for passion.
McKenzie's Turn to Fall
A holiday romance where a romance author falls for her neighborhood butcher.

ACKNOWLEDGMENTS

The Gibson Brothers are DONE! It feels incredible writing this, but even more so because my readers—YOU ALL—trusted me on this creative journey and supported these stories with enthusiasm and loyalty that I will be forever grateful for.

Because of you, I am able to take this writing journey to a new level next year, giving you audiobooks galore, AND a new small town series that has also been in my mind for years.

Willow, Shauna's best friend, will find her happily ever after in the first book of my new series, Somewhere You Belong, Carrington Cove Book 1, coming in June 2024.

Stay tuned for alerts and news related to my next releases! Make sure you're signed up for my newsletter so you don't miss out on updates.

To my husband: When you attended the HEA Reader Event with me this year, you got to experience first-hand how much joy this writing gig brings me, and the pride you showed for me makes me love you even more. I COULD NOT DO THIS WITHOUT YOUR SUPPORT. I know I am one of the luckiest women on the planet because of how fiercely you love me and support me. I thank God for you every day.

Thank you for cheering me on and celebrating my success with me as I release each book. Thank you for understanding how much joy this hobby brings me. Thank you for listening to me vent when I'm struggling, and helping me turn this into a business now, including being my "book bitch." 😉 Thank you for trusting me with investing in my audio books because I know it's expensive, but my readers are going to be SO happy.

Here's to our adventures this next year doing signings and staying in many hotel rooms with no kids. And thank you for being my real life book husband and giving me my own true love story to brag about.

To Lizzy: I remember sitting on the beach, plotting this series, and now it's finally come to life. You were right. It just wasn't the right time back then, but now, the Gibson brothers are done. For almost five years, you've been my rock, my sounding board, and the person who listens no matter what. You help me plot, cheer me on, and get excited about my ideas just as much as I do. I love you and couldn't do this without all of your support along the way.

To Melissa, my editor: I am SO grateful for our working relationship. I always know that my book is in great hands with you. Thank you for your dedication to this series.

To Abigail, my cover designer: For almost four years now, you have brought every vision of mine to life, and this book was no exception. I LOVE working with you. Thank you for putting in so much time and love to my books, and giving me those voice messages with your accent that makes me smile every time. I think these might be my favorite covers yet!

And to my beta readers (Keely, Emily, Kelly, Carolina—I love you all SO much!), my ARC readers (The BEST team on the planet!), and every reader (both old and new):

Thank you for taking a chance on a self-published author.

Thank you for sharing my books with others.

Thank you for allowing me to share my creativity with people who love the romance genre as much as I do.

And thank you for supporting a wife and mom who found a hobby that she loves.

ABOUT THE AUTHOR

Harlow James is a wife and mom who fell in love with romance novels, so she decided to write her own.
Her books are the perfect blend of emotional, addictive, and steamy romance. If you love stories with a guaranteed Happily Ever After, then Harlow is your new best friend.
When she's not writing, she can be found working her day job, reading every romance novel she can find time for, laughing with her husband and kids, watching re-runs of FRIENDS, and spending time cooking for her friends and family while drinking White Claws and Margaritas.

<u>Connect with Harlow James</u>
Follow me on Amazon
Follow me on Instagram
Follow me on Facebook
Join my Facebook Group: Harlow James' Harlots
Follow me on Goodreads

Follow me on Book Bub

Subscribe to my Newsletter for Updates on New Releases and Giveaways

Website

Printed in Great Britain
by Amazon